Jessie locked his eyes on her face and began. "Outta the box, you gotta know how the dream came to me through Uncle Willie. Before I knowed him I ain't doubted just a teeny mean look from a Mafia man woulda dreened pee down everybody's legs from the police to the president and me even. But no, not Uncle Willie, and 'cause I worshipped him I kilt one and lost my fear of Mafia men.

"After Unc was buried I rounded up more'n three hundred of the baddest niggers on the Westside to heist and shake down numbers banks and dope dealers for the geeters to but artillery to waste all the Mafia men in Chicago for killing Uncle Willie. We training an army of commandos! After Chicago, we gonna waste them in New York, Detroit, Cleveland and everywhere cross country.

"Ra, the people gonna know Jessie Taylor livin' and dyin' and dead even, and even white folks eating, crapping or screwing they gonna take time and feel sad when Jessie Taylor's leavin' and gone. Ra, that's my dream. What you think?"

—*DEATH WISH*

**Holloway House Originals
By Iceberg Slim (Robert Beck)**

THE NAKED SOUL OF ICEBERG SLIM

MAMA BLACK WIDOW

TRICK BABY

PIMP: THE STORY OF MY LIFE

DEATH WISH

AIRTIGHT WILLIE & ME

LONG WHITE CON

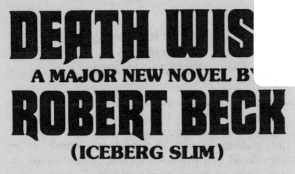

DEATH WIS

A MAJOR NEW NOVEL BY

ROBERT BECK

(ICEBERG SLIM)

An Original Holloway House Edition

HOLLOWAY HOUSE PUBLISHING CO.
LOS ANGELES, CALIFORNIA

An Original Holloway House Edition
DEATH WISH

ISBN 0-87067-934-1

CHAPTER ONE

Loudmouth hoodlum winds lunged across the Chicago heavens and muscled away a mob of sooty clouds. Frosty stars suddenly spangled the black Caddie that cruised the snow-gutted ghetto.

Four-hundred-pound Lollo "The Surgeon" Stilotti stuffed chocolate cashews into the vulgar hole in his face. He broke rotted chocolate wind on the Caddie's rear seat.

He complained, "What a fucked-up Christmas morning!"

Angelo Serelli, at the wheel, said, "Mr. Collucci ain't gonna postpone justice for a guy who rips off eight kilos of Family merchandise."

Phil, the Surgeon's first cousin, sitting beside Angelo, blew an impatient gust of cigarette smoke against the windshield. "I hope we wind this guy up before daybreak so I don't miss my twins tearing open their first Christmas score."

Lollo groaned. "I got a broad waiting in my bed with size forty-two tits." He sighed. "And she sucks like a milking machine."

There were bumping, choking sounds coming from the trunk behind Stilotti.

Phil chuckled and said, "Lollo, Angelo can pull over and you can do a sixty-nine with the Bone's Mexican bitch."

Stilotti said, "Fuck yourself, Phil. I respect my prick. You can get hard for even the coloreds."

Angelo thought about his daughter Stella who had passed away at about the age of the teenage girl in the trunk. He pulled the Caddie to the curb and said, "I have to check her gag. I didn't like that sound."

Stilotti sneered. "You worried about a chili-gut?"

Angelo said as he got out of the car, "Asshole, you want Mr. Collucci's witness against the Bone to croak on our hands?"

Angelo unlocked the trunk lid and saw that the girl's brown skin was nearly black. He removed the choking wad of Stilotti's handkerchief from her mouth.

She gulped air and gasped. "Please let me out of here. I won't make trouble. Please!"

Angelo loosened the rope that had rubbed her ankles and wrists raw.

He said gently, "I'm sorry you let Bone trap you in his trouble. Like a father, I advise you to tell the truth when you get the chance."

Tears welled in her brown eyes and she said, "When?"

Angelo removed a steel bumper jack from beneath her side.

"Soon," he said.

"You will speak good for me?" she asked in a voice that staggered the rim of hysteria.

Angelo nodded and re-gagged her with a smaller wad of Kleenex tissues from his pocket. He shut the trunk lid and got beneath the wheel of the Caddie. Angelo passed Mack Rivers' Voudoo Palace Cabaret just before he turned off Forty-seventh Street into Calumet Avenue.

Stilotti said, "I'm so fucking tired and bored, I feel like pissing my pants just for the action."

Angelo snickered. "Beat your meat, Stilotti."

Angelo slowed the Caddie to a crawl and said seriously, "Bone is pretty strong, and he's got a guilty conscience, maybe I should put him up front between Phil and me. Stilotti, you could calm him down with a twist of your choker if he got frisky. Whatta you guys think?"

Stilotti said, "It ain't what we think. You heard Mr. Collucci lay it all out sweet and smooth yesterday. A guy is always relaxed with nobody behind him. Besides, he trusts you like you're his old man."

Phil said, "Angelo, you been edgy all night. You got a sucker soft spot for the guy or what?"

"I shortened my life mothering the sonuvabitch around the clock, running the cunt-lapper down before big fights. Hah! A soft spot for Bone? I woulda put a slug in his noggin a thousand times except Mr. Collucci owned him," said Angelo.

Angelo cruised the Caddie into the next block and said softly, "There's the Bone's Eldorado in the slot."

Angelo pulled past the rickety trio of carports

beside Larry "Love Bone" Flaubert's ancient two-story apartment building and coasted the Caddie to a stop in front of it.

Angelo had stepped to the street and was pushing the car door shut when Stilotti leaned forward and said seriously, "Don't forget what Mr. Collucci said about eyeing through his joint so we don't leave nobody up there."

Angelo pushed the door shut and nodded through the dark-tinted glass. A freezing blast of wind ripped at the hem of his blue Russian-front greatcoat. He hunched his beefy shoulders and sloughed his big rubbered feet through the snow to the sidewalk. His bare gray buffalo head wore a dull halo of silver light for an instant beneath the street lamp. As he went across the sidewalk toward the vestibule door, a corner of his eye snared a flutter of Bone's curtain.

He stepped into the shadow-haunted vestibule and held his breath in an eye-stinging smog of disinfectant and the rotted-meat stink of a pygmy junkie whore "coasting" on the steps before him.

She huddled her frame inside a fake fur jacket. She sprawled out bird legs pocked with sores oozing pus. He saw a rope of dried semen looped on her chin when she walled her piteous eyes up at him.

She clawed at him in slow motion as he side-stepped past her. She half swiveled her chicken neck and slurred, "C'mon sweetie and have some fun. I got one tighter'n mosquito pussy, and hot and good, ooooooeee! No shit baby, I ain't but twelve. C'mon back here and give your pretty

8

white dick some Christmas sport."

Angelo went up several stone stairs and heard the hornet's-nest buzzer unlocking the glass door ahead.

Upstairs, Love Bone draped angel hair on his Christmas tree. He had not been alarmed, he was only mildly surprised and curious at the sight of Angelo coming to visit him on an early Christmas morning. Angelo had been a tried and trusted friend through the years.

However, Bone had, after buzzing open the downstairs door, pushed a vial of powerful Tuinal sleeping pills and an almost empty glassine bag under a chair cushion. The bag, earlier in the evening, had bulged with a half-ounce of pure cocaine.

As Bone opened his front door he felt his head cloud. He, ten minutes before, had gulped a gob of the Tuinals. He wanted the most to descend from the leapy frozen peak he had climbed in a twelve-hour freak-in with a cocaine-banging trio of bitches in a far Southside hotel suite.

Angelo came slowly through the mildewed murk of gray-carpeted stairway to the second floor. He paused on the dim landing for a long moment and gazed at grinning Love Bone lounging in his doorway ashimmer in a black satin wrapper.

Why must I be the fucking Judas Goat? Angelo thought as he moved toward Bone, with a warm con smile on his cratered moon face. How he hated this, his tenth mission of death for the Family. Just this one . . . With the others he had felt absolutely nothing. Possibly even pleasure on two of them. He

9

felt his sick belly quiver in the poisonous bile of his rage against stupid Bone for stealing Family dope. How he hated, at this moment, the whole Family, from Top Boss Tonelli all the way down to himself. Himself most of all for the debt of life he owed the Bone that now he could only pay off in Collucci's court of death.

Three feet apart, Bone and Angelo hollered at each other. "Well I'll be Raquel Welch's tiddie baby if it ain't my favorite wop. Merry Christmas, Pappy, and all that other jazz."

"Hi ya Bone, sweetheart! Merry Christmas and a hundred more, you pretty black mother you."

They flung themselves violently together. Then, like Mutt and Jeff faggots reconciling, jigged a prancy rigadoon into the living room. Bone took Angelo's coat and flung it across the end of a dazzling white silk sofa. A cunty zephyr wafted up Angelo's nostrils as he followed Bone.

Angelo dropped loosely onto the couch. He shot a glance into the gold and purple bedroom. He mulled mission changes if some fucked-out broad was present. If so, she must, as his boss Collucci would say, "be put to sleep" with Bone. Bone sat on a giant red cushion beside a round alabaster coffee table facing Angelo.

Bone uncapped a bottle of Harvey's Bristol Cream. As he poised it above a pair of crystal glasses, he asked with a light overlay of sarcasm, "Pappy baby, you still go for the usual with me?"

Angelo took a deep breath to unload tension that might fink through to Bone in his voice. Bone chewed his bottom lip as he studied the gaudy anguish etching Angelo's brow.

Angelo's heavy palms jiggled reproach above the coffee table. "Ain't this a bitch? Brother, you gotta ask after the vat of Harvey's we hoisted together through the years?"

Angelo smiled to hear himself say it so smoothly, laced with disarming soul shit. Bone poured the wine. His scar-crusted face was cocked impassively. His eyes burned with the ultra-alertness of those of a priest of Voudoo in his native Haiti, intently listening for voices of the all-powerful Loas, or Spirit Voudoo Gods, to speak through a freshly severed human head in the flame and blood-stained night. The musical splash of the sherry was a baleful gurgle in the whirling silence.

Bone finger-stroked across the twenty-five automatic in his robe pocket. He pulled a cigarette from a pack and thought, *This Dago is flinging some weird vibes this morning. I feel them Tuinals kicking my ass fuzzy. Ain't this a bitch! I wish I could cop a few blows of the Miss Pure White Lady stashed under that cushion to clear my skull.*

Bone grinned. "You know you my main man. But damn, you ain't called. You ain't been back to the pad since I let my three-way Hawaiian freak blow your mind Thanksgiving night. Pappy, I woulda bet a C-note against a jug of snot you wouldn'ta done me like that."

Angelo averted his eyes and hula'ed the wine in his glass. He was weary and must use the first natural cue and serve Bone with Collucci's summons.

"Bone sweetheart, I missed you," he said. "But

11

Mr. Collucci has got my ass dragging with all our troubles with Tat Taylor's Warriors and other serious trouble I can't talk about. *Capisce?*"

Bone blew a barrage of lazy smoke rings at the face across the coffee table. "I understand, Pappy baby. You know I love ya. If I was a broad I'd let you wear my pussy like a football helmet . . . year 'round."

They hee-hawed together.

Angelo swept his eyes about the seductively blue-lighted red and white living room.

"Bone, now you really got some kinda trap for broads," Angelo said as he caressed his fly.

Bone gazed at a painting of his beauteous sister Mayme above the fireplace. "Yeah, I been catching and holding good since my sister freaked the pad off. We going to redecorate every pad in my building by spring."

Then he pulled back his punch-thickened blue lips in a white-fanged dazzle of black leopard grin. He locked Angelo's eyes in the cold gray stare of his own.

Bone almost whispered, "Man, what's happening?"

Angelo asked with terminal pain on his face, "Whatta ya mean, Bone?"

"I mean, man, on Christmas you ain't gonna neglect your old lady's big sweet lollipop tits for no light chitchat with even your boon spade."

"Mr. Collucci wants to see you this morning," Angelo said quietly.

Bone asked softly, "He downstairs?"

Angelo shook his head.

Bone fiddled with the lapel above the automatic and said harshly, "Man, what is all this shit going down on Christmas morning?"

"Whatta ya mean, Bone? Bone, this morning it's like we don't know each other. Mr. Collucci sent me with a message." Angelo shrugged helplessly and shook his big head in apparent puzzlement.

Bone exploded off the red cushion to his feet and towered over Angelo, slit-eyed. He leaned his smashed nose down close to Angelo's face.

Bone's index finger slashed the air before Angelo's upturned face like an ebony stiletto as he mimicked with whispered ferocity, "*Whatta ya mean, Bone? Bone, this morning it's like we don't know each other.* Dago motherfucker, I mean is everything cool? I mean level with me, man! I mean you owe me! It's like you don't know me, gray ass.

"I mean have you forgot those slugs I took in the gut outside the stadium because you couldn't keep your pecker outta that Swede's broad? I coulda laid back and let him blow a few extra holes in your head. How's the weather, man? Is Mr. Collucci upset or something? This is Christmas morning, man!"

Angelo smiled weakly, "Hell no, he ain't salty about nothing. He was a creampuff just a few hours ago. You know, with smiles and a good mood."

Bone stood lie-detecting Angelo's face, softened now into a con mask of righteous innocence in the blue cathedral glow of the table lamp.

Angelo baited the hook. "Bone, I swear by the

Holy Mother there ain't nothing to be up tight for. All right, I'll risk my balls in the fire 'cause you're my friend.

"I'm gonna tell you what I ain't supposed to know." Angelo paused for a long moment and then threw the hook. "Mr. Collucci is holding two black guys he wants you to look at . . . at his roadhouse in Skokie. He's pretty sure they heisted the eight kilos from you and Mack Rivers."

Bone was dizzy with relief. Collucci couldn't have the guilty heist men waiting to finger him into the grave! Couldn't know that he, Bone, had set up the heist! He had talked to Charming Mills, one of them, on the phone just five minutes before Angelo showed.

He flung himself on the couch beside Angelo and pounded Angelo's back. "Baby, why you dangle me like that? Pappy, you gonna overlook my uncool? Right?"

Angelo grinned, bear-hugged Bone and said, "I ain't no fucking friend if I'm gonna tally a small misunderstanding between us. Right?"

Bone stood up and felt the Tuinals reel him for an instant. His fingers roughhoused through Angelo's mane of coarse gray hair. He weaved toward the bedroom and slurred, "Pappy, last night's juicing is kicking my ass, so I'm just gonna slip a coat on."

A bolt of cunning lightning flashed through the darkening Tuinal overcast. He'd finger Collucci's prisoners and close the eight kilo case! He turned and still-lifed himself in the bedroom doorway.

Finally he found his voice and croaked, "Ain't it

a bitch, Pappy, I just got a helluva powerful vision. Mr. Collucci's probably right on the money with them two jokers he's got on ice. Pappy, I'd bet a C-note against the clap they the ones."

Angelo nodded, drained his glass, and stood up. He caped his overcoat across his shoulders. He went to the bedroom doorway to make sure there wasn't the usual broad in Bone's bed.

Alarmed by Angelo's sudden presence, Bone's hand froze on the automatic he was stashing in a dresser drawer. Bone recovered and slipped into a fur-trimmed black suede coat. They moved toward the door.

Bone stopped and turned, looking about the living room. "I'll be back before daybreak, so I won't kill my lights."

Angelo shrugged and said, "Yeah, the lights might keep some hustler from shimming open your door for a score."

Bone turned and stood facing the wall beside the door, covered with a photo of Bone in his fighter's trunks and, surrounding it, Polaroid shots of broads of almost every race and hue. Angelo remembered the long years of misery and pressure as Bone's handler. Bone gazed with pride at the freaky rogue's gallery of groupie sexpots. They had drained away the steely ballet in his legs. The rattlesnaking instant oblivion coiled in his fists had crawled these caves of easy slime and died.

Bone stumbled twice on the way down the stairs to the vestibule. The child junkie was shivering as she huddled over a large coffee can in a corner on the stone landing. She stared hypnotically at dragon tongues of fire licking into the chilled vestibule air from a tight roll of newspaper inside the can.

Bone scrambled past her through the street door. He went to a snowbank at the side of the building and scooped up a mound of snow. He came back and flung it into the can. A steamy genie hissed angrily and escaped into the air.

Angelo stood on the landing behind Bone, smiling crookedly. Bone squatted, clucking concern before the scarecrow clump sobbing and snotting guilt and fear of eviction.

Bone patted her humpy back and she cringed away and wailed. "That ain't my fire. One of them Forty-seventh Street hypes musta made it. Bone, I swear it ain't mine."

Bone said, "Easy, girl, you know your play. Uncle Bone wouldn't put no hurt to you. Li'l Dee, why you in these streets like this on Christmas morning? Pearl know you out here?"

She blotted a bubble of snot with her sleeve and said plaintively, "I been had a habit two months. Mama threw me out. Ain't no room and food for no junkie with them ten squealers still at home."

Bone shook his head and said, "Go home, li'l Dee. Ain't no way Cecil wouldn't take you in tonight with that bad hawk screaming and blowing instant T.B. out there. Li'l Dee, use your outs."

She said sadly, "You ain't heard? The cops wasted Papa hiding in Sam's Baby Store just before midnight last night."

Bone sighed and fumbled with a ring of keys. He unlocked the glass door and held it open.

He ordered in mock anger, "Li'l Dee, take your

skinny ass to the shower in the basement and throw them clothes in the furnace. Tell old man Franklin, the janitor, I said give you a old shirt and a sandwich and let you sleep on that cot by the furnace. Uncle Bone will hustle up you a jive wardrobe in a coupla days. G'wan, girl, before I throw you to the hawk."

She got up laboriously like a decrepit crone, her child eyes brimming tears of gratitude. She squeezed Bone's hand and kissed it.

Bone tenderly slapped her bony behind and said, "Li'l Dee, stop playing that jive on Love Bone Larry Flambert. Girl, I'm hard and cold as a bandit squad roller at Eleventh Street Station."

She grinned wanly and started through the door.

Bone held her arm for a moment and his glazed eyes looked down seriously at her. "Li'l Dee, Uncle Bone gonna help you kick that thing you got. You gotta get back to your school books."

She nodded. The Tuinals wobbled Bone's legs as he turned away and followed Angelo to the sidewalk. Angelo felt it unnecessary to play the disarming game of "you follow me in your El D." He steered Bone directly to the yawning maw of the opened rear door of the black sedan.

Bone stooped and swiveled his head inside the car for an instant and recoiled back against Angelo. "Man, who. . .?"

Angelo cut in smoothly. "Mr. Collucci is gonna have a Christmas dinner, fun and games kinda thing, around noon at the roadhouse for some friends and their kids. The guy in the back is a chef, and the guy up front is his helper and waiter."

Bone mumbled and flung himself onto the back seat beside beaming Stilotti. Angelo slammed the door shut and went to the driver's seat. He started the Caddie's engine and pushed a button on the door armrest. Bone didn't hear the faint click inside the door next to him as the sedan pulled away. Bone was sealed inside a two-inch-thick bulletproof glass-and-steel-plated rolling prison.

Bone leaned across the seat and stared filmy eyes at Stilotti. He sniggled a spray of spit full into the round, kindly, stunned face and babbled, "Chump, you ain't no cook. You got no whiskers and red vine, but I'd know your lard ass anywhere. Shiiiiiit! You Mr. Santa Claus. I got a last-minute list to lay on you. I wanta . . ."

Bone's head dropped back against the cushion in open-mouthed, growly sleep. Phil guffawed. Angelo grunted and gripped the steering wheel. The Surgeon giggled tears down his fat, pink cheeks.

CHAPTER TWO

Angelo sped the black sedan and its prisoner toward Collucci's roadhouse in suburban Skokie.

Nude Collucci thrust anxiously on silk sheets in his mansion in posh suburban River Forest. He felt himself go limp against the vulva's pink lips pouting through the silky brambles. He had failed miserably once again between the alabaster thighs of Olivia Tonelli Collucci.

He rolled away to his side and watched her violently undulate her round dimpled butt in the fading glow of a fat yellow moon. She impaled herself on his long index finger. She hissed hotly as she rode and humped the wet stump. She jackknifed her thighs as he suckled at her breasts. She galloped madly for the finish line. He vised her nipples together under his big hand. He chewed, bit, sucked, gnawed and stabbed her into orgasm.

In a raging storm of guttural joy she flip-flopped in great voluptuous spasms of starved release. Then immediately she was hurt, furious that again he could not stay hard for her. At this moment she hated his mechanical finger-fucking that had, after all, done nothing for her that she couldn't have done for herself. She scooted off the punching dildo and sank her nails into his crotch. She drew herself into a fetal ball, panting and glaring blue fire at him.

Collucci reached for her. "Angel Doll, I'm. . . ."

She uncoiled and knifed her teeth into the tender web between his thumb and index finger. He gasped in pain and sucked at the wound. She taunted him with a wicked grin.

He said harshly, "You treacherous witch, I'll beat the pee out of you."

She laughed mirthlessly and needled in her throaty voice, "You do, Rubber Dick, and I'll scream the whole neighborhood and Papa into this house."

She moved away and turned her back. She barbed over her shoulder in Sicilian, "You horny Westside scum, why don't you beat the pee out of your new black whore you must be screwing? They have been why you can't get hard for a decent white woman any more."

He was enraged to be reminded of his slum beginnings. And he was always infuriated when she mentioned his wild hang-up on coal-black sexpots.

He choked back the angry words, the truth to shake her clean serene little world of teas and kid-glove hustling for worthy causes. The truth that Joe Tonelli, her precious father, had swum a river of blood to his present wealth and image of the respectable retired business man.

After a long silence Olivia said softly in a breaking voice, "Please forgive me . . . You know I don't really mean to say those awful things. I just feel sorry for you, I really do. You're going to lose me, lose Petey . . . everything."

Collucci scooped his yellow silk pajamas off the Persian rug. He slipped into them with a wry smile. He pillow-propped himself against the headboard and glanced at the Patek Phillipe's diamond face winking four A.M. on the nightstand.

He lit a cigarette and sucked deeply, exhaled and watched a poltergeist of smoke float across the bedroom and suicide against the frosted floor-to-ceiling windows overlooking the frozen grotto-garden. The garden sparkled like a crystal Shangri-La in the blaze of security spotlights ringing the mansion.

He glanced over at Olivia's silky mane firing golden skyrockets on her pillow. He idly thought that the Golden Fleece with the dragon bodyguard he had read about somewhere must have had the pulse-leaping magic of his Olivia's hair. He tried to remember the names of the two heisters with the balls to rip it off. He bit his long bottom lip rummaging his memory.

Yes, he'd get back to his reading of the classics on a regular basis. He had to keep his respectable, upper middle-class role-playing free of telltale flaws. That and other self-improvement things he would do as soon as he managed to put Tit For Tat Taylor and his Warriors to sleep in Rosedale Cemetery, or wherever.

He whipped the satin quilt over Olivia's splendor. He thought what a beautiful no-suck, one-way, hung-up Catholic, lousy lay she was. And for the thousandth time he wondered what the ungodly sexy Mayme Flambert would be like to lay.

He remembered when sex with Olivia had become a bore. It had happened when he started handling a big buck. He had showcased his impeccably groomed six-six frame in the posh watering and feeding establishments on the near Northside. Then a succession of foxy high-fashion nymphs and three-way society whores freaked his tongue and nose wide open for licking and rooting into pungent valleys.

He had gotten hopelessly jaded over the years. While Olivia remained the invincible one-way lady who could not be even a two-way bitch in the bedroom.

He gazed at her realizing that the sexual and spiritual love he had felt for Olivia in the beginning, thirty-five years before, had not been really lost, but rather it had transformed itself. Now he felt for Olivia only proprietary lust. Perhaps the infatuation, that trapped orgasm-of-the-eye kind of cold passion that an art fanatic lavishes upon the most fabulous piece of his collection.

He puffed his cigarette and got a whiff of Olivia's vaginal fragrance on that finger. But oddly he thought not of Olivia, but again of the haughty and mysterious Haitian temptress, and wondered what her scent would be. He sure as hell was going to find out. Like all the others, she was going to spin and dance her crotch on his stiff organ like an ecstatic yo-yo. Willingly, or by violent force. His. Soon!

He had always gotten the choicest of the coloreds. He visualized the last one he had played with. She had been a strikingly unique beauty, as all the other black ones had been. She had been haughty and aloof at first, like Mayme. She had belonged to a trigger-happy black numbers banker. She had had an absolutely fantastically curvaceous body. But the awesome oddity that Collucci could not resist was that her skin, eyes and hair were one color. Rich, ripe, radiant apricot.

The love-crazed banker had threatened Collucci with a foamy mouth and had to be put to sleep. The apricot beauty joined him six months later. She killed herself when Collucci's inferno yen consumed itself. He smiled. At least the coroner had recorded her death as a suicide.

He always got what he wanted, did whatever he wanted with any of them. Mayme was no different. Except that he was going to put her brother to sleep.

Now he gazed at Olivia's face, still holding so much of the soft beauty of her girlhood. He remembered that first time he saw her thirty-five years before on a star-infested summer night in the late nineteen-thirties. He had been twenty. She fifteen.

He was standing by the merry-go-round. The sight of her trembled his legs with desire and awe.

She moved like a ballet prima donna across the carnival sawdust and through the rubbernecking crowd. Her thighs were sculpted against the clingy organza gauze of her snowy dress. The lilting music of the merry-go-round synched with her sensual walk, shook him like a percussion of drums.

At a distance her face had a striking resemblance to Loretta Young's. But as he followed her, close up he saw she was taller and prettier with long shapely legs and her waist-length hair was ashimmer beneath the lights.

She stopped and vainly pitched pennies at a saucer floating in a tub of water that reflected a rack of smirking kewpie dolls. He was standing behind her and watched her shake her head in refusal of a kewpie doll gift from the bowing and scraping concessionaire.

She turned abruptly, and he was stricken by the great blue eyes, electric in the fawn face.

She said, "Why do you follow me and look at me so strangely?"

Her voice and presence blanked out the raucous carnival noises and moil of people. He was alone with her in the moon-tinted night. He tenderly imprisoned her white hands in the cups of his huge palms. He felt them flutter and twitch and cuddle like doves in love, in heat. They stood there speechless, swaying drunkenly for a long moment.

He whispered in dulcet Sicilian, "I follow you and look at you in this wild way because I fear to lose sight of you. I need you. I will not live without you. I have been alone searching for you, dreaming about you since my mother and sister

24

went to Heaven when I was six years old. I love you, angel . . . saint of my dreams. I want you to be my wife."

She tore her eyes away to the sawdust and escaped her hands. The snakepit world of people and reality crashed through the shattered spell.

Her bottom lip quivered uncontrollably as she laughed and said flippantly, "Marry you? I don't even know your name." She paused with her eyes dancing mischievously. "Is it Jack the Ripper?"

He frowned annoyance. "I'm Jimmy Collucci. You?"

She moved away a bit and glanced over her shoulder toward the street. "Olivia Tonelli and it's been pleasant meeting you, Jimmy."

Some familiar reference to her last name snagged on his memory. He moved close to her and saw the large vein at the pit of her white throat balloon.

"Beautiful, what I told you . . . I was serious as hell."

She glanced over her shoulder again. "It's Olivia. Remember? Don't be serious, Jimmy."

"Why?" he asked.

The tip of her valentine tongue stumbled nervously across her confection lips. "For several good reasons," she said with an unconvincing quaver in her voice.

He lifted his eyes from a slow deliberate scanning of her upturned face. He looked past her and saw a heavy-set guy step from a new black Lincoln sedan across the street. "Heavy Set" lumbered up a cobblestone walkway to the front door of a brownstone house.

"Like for instance?" Collucci's strangely lupine eyes narrowed as he watched the heavy-set guy cross the street and stride into the carnival lot.

She said, "Like for instance, I'm too young to be anybody's wife. Or should I say slave?"

He frowned and said in Sicilian, "Look at my jewelry, my clothes. Do I look like a penniless 'Mustache Pete' fresh off the boat? See! The corners of your mouth quiver at this moment for my kisses."

She bit her bottom lip and shook her head, "You're crazy. You . . . it's impossible. I can't marry you."

He made a sound deep in his throat and continued in caressful Sicilian. "So, you heavenly cock teaser, you will date me a coupla times. Then I guarantee the secret fire in your heart and between your thighs will burn only for Jimmy Collucci. Test me. You'll marry me."

She blushed and said with a little-girl whine of helpless confusion, "Please! Don't say things like that. Respect me . . . Let me . . ."

She glanced back at the heavy-set guy coming through the crowd, aiming his seamed face at her.

Collucci said in English, "Your old man?"

She shook her head. "No, his chauffeur." She touched her fingertips lightly against Collucci's hands and said softly, "My father thinks I'm . . . well, at least two years away from dates with boys. Besides, I won't be available. He's sending me to a fancy girls' school out East with a twenty-foot wall just to keep hot fast talkers like you out."

She lowered her eyes and said, "I'm sorry, nice

Jimmy Collucci."

She turned and walked quickly away.

He bellowed his despair and loss at her back, "Olivia! I'm here with the carnival for a week. Come back soon, Angel Doll. I gotta see you again. Okay?"

She stopped for a pounding instant and smiled over her shoulder. Her blue eyes gazed at him dreamily as her lips mutely said, "Maybe."

He didn't take his eyes off her until the heavy-set guy disappeared her away in the Lincoln. And for the next three nights he haunted the carnival where he had never worked, hoping she'd come. Then hollow-eyed he dragged to bed, tossing sleeplessly until daybreak, raging and cursing her for letting him know she existed.

On the fourth evening, the Lincoln came. She got out and went into the brownstone house where, as it turned out, lived a sick relative that she visited. To Collucci it seemed like forever. But within ten minutes she came across the carnival lot to him with her hair like a golden banner flying joy, flying love!

They concealed their affair from Joe Tonelli. And Collucci concealed from Olivia the strong street rumor that her father was underboss to the top boss Louis Bellini. And of course he concealed from Olivia the grisly proof he witnessed with his own eyes that Joe Tonelli was one of the Mafioso.

Collucci got his confirmation the first night he set foot on the grounds of the Tonelli estate in suburban Oak Park and Olivia Tonelli gifted him with her precious maidenhead.

Since their first meeting two months before in June they had spent countless hours cooing love and banter on the telephone. Many times during this period Olivia, dropped off by the chauffeur, would meet Collucci in the cool balconies of movie theaters to enjoy deep tongue kissing and to fondle themselves into a state of near nervous collapse.

Finally Olivia would look at the radium dial of her wristwatch and flee to the black Lincoln gleaming outside the theater. Collucci would follow and watch the chauffeur take Olivia away again.

Collucci would reluctantly take his iron hard-on and blow the achey pressure in his balls into one of a dozen young girls waiting eagerly to receive it.

Finally Olivia and Collucci found themselves together in the guest bungalow behind Joe Tonelli's mansion on a night when he was out of town.

The servants were off and the estate apparently had only the usual two resident guards in the mansion, plus three killer Dobermans guarding the rear of the estate, that Olivia had locked in the basement.

Collucci had slipped through a ten-foot-high steel gate, unlocked by Olivia, to the bungalow. Soon they lay nude, face to face, kissing and fondling. For the first time he put his shaft between her thighs. She squeezed herself around it and rubbed its heady gristle against her stiffening little dingus.

In the midst of their ferocious tonguing and wild bumping and grinding in the slippery creaming frenzy, she groaned, "Jimmy, I lied on the phone, and I feel so whorish and ashamed. I wanted . . . to give you my . . . cherry. Don't hurt me. Don't be rough. But please Sweet Jimmy Collucci, take it now, it's yours. I might die before I reach eighteen."

He started to protest and she muzzled his mouth with her palm.

"Don't speak. Take it!"

He obeyed her wish with exquisite tenderness.

When he left the bungalow hours later, he saw a sliver of light flash from a root cellar door in a far corner of the deserted grounds. Curiosity pressed his eyes against the rotted-out crack in the door. At first he thought the two young guys laughing and joking around in Sicilian were undressing a realistic clothing store mannequin. But it had a weirdly familiar face that seemed splashed or daubed with red paint. It lay hideously realistic on a table covered with sheets of tar paper dripping scarlet.

He almost cried out in shock and betrayed his presence. He realized the thing on the table had been likeable Tarantino, a wholesale grocer!

Then he saw one of them sawing off sections of arms and legs while the other guy rolled the sawed-off parts into neat tar paper packages.

Collucci ear trapped enough of the rapid Sicilian chitchat to learn the guys planned to mail the packages to friends and relatives of their butchered enemy as grim warning from Tonelli. He puked all the way to his car until his guts dry locked.

Collucci led Olivia to believe he was on the legit

as part owner of the carnival where they first met. He concealed from Olivia the fact that he was leader of a hot car ring.

Mafioso Frank Cocio, behind the scenes, controlled Collucci, a non-member, in the operation of the stolen car ring. And Collucci concealed his affair with Olivia Tonelli from Cocio, who adored even the ground that Olivia walked on.

Olivia told Collucci that she was frightened by the naked lust and desire in Cocio's eyes for her.

The grotto-garden lights that reflected on the frosted windows in the Collucci bedroom suddenly snuffed out and moved Jimmy Collucci from his reverie of Olivia.

He wasn't alarmed as he saw it was five A.M. The spotlights came on at that same instant he told himself that it was Henrietta, the live-in maid and cook. She lived in quarters above the five-car row of garages on the other side of the garden. She often accidentally pulled the wrong switch on the service porch off the kitchen, downstairs.

Now he faintly heard her clattering pans and her resonant humming of a Christmas carol as she started breakfast for the Colluccis.

Collucci glanced at Olivia's sleeping form and sprang out of bed. He went to the windows overlooking the garden and noticed that the white stone duplex at the edge of the garden, shared by bachelor Lollo Stilotti and married Angelo Serelli, was completely darkened. He wondered if they would have Bone ready for trial before he went to early Christmas Mass with Olivia and their ten-year-old son Petey.

Collucci and Olivia had not missed this Mass together in thirty years. Olivia and Petey always in devout sincerity, Collucci always as ritual camouflage for his secret atheism, and in that fiercely respectable "role play" of Mafiosi with families.

Naked Collucci jogged his steel spring shadow on the frosted bedroom windows for fifteen minutes. Then he stretched out on the carpet and did fifty pushups. His wide chest was dewy with sweat but heaving smoothly when he finished his daily morning exercise.

He took his pajamas to the hamper in the mirrored bathroom off the bedroom. He sat on the stool smoking and reading intently a long article in the *Tribune*.

The article posed the question: "Are the Mafia Families in large cities across America attempting now in the Seventies to eliminate Black, Cuban and Puerto Rican competition and regain a total narcotics monopoly?"

Collucci smiled grimly as he read on about narcotics history that he had experienced. And he was determined to make history himself despite Tonelli and Cocio.

He rose and flushed the commode. He stood and watched serpents of blood wiggle down the hole with his stool. *Pressure!* he thought, *I got Taylor and his fucking mob of Warriors stacked on top of the Cocio and Tonelli grief. I've gotta put the cocksuckers to sleep soon.*

He showered and stood terryclothed before a

mirror. He razored away a graying cave of blue-black stubble inside the deep cleft in his strong chin. *That cleft*, he mused, *is my Kirk Douglas cunt catcher.*

He thought about his upcoming urgent meeting the next day with Tonelli and underboss Cocio at the fifty-story Tonelli penthouse fortress. He was almost certain he was being summoned to be told that the bosses had made a decision to end the Family's involvement in the narcotics business.

A smug little smile flickered across his mouth at the thought that he had anticipated the Family's narcotics pullout a year before.

Fuck the bosses, he thought. He, with the help of other relatively young Family turks would bury the bosses and the niggers and build a billion-dollar drug business.

How? Simple, he thought, with carefully established networks of "mules" to bring it into the States. And his "Italian Connection" would refine his bountiful supply of raw opium from his "Iranian Connection." The refinery would be a licensed pharmaceutical house which he would secretly control in the near future. It would be protected by high government officials who would share in the profits.

He slapped after-shave lotion on his lean jaw and mulled the state of affairs.

Olivia would be Tonelli's only heir to his material wealth. He would fall heir apparent to the Tonelli and Cocio mob power and prestige if he exterminated them in a manner that left him beyond the suspicions of the National Commission of ruling Mafiosi, of which Tonelli was a most respected member.

Collucci's mouth drooped in a bitter half smile. Even after that he would face a problem. Consuella Bugatta, an Italian aristocrat, beautiful but broke, and her infant twin girls lived with Tonelli in the penthouse. Love-whacked Tonelli was certain to marry her when her divorce was finalized in the early coming spring.

His odd yellow-tinted green eyes hardened in the mirror. Olivia's old man would have to be put to sleep before spring. Collucci would put a thousand people to sleep to realize his dream.

He was leaving the bathroom when he heard Petey's excited voice at the Christmas tree downstairs, opening one of his mountain of presents. The rest were to be opened after he returned from early Christmas Mass.

He went into the bedroom and got into bed. Tenderly he kissed Olivia's eyes open. She looked into his eyes for a long moment before kissing him and embracing him warmly.

"Merry Christmas. I love you," they chorused together and laughed merrily. He opened his nightstand drawer and gave Olivia her major present, an extravagant diamond bracelet from Peacock's. Olivia squealed with joy and smothered him with new kisses.

Collucci left the bed to go downstairs to get his own thrills. Every Christmas he would stand back and watch Petey's radiant happiness to see the rainbow of treasure boxes beneath the tree. And he would remember how bleak Christmas usually was in the countless foster homes when he was a child.

The phone rang and stopped Collucci at the bedroom doorway. He looked right into Olivia's eyes as he went to the nightstand and lifted the receiver. He listened to Angelo tell him in code that Bone was secured in the big combination garage and storage barn behind the roadhouse, and he would come within the hour to take the Colluccis to church.

Collucci said, "Yes," and avoided Olivia's eyes as he cradled the receiver.

Olivia said in a low voice, "What the hell was that?"

He said with a faint frown of irritation, "Business."

She sprang out of the bed nude, her long trim body twanging emotion. "What kind of business on Christmas morning, Jimmy?"

"Your father's business," he said sharply.

"Baloney! Rubber Dick!" she spat.

His face congealed into a hard leering mask. He darted his hand through the front of his robe and jerked out his long limp organ.

He waggled it violently before her captive eyes, and jabbered in Sicilian, "Suck it! Suck it! You old-fashioned hung-up bitch. Everybody on this planet sucks. I'd lay big odds even your goddamn precious Pope sucks. Here! I'll choke you blue with its hardness."

He turned away and flung over his shoulder, "Olivia, mind your own fucking business. I'm your boss. Don't quiz me again."

She seized the back of his robe belt and ripped it

from his middle. He whirled and glared venomously at her. His fists were knotted clubs shaking at his sides.

"Hit me! Hit me!" she exploded. "You blasphemous filthy bastard pervert. For twenty years you have brought the stink of your black whores into my house. My legs are still sexy, my ass firm and round to excite the eyes and hands of a handsome lover. To hell with my church vows! I'll squeal like a horny sow in my lover's arms."

Collucci lunged across the carpet at her with his long powerful fingers clawing air. She recoiled from his fearsome face and sank to the floor when her knees buckled. He hurled himself down on her. He vised her shoulders with his hands. His biceps writhed and lumped against the terrycloth as he shook her like a doll. Then he banged her head against the carpet until her eyes clouded.

He stuck his face against her shock-dampened face and shouted in a whisper, "Take it back! Take it back! All of it!"

She gasped, "Jimmy, please! I didn't mean any of it. You know I wouldn't let another man know me. Please let me go!"

Collucci released his crushing grip on her shoulders and said in a low deadly voice, "You realize that Petey will lose his mother? That I will put you to sleep if I ever catch you unfaithful?"

She nodded frantically with blue eyes enormous.

Collucci went on savagely, "You understand that you're going right down to the gray ass, saggy tit finish like with me?"

She nodded again, frantically.

Collucci was getting to his feet when he heard Petey sobbing behind him. He quickly reached out to help Olivia to her feet as he shot a look over his shoulder.

Petey, clutching a monstrous wedge of whipped cream-topped coffee cake, stood in the bedroom doorway. Sparkly tears flowed from his big eyes, blue and tragic. A wet web stained the front of his red bunny pajamas.

Collucci rushed to the boy and lifted him as tenderly as a mother comforting her new baby.

"Petey, Petey, don't cry any more. Livvy and Daddy were only play acting. Look at Livvy smiling. See, she's not hurt or mad," Collucci said in a gentle voice.

"We were fighting just like the game we have played together. Remember? You would hit me with a strong punch and Daddy would play knocked silly?"

Collucci sat down on the bed beside Olivia with his considerable burden. While he rocked Petey in his arms, Petey swung his eyes to and fro between the fake togetherness beaming on the faces of his parents.

Finally Petey's eyes were dry and he was chattering gaily about Christmas. And shortly they all started to dress for church.

Angelo pulled up at the curb as throngs of worshippers were going into the triple-steepled old church. Collucci, riding beside Angelo, touched his wrist lightly and got out himself to open the car door for Olivia and Petey.

After he helped Olivia to the street, she raised her lips. As he pressed his lips against hers, she whispered through her teeth, "Happy, happy with her, Rubber Dick," and knifed his bottom lip with the sharp edge of her upper front teeth. She moved toward the church.

He helped Petey from the car, squeezed him close and whispered huskily, "I love you, Petey boy. Light a candle and say a rosary for your old man."

Petey kissed Collucci's mouth and said, "Sure. Wanta know two big secrets?"

Collucci nodded.

"I love you, Daddy dear. I'm very very glad you and Livvy were only play fighting. Hurry home please so we can play with my toys like every Christmas, will ya?"

Collucci squeezed Petey close and said gently, "I'll be home before noon. That's a promise, Petey."

Petey sprinted away after his Livvy.

The Caddie was only a half-mile from the roadhouse before Angelo broke the heavy silence. "Mr. Collucci, I oughta . . ."

Collucci cut him off. "Start over, and remember you don't call me Mr. anything. Angelo, you've been my best friend for forty years, so when none of the others are around you can call me 'Lupo' even."

They laughed together at the sound of Collucci's kid gang moniker.

Angelo said, "Jimmy, what I was gonna say . . .

Maybe on the eight kilos, Mack Rivers is makin' Bone the patsy for some reason . . . and some kinda way . . . Rivers is slick and tricky . . . Maybe if it comes out Rivers conned him . . . you could give Bone a break. He . . ."

Angelo was cut off from a further mercy plea for Bone by the grim expression on Collucci's face.

Collucci said, "Angelo, forget it! Bone was dead yesterday. Mack Rivers told me a Mexican broad was dealing pure coke on Sixty-third Street. That was three days after those jigaboo dope jackers muscled Mack and Bone while they were delivering the eight kilos to Southside wholesalers.

"Rivers is old and already nigger rich, as they say. That punch-drunk jack-off was getting paid to protect Rivers and the merchandise. Bone used my trust to tear me off . . . that was dirty . . . So, I put him to sleep dirty."

Collucci stared sternly at Angelo and intoned, "*Capisce?*"

Angelo said, "Sure, Jimmy, I understand . . . He should get the worst."

Collucci continued. "Believe me, old friend, every guy and broad that you have to put to sleep is really the guilty, responsible one. No pun intended, but I've convinced myself to the bone that it is and will always be the goddamn stupid bastard who is slain and not his slayer who bears all guilt and responsibility."

CHAPTER THREE

Bone's sister Mayme, exotic dancer and secret priestess of Voudoo, leaped awake in her apartment atop Mack Rivers' Voudoo Palace. Her gray cat eyes were wide in the elfish black face. Had she heard screams of terror through the funky pound of the jukebox downstairs where Mack Rivers was throwing a private party? Or had the sounds been the keening voices of the Loas, her Voudoo Gods?

Mayme heard someone stumbling up her back stairway leading to the cabaret. Someone banged on her back door. She slid out of bed and went and opened it on chain.

Mayme peered out at ebonic Mack Rivers. His arms were loaded with presents. His lemon suit, shirt and shoes were a noisy symphony draped on his cadaverous frame. His long head was swathed in bandages. He and his chauffeur-bodyguard, Love Bone, had four days before been pistol-whipped and robbed by killer bandits, known throughout Chicagoland as the dope jackers.

Rivers pushed his gullied face against the door crack and flashed his solid gold grin. "Merry Christmas, Lady Fine Frame."

Mayme recoiled from gusts of rank whiskey breath. She wrinkled her nose and said almost pleasantly, "Merry Christmas, Mack." Then she said sharply, "Why the hell did you wake me up?"

Rivers flinched. He sweet-talked, "So I could give the beautifulest lady on the Southside all this pretty stuff . . . lemme in!"

Mayme said, "Mack, I thought we had an understanding . . . I will accept from you only my weekly salary as star and producer of the shows downstairs."

Rivers' bloodshot eyes narrowed. "Why? . . . 'cause I ain't young? . . . or maybe 'cause I ain't white?"

Mayme slit-eyed him and thought, *The time is here to put old Baboon Face in his permanent place.*

She said wearily, "Mack, you're not the worst, I guess . . . but you're a damn fool to dream you could hook Mayme Flambert to that daisy chain of chippies you abuse in that bedroom downstairs."

His fat bottom lip quivered, "You cold-blooded black bitch, lemme in there or I'll fire you!"

Mayme laughed in his face, "Mack, you're full of shit. The owner . . . the real owner told me a week after I started that only he could fire me. Which means you are only fronting as owner of the Palace, right, Mack?"

Rivers' face ashened. "Mr. Collucci ain't told you no motherfuckin' lie like that!"

Then Rivers stared into Mayme's amused eyes for a long moment before the truth hit him.

He staggered back with fearful eyes. "Mr. Collucci fuckin' you?"

Mayme said, "No! But he's still trying. So get out of my face and stay out, Mack. Maybe I can get you fired without Mr. Collucci having me . . . You think I don't know my shows pull, into the Palace, more big white spenders than any black cabaret in Southside history?"

She started to ease the door shut in Rivers' face.

He screamed, "Mr. Collucci ain't gonna take no! I hope he rapes you with a baseball bat—rolled in barbed wire!"

Mayme slammed the door shut and went to a front window. She looked down on bleak Forty-seventh Street. She felt frigid wings of danger and death flutter up her spine.

Mayme remembered how her friends, the all-knowing Voodoo Spirits, had banshee'd alarm to her about her brother the year before in the mountains of Haiti. She had rushed to Chicago to save Bone from nearly fatal exploitation in the fight game by manager James Collucci and trainer Angelo Serelli. They had, too quickly, thrown Bone into the canvas pit with a tigerish World's heavyweight contender. She had only napped for a week in a chair at Bone's bedside. Before he came out of coma, she had stood up to Collucci and forced Bone's retirement from the ring.

Mayme moved toward the double-locked steel-barred walk-in closet that served as her temple. She unlocked the door and swung it open.

She paused at the threshold and gazed into the murk of the temple. It was lit by a red bulb inside the shriveled head of a mad witch doctor. The head was shrouded with layers of webbing spun by a black widow spider nesting inside it. The head sat on a small altar covered with the skin of its owner. This scarf was fringed with the spines of cobras.

Her lips shaped a cold little smile as she remembered how the maroon eyes had oscillated inside the living head that steamy summer afternoon long ago in the mountains in Haiti. She had pulled her body, already lushly rounded at twelve years of age, from a cool pond. She remembered standing naked and spellbound in the stare and caress of the most feared of all sorcerers, *Poteau!*

His toothless mouth gibbered excitement as it explored her incredibly unique sex nest.

That very night Poteau had visited the family hut. Mayme remembered the shocked eyes of her parents in his awful presence. Poteau claimed that in the past the Flambert hut had been protected against demons and death only by Poteau himself. Poteau's soul had suffered an invasion of love for Mayme. Soon Poteau's soul would be seized and tortured by demons unless they gave him Mayme for his wife. Only this gift would prove their good faith necessary to continue Poteau's gift of protection.

Now, again, Mayme saw her father's defiant eyes as he refused Poteau's request in his polite peasant manner. He threw Poteau from the hut when Poteau tried to seize Mayme and escape into the night.

Poteau screamed curses on the Flambert hut until daybreak.

On a late afternoon only a week later, Mayme and four-year-old Larry returned to the hut from Port-au-Prince where they sold trinkets made by their parents to tourists. They found their parents dead at a clawed-out hole in the hut wall. Their fingertips were shredded and bloodied. Their parents' faces were frozen hideous with terror. Poteau had apparently conjured up a spectacle of such horror that the elder Flamberts had been frightened to death.

Mayme and baby brother Larry fled into the most desolate depths of the mountains. They lived in the trees and caves with wild birds and animals who befriended and warned them when Poteau was about.

One afternoon in the third summer, they fled deep into a secret network of caves to elude Poteau. It was the home of the Queen of Voudoo, Bhaleur, the most esteemed and powerful of all priestesses. Ancient Bhaleur wept at the sight of their pitiful neglect and vowed to protect them against Poteau.

Bhaleur nourished them and taught them the three R's by candlelight. Bhaleur began to reveal the secrets of Voudoo to Mayme on her fifteenth birthday.

Bhaleur died shortly thereafter. She was said to be one hundred and forty years old at her death.

Mayme won esteem and power as a priestess of Voudoo at the age of twenty-five.

Larry blossomed into a black Apollo, renowned for his prowess as a fistfighter in the alleys of Port-au-Prince. The peasants dubbed him "Love Bone" because his sugary persuasion was fatal to maidenheads for miles around.

One afternoon Larry almost killed, in a brawl, the most feared street fighter in Port-au-Prince over a Haitian sexpot. Tourist Mario Rizzio, James Collucci's cousin and employee, was mesmerized by Larry's granite physique and ferret reflexes. Over the years Collucci had failed a half-dozen times to develop a fighter who could win the heavyweight crown.

Mayme respected the warning of the Voudoo Spirits that Larry's legion of enemies planned to trap him and lop off his love bone. So she gave her blessing to Larry's departure for Chicago for Collucci's evaluation.

Mayme remembered the ecstatic day of revenge on her thirtieth birthday. She let feeble old Poteau fondle the bait of his death trap. Then with his own machete, she cut his throat and beheaded him beside a mountain pool. Ironically, it was the same where Poteau had abused her as a child.

Now in her closet temple, Mayme chanted and hurled powder into an urn that burst indigo fire to summon the Loas. Her hand blurred as she repeatedly stabbed a dagger into the eye sockets of Poteau's skull.

Mayme stripped and placed the urn on the bedroom floor. She humped and belly danced around it until her sweat-glistened body reflected the blue flame.

Suddenly she groaned ecstatically. She collapsed and lay panting on the floor. Her thighs quivered violently in orgasmic release.

She stiffened and sat up as she heard the satin whispering of the Voudoo Spirits rise to shrill chanting: *"Larry's lost! Study the entrails of a beast! Larry's lost! Study the entrails of a beast!"*

Mayme went to the phone and called Bone's apartment. She listened as it rang unanswered. She hung up and felt guilty because she had half expected him to answer after the Loas' notice of Larry's death. She called Central Police Headquarters and the City Morgue. *No Larry!*

She heard hubbub on the street. She went to the front window and watched Mack Rivers' guests start to spill out to the sidewalk.

The two dozen or so guests were the Southside numbers bankers and their bank managers with their women. These bankers were under the protection and control of Mafia enforcer James Collucci.

Mayme left the window and went to a giant tomcat glaring at her from its cage in the bathroom. She baby talked the cat as she reached behind her back and gripped the butcher knife she would use to disembowel the beast. She must read its entrails as commanded by her beloved Voudoo Spirits.

Downstairs in the Palace, Mack Rivers beamed his crooked little smile on the last of his guests and locked the door. He stood at the door glass watching several smile and wave back from their flashy machines as they gunned away.

Chumps! he thought, *they ain't never gonna*

wake up that Old Mack fingered them and their banks to the Mafia. Mr. Collucci fucks them for sixty percent off the top. Old Mack, the genius and president of the chumps' organization, gets a freebie pass to run his own bank.

CHAPTER FOUR

Angelo drove down an unpaved driveway past Collucci's darkened Sweet Dream Roadhouse. He stopped at a rambling barnlike building a hundred yards behind the roadhouse. Phil and Stilotti rolled back wide doors. Angelo eased the Caddie into the dim building.

They got out of the Caddie. The four of them stood talking in low voices. The bright eyes of the Mexican girl stared at them from the open trunk of Phil's Pontiac. They walked to a far corner of the building. They stood in a semi-circle before Bone. The only light in the big barn was a yellow glow from the parking lights on an old truck near Bone.

Bone was naked, gagged and bound to a metal office chair with baling wire. His eyes stared up at Collucci. He made grunty noises behind the gag.

Collucci was dressed all in black right down to a black turtleneck sweater. He stood with his hands jammed into his overcoat pockets. He studied Bone with a blank face for a long moment.

Collucci's three underlings all watched Collucci's face for the subtle signals that would be flashed there. Collucci was a past master at this kind of fatal choreography.

Collucci raised his right eyebrow slightly. Angelo stooped and removed the gag. Bone coughed and opened his mouth to speak. Collucci glared at him and flung his palm into the air like a Nazi salute to silence Bone.

Collucci said softly, "Where are the eight kilos?"

Bone's mouth gaped open. He stuttered, "Co . . . co . . . come on now, Mr. Collucci, don't do me like this. You know I told you the truth about them kilos."

Collucci smiled thinly and winked his right eye. Phil and Angelo quickly left the scene. Stilotti shucked out of his overcoat and Bone's eyes were trapped by a glittery apron of knives around the Surgeon's middle.

Angelo and Phil came back and unloaded Bone's girlfriend and the four kilos, plastic wrapped, on the floor before Bone. Bone swung his eyes from her to the kilos of cocaine. Bubbles of sweat popped out on his face.

Collucci stroked his index finger across his right cheek. Angelo, wearing brass knuckles, took a step toward Bone and their eyes met. Angelo cocked back his arm. But he hesitated, bit his lip, shot a look at Collucci who raised his eyebrows. Angelo clenched his teeth and smashed his fist against the side of Bone's face. The brass gouged a red rill from chin to ear lobe. Bone's face was a fright mask of hate. His mass of muscle corded and puffed against the baling wire.

He screamed up at Angelo, "You cunt wop, stinking motherfucker!"

Collucci nodded at Phil. Phil stepped in close and like an unhorsed picador grunted and plunged an icepick to the hilt into Bone's upper thigh muscles and spun away leaving it buried. The shock of the thrust relaxed Bone's angry face to childlike awe. He stared down at the icepick handle.

Collucci said casually, "Look at me, Bone. Look at your good friend that you double-crossed."

Bone raised his glowing eyes and his head shivered a spray of sweat.

Bone stammered, "I ain't . . . double-crossed . . . uh . . ."

Collucci widened his eyes in threat to cut Bone off and said softly, "Where are the other four kilos?"

Bone licked his grayish tongue across his lips and dipped his head. He said with a quaver, "You ain't gonna let them fuck with me no more?"

Collucci shook his head.

Bone blurted, "Mr. Collucci, I been doing my own secret thing on them bastards that heisted me and Mack Rivers. I Dick Tracy'd to one of 'em and copped back four kilos. I kicked the shit outta him and he put the finger on a young dude they call Charming Mills."

Bone shook his head mournfully at the cruel irony of it all. "Mr. Collucci, I was gonna run Mills down and them other kilos. All your stuff woulda been safe back in your hands before the New Year."

Collucci shot a look at his men. His mouth exploded a scornful laugh. Stilotti, with surgical knife in hand, stepped in and scalpeled off Bone's right earlobe. The lobe fell and glistened in Bone's crotch hair. He gazed down at it with mouth agape.

Collucci said, "Bullshit! I've got mug shots of most of the Warriors. Mills is one of them. Taylor executes them if they don't immediately destroy all narcotics they confiscate."

Bone said, "Yeah . . . but lemme . . ."

"Where are the four kilos?" Collucci intoned.

Bone strained forward against the wire across his chest and said, "I ain't lying. Taylor don't know Mills is doing his side thing with a gang of dope jacking pushers. They already killed over twenty dope dealers all over the state. You got to be dealing their dope or paying them two bills a day to deal your own dope . . . if you don't wanta die."

"How do you know they aren't all Warriors?" Collucci said.

Bone said, "I know the rest ain't Warriors 'cause Warriors don't kill no outside black people, and no poor people at all."

Collucci glanced down at his feet and nodded at Angelo and said, "Where can I put my hands on Mills and the four kilos?"

Bone swallowed and bit his lip. Angelo pulled back his right leg and kicked Bone in the side. Bone swayed his head, closed his eyes and groaned.

Collucci said, "Bone, you got a terrible memory. You told me a moment ago you were going to bag Mills and check in the kilos by New Year's Day."

Bone gazed down at the blood oozing down his

chest from his wounded ear into a gooey pool between his thighs. He had a seizure of bellowed retching.

Collucci stared down at the girl. Her pink dress was wrinkled, stained and soggy with urine and feces. Phil and Stilotti removed her gag.

She spurted words. "Sir, the black bastard lied to you. He lied to me. He never meant to give the stuff to you. I sold many, many fifty-dollar bags from the kilos for him. Please! Please let me go back to my mama and baby in San Antonio. I will keep my silence about everything."

Collucci said, "You think Bone is a Warrior?"

She said, "No, too much pig for dope and *punta.*"

Collucci shrugged and said, "Where can I find Mills and the four kilos?"

She wailed, "Please! Let me clean myself and give me one day and I will find Mills for you."

Collucci closed his eyes, shook his head and pursed his lips. Angelo stooped and re-gagged her.

Bone surged in the chair with excitement and the killer instinct he'd had in the ring. He noticed that a section of the wire strung across his chest was rusted thin between his right chest and right bicep. They had used one long piece of the wire to quickly tie him into the chair while he was still groggy.

He stole a glance at a vertical section of the truck's front bumper, just two feet away. If he could tilt the chair and fall forward at exactly the right angle he could snag the weak section of wire on the bumper and snap it with his two hundred and fifty pounds.

His arms and hands would be instantly freed.
They were not tied together, but against the back
of the chair by the same half-dozen strands
criss-crossing his chest. The wire around his
sweat-greased feet he was certain he could slip or
snap with his hands in the blink of an eye. His
heart boomed at the thought that before they
killed him he'd get a chance to spill some of their
blood.

Collucci said, "Bone, I want Mills and the kilos."

Bone closed his eyes, flopped his head from side
to side and said weakly, "Mr. Collucci, it's . . . so
hard . . . for me to hear. I feel . . . fun . . . ny. I
need . . . a croaker."

Collucci looked at Phil, who dangled a cigarette
from his lips. Collucci brushed his index and
middle fingers across his lips and dipped his head at
Bone.

Phil grinned and stuck the fiery cigarette tip into
Bone's ear. Bone cried out and reared against the
wire. He tilted the chair toward the bumper and
balanced it for an instant on two front legs. He
scraped his toenails against the concrete for a bit of
thrust. He plunged down toward the bumper.

He heard the wire zing when it snagged on the
bumper. He heard it snap and uncoil from his chest
and arms. He crashed to the concrete. With
flesh-peeling violence he jerked his feet free of the
wire. He kicked up into Phil's crotch and collapsed
him into a half-conscious heap.

He ducked his head down as Stilotti chopped a
knife at his throat. Stilotti slashed his forehead to

the bone. The buried iceprick in his thigh made a sucking sound when Bone jerked it out and scrambled unsteadily to his feet.

Bone felt a sharp stinging sensation on his neck and back. He whirled and through a fog of blood flowing from his forehead saw Stilotti's hand holding a knife high to hack him again. He sighted for Stilotti's temple and rammed the icepick at it. Stilotti slipped in a puddle of Bone's blood. As he fell backward the point of the icepick went into Stilotti's cheek and punched out under his ear.

Bone heard an explosion behind him. He felt a blow like a sledgehammer against his shoulder that knocked him violently against a wall. He turned and through a wavy red mist saw Angelo fumbling with a jammed automatic. Beyond Angelo he saw Collucci pull his magnum pistol from its shoulder holster.

He hurled himself blindly at Angelo's throat, but found his hands clutching Angelo's face. He hooked the fingers of his hands into the corners of Angelo's mouth and ripped the corners loose into the cheeks.

He hopped on one leg and rushed Collucci's vague shadow in slow motion. He saw orange fireflies in the distance. His bloody face grinned as he fell to his knees and thought, he'd sure as hell top all the liars in the barber shop on Forty-seventh Street. He'd throw them his true tale about the fireflies that flashed miles away and at the same instant knocked him flat on his ass.

Bone knelt like an ebony buddha on the concrete. Flaps of flesh hung from his blood-soaked body. Collucci, standing over him, with gun in hand heard the Bone mumble his last words, "Mayme! Mayme darling! They kilt your baby brother!"

Collucci turned away and glared at his wounded and bloody troops moaning in a cluster beside the truck. "You careless, stupid bastards almost committed suicide. Phil, you feel in shape to drive yourself and those two to our doctor?"

Phil nodded and pressed his hands tightly against his crotch as he hobbled toward Collucci. Phil swept his eyes across Bone and his girlfriend, who had rolled beneath a dilapidated table.

He waved an arm and said, "What about this? Her?"

Collucci slashed an index finger across his throat and said, "Before you leave."

Phil said, "Up there with them?" He tossed his head towards the secret graveyard two miles beyond the barn on a wooded hill.

Collucci thought for a moment and said, "What was the layout where you picked her up?"

Phil said, "A three-room dump off an alley on Division Street. Condemned houses on both sides of her building."

Collucci said, "Bone was a notorious cock mechanic. Call Freddie and Marty before you leave and tell them to scrub this joint and plant Bone and the broad in her bed tonight. I can get it on the record and into the papers as an ordinary double murder by a jealousy-crazed undisclosed suspect, not apprehended. Let's get out of this stink."

Collucci locked up the building himself. Stilotti and Angelo had to be helped into Phil's Pontiac.

Collucci let Phil and himself into the roadhouse. While Collucci used the toilet, Phil called Freddie and Marty and gave them Collucci's message. Collucci went behind the bar and poured himself a glass of Courvoisier.

Phil said, "Freddie says Mack Rivers wants to talk to you. He has put together a cinch setup to hit Tit For Tat Taylor."

Collucci got Mack Rivers on the bar phone. He nodded and smiled as he listened.

Collucci hung up and Phil asked, "Who and how many guys should I round up? What kinda equipment, shotguns?"

Collucci said, "Phil, you nuts? You think I'd let anybody share the pleasure of putting that cocksucker to sleep? Get me a fine-scoped rifle before the twenty-eighth of December."

Phil nodded and went toward the door.

He turned and said, "Lollo and Angelo are pretty bad. What if the croaker says they gotta have a hospital. The cops . . . ?"

Collucci cut in. "I'm going straight from here for some of Hilda's blueberry pancakes on Kedsie. Remember the joint? Then I've got to rush home to keep a promise to Petey. Any problems come up, call me."

Collucci followed him through the door and locked it. He watched Phil drive down the highway with Angelo and Stilotti. He got behind the wheel of his Caddie and sped toward Hilda's House of Pancakes.

Later in the early Christmas evening, Angelo, with his split cheeks bandaged, sipped coffee through a straw with Collucci. He insisted that he felt good enough to drive Collucci to his appointment with Joe Tonelli. But Collucci would have none of it and ordered Angelo to bed.

Collucci felt a persistent uneasiness about the meeting while dressing. He decided that he would try to persuade Olivia to go with him. She was propped up in the bed reading a book.

Collucci leaned over and kissed her forehead and said, "Doll, I'll have to drive myself to the penthouse. How about you and Petey going along to keep me company?"

She lay the book in her lap and smiled up at him, "I can't expose Petey again to that mob Papa invites every Christmas. Petey caught the flu up there last Christmas, and I have a raging headache."

Collucci said, "The old man is going to be very disappointed."

Olivia picked up her book and said, "He won't be. I called him and told him Petey and I were under par."

Collucci went into his closet and got twin double-barrelled derringers with lengths of elastic attached. He finished dressing in the bathroom and kissed Olivia and Petey good-bye.

CHAPTER FIVE

On the way to Tonelli's penthouse Collucci stopped the Caddie at a stoplight. He stared at a two-headed python ad, writhing and coiling in a fancy pet store window. *Cocio and Tonelli are human two-headed snakes*, he thought.

He pulled away and passed a honking caravan of wedding cars. He remembered his marriage to Olivia and how Joe Tonelli had tried to strike young Collucci out of Olivia's life before their marriage.

It had been just three days before Olivia was to leave for the exclusive girls' school in the East. He remembered lying in his bed on a dazzling September evening. He was childishly fantasizing the plunder of the Big Dipper pendant blazing in the midnight sky. He saw himself toss it casually at Olivia's feet as a going away gift so she couldn't forget him for one moment until they got married.

The phone rang and Olivia blurted out her loneliness, "Just come and hold me a little bit. Please come and stay a little while so I can go to sleep. Please! Sweet Jimmy Collucci!"

He said, "But your father is in town. How about a movie tomorrow?"

"I can't wait that long. Don't worry about Papa. He's busy playing host to a lot of his Old Country friends. They are having one of those wild drinking and gambling stag things in the front house. Hurry over! I'll lock the Dobermans in the basement and unlock the gate like the last time."

There was a long silence before Collucci chuckled and said, "Olivia, I should get help for my head." He hung up.

Collucci slipped clothes on over his pajamas and drove to a side street in Oak Park and parked his new nineteen thirty-eight Buick Limited. He went through the unlocked steel gate and into the bungalow.

Collucci did not know that a Tonelli bodyguard, clearing his head of too much vino on a bench near the bungalow, spotted him and rushed to notify Joe Tonelli.

Five minutes later Olivia grunted naked joy under Collucci's sweet punishment. Soon, under Collucci's deep strokings, Olivia's pleasure yowled the dog-fashioned shadows.

And seeing and hearing all through a tear in a drawn shade was Joe Tonelli. He waggled his head and his three button men followed him down the walk away from the peephole.

Collucci at that moment climaxed. After a moment he went to the bathroom. He stood relieving himself. He heard muffled voices beneath the partially open bathroom window. He peered out and saw Joe Tonelli's handsome features contorted into a mask of rage and hurt.

Collucci noticed two of the button men were the two young guys he had seen in the root cellar chopping up and packaging the body of grocer Tarantino.

Tonelli whispered in hoarse Sicilian, "That criminal raper of children must be punished for his crime against my daughter's innocence. You, Antonio, give me five minutes. Knock hard on the front door like a big emergency. You say I got a bad attack, big pain in my chest. She's got to come right away to my bedroom. I will be very sick. She will not be allowed to come back here to him.

"Emilio, Mario, Antonio, conceal yourselves and get him when he leaves."

One of the root cellar pair said, "Mr. Tonelli, should we . . . ?"

Tonelli waved his hands in disgust that Antonio had no perception of the need for less than fatal chastisement in the case at hand. "Antonio, we must not be too extreme in this matter."

He shrugged. "But she must be protected against her weakness for his filthy abuse. Break him up. You know, stomp his face and his private parts to jelly. Change him so all young girls will scream and flee at his approach.

"There is no trouble for me from my daughter. I knew nothing of the burglar discovered on my property. We must be very careful that no suspicion of me will shock her soft loving heart and harden it against me. Understand?"

Tonelli went down the walk and the others faded into the shadows. Collucci heard his heart pounding as he went and lay beside Olivia. He made his decision quickly. He wouldn't hide behind Olivia's skirt for safe conduct out of Tonelli's trap. He would say nothing about her father to hurt her.

He wasn't afraid of the button men because he knew he had a vital edge on them. They were handicapped. They had orders only to disfigure and cripple him.

But young Collucci's decision to ambush the ambushers rather than use Olivia to shield him from harm was really influenced by a deeply rooted terror of personal cowardice. Deadly danger always generated his reflex ferocity to attack, maim and destroy the enemy.

His fear of cowardice was tied in with his poisonous hatred for his father. Collucci lay embracing Olivia, waiting for Antonio to bang on the door.

As they lay there waiting for the knock, he trembled with emotion. As always in situations of personal danger, he remembered the awful cowardice of his father. His father's face, dripping sweat. He remembered the terror stink of his father's breath behind a barricaded door in the attic of the Collucci home.

His father held him in a death grip and muzzled his mouth. They listened to his mother and sister begging for mercy. Then he heard them screaming for help. The sex murderer hatcheted them into silence. And then worst of all, after their voices stilled, he heard the fiend grunting joy as he violated the dead. He saw his father feel his way down the attic stairs with his arms locked across his eyes against the carnage. He saw his father go out the front door and disappear forever.

He thought about his first foster home where he was burned with cigarettes and locked in the pitch-black basement for two days because he ate a sausage from the icebox without permission.

Antonio knocked. He patted Olivia to calm her. She said in a sharp voice, "Who is it?"

Antonio said loudly, "Antonio, Miss Tonelli, your father fights for breath in his bedroom and calls you."

Olivia went to the door and told Antonio she would come in a minute or two. She kissed Collucci good-bye with a promise they would meet at a downtown theater the next day.

Collucci was a blur of silent motion. He speed-dressed and chain-bolted front and back doors. He drew a giant kettle of scalding water. He found a nearly full half-gallon container of bleach. He emptied the bleach into the kettle with the water. He found a heavy industrial wrench under the kitchen sink.

He eased the front door open and stepped out on the front porch with the kettle. He threaded the end of a bath towel through one of the holes in the latticed walls enclosing the porch. He tied the kettle by its wire handle near the top of the porch roof.

He chinned himself to the roof and reached down and got the kettle. He went silently across the roof to the rear of the bungalow. He got on his belly. He peered over the rim of the roof at the three button men. They crouched among lilac bushes on both sides of the steps leading from the back porch. All three had baseball bats.

Mario, a muscular giant, on one side, Antonio and Emilio on the other side. He stood and hurled the scalding contents of the kettle down in a sweeping motion. The trio's screeches of pain reverberated in the night like mass murder.

In one motion he slipped the wrench from his belt and plunged down. Emilio and Antonio were screaming and scrambling out of the bushes. Emilio, fleeing the bushes behind Antonio, stumbled and fell on his knees on the lawn.

Collucci's rage was at its uncontrolled peak. He gripped the wrench with both hands. He raised it high above his head. He sighted for the top of Emilio's shiny skullcap of hair.

He growled for velocity and whistled the wrench down. Emilio's eyes were phosphorescent. He rolled to his side and flung his arm up to shield his head.

His elbow took the crunch of the steel blow and the arm burst blood and shards of bone. Collucci swung the wrench rapidly, breaking Emilio's wrist on his other arm and his right ankle.

Collucci saw Antonio fifteen feet away with a wicked-looking forty-five automatic in his hand. He waved it aimlessly as he frantically wiped the back of his other hand across his eyes to clear them of the scalding water.

The stench of Emilio's loosened bowels pulled a spurt of vomit from Collucci's guts. He leaped across the unconscious Emilio toward Antonio.

But, too late, he saw the shadow of Mario on his right swinging the baseball bat. The blow struck the wrench upraised at the side of Collucci's head.

The bat splintered and banged the wrench against the side of Collucci's head. His legs went rubbery for a moment. He viciously backhanded the wrench at Mario's throat and busted his jaw instead. Mario fell and rolled into the lilac bushes.

Collucci smashed down Antonio's gun arm as he was leveling it. The automatic skittered across the grass. Antonio, dangling his useless arm, bombed his foot at Collucci's crotch. The toe of his shoe sank into Collucci's navel and doubled him into a knot on the grass. Antonio rushed and snatched up the wrench with his good arm. He grunted as he brought it down. Collucci turned a saving fraction in time. He heard the whoosh and dull impact of the wrench against the grass.

Collucci reached up and seized Antonio's broken wrist. He twisted it and wrung it like a chicken's neck. Antonio's hand hung crookedly on tendons and skin. Antonio whimpered and staggered away toward the main house. Collucci got to his feet. He gripped the wrench and went in pursuit. Antonio screamed for help.

Olivia sat on the side of Joe Tonelli's bed stroking his temple. She heard the scream above the bedlam singing of an old Italian Army marching song.

She flipped the floodlight switch and saw the scene. Collucci was wild-eyed, chasing Antonio. Mario pussyfooted, thirty feet behind Collucci, gripping a length of lead pipe. Olivia screamed the house quiet. Tonelli's guests followed her to the yard.

Collucci knocked Antonio senseless. Mario was swinging the pipe down on Collucci's head when Olivia screamed, "Jimmy, behind you!"

Collucci threw himself forward and the pipe struck only a glancing blow. Collucci whirled and grappled with Mario. Mario fell and pinned Collucci to the ground with his great weight. He fumbled a stiletto from his pocket. He stabbed down at Collucci's throat. But the point missed and sank into the flesh above Collucci's collar bone.

Olivia flung herself over Collucci's face and chest and screamed, "Stop it, Mario! I love him! I love him!"

Louis Bellini snapped his fingers and a gang of his button men and bodyguards pulled Mario away. Joe Tonelli came slowly on a cane to the scene. He held his hand over his heart.

Olivia ran to him with tears flowing and sobbed, "Papa, they were trying to kill Jimmy Collucci. I love him. Papa, we're going to be married!"

Tonelli embraced her and patted her back. He released her and went, with a furious face, to Mario cowering in bewilderment.

Mario mumbled, "Mr. Tonelli, we thought he was a thief."

Tonelli flailed Mario's head and shoulders with the cane and shouted, "*Stupida!* You have hurt my daughter's innocent fiance."

Tonelli went and put an arm around Collucci. He turned to several of his men and said, "Take this boy to the finest hospital. He must have the best of everything. He's going to be my son-in-law. Understand?"

Louis Bellini chuckled and said, "That skinny kid has the balls to be important. Tonelli's guys look like a whole mob worked them over."

Then moments later Bellini stuck his head into the limousine about to pull away for the hospital and said softly to Collucci, "Jimmy Collucci . . . I like you. Are you Sicilian?"

Collucci nodded.

"What is your mother's maiden name?"

Collucci said, "Why?"

Bellini frowned and said, "I'll overlook your ignorance this time. But never ask Louis Bellini *why* again."

Collucci said, "I'm sorry. Her maiden name was Saietta."

The limousine pulled away. Collucci stayed in the hospital for a week.

On the sixth day Frank Cocio came into his room and said, "Congratulations, you are to marry Olivia Tonelli thirty days from today."

Then Cocio smiled. "Mr. Bellini wants you to join the Family. He told me to see that you make your bones. I have the guy you need in mind already."

Collucci said, "Who do I . . . ?"

Cocio grinned and said, "Bobo Librizzi," and went through the door.

Collucci lay in shock. His joy at the prospect of becoming a Mafioso wiped out as he wondered how he would manage to kill his friend.

And now, the recollection fading, Collucci glided the Caddie into Chicago's exclusive Gold Coast section. Refuge of the rich and the powerful.

Collucci sighed as he gazed up at Joe Tonelli's fifty-story apartment building. The crown jewel of his vast real estate holdings.

He swung the Caddie off the street to halt before the eye of an infra-red TV monitor. The monitor swept above a wide steel door at a ramp leading into Joe Tonnelli's private underground garage and elevator.

The steel door rolled up and the Caddie's headlamps spat light into the ramp's inky mouth. Shadows darted and leaped as the Caddie crooned down the ramp and into the tunnel. He drove into the brightly lit garage and parked.

Two guards, in shirtsleeves, waved from their gin rummy on the rear seat of a Tonelli limousine. He went across the concrete to the self-service elevator in the rear of the garage. He glanced up at the bulletproof dome jutting out above the elevator. He nodded to the machine gunner, who waved.

He reached to punch the "up" button. The cage opened, and out stepped Lieutenant Paul Porta. He was commander of the special gang squad headquartered at Eleventh Street Central Station.

The chunky cop shook Collucci's hand warmly and said, "Maybe you're lucky I preceded you up there."

Collucci said, "Why, Paul?"

Porta said, "A half-hour ago, Taylor's Warriors hit Mullins' policy bank check-in station and safe for seventy-five grand."

Collucci said, "Uh-uh, maybe I better go up another time."

Porta leaned close and said seriously, "Jimmy, I think I've finally done it. In fact I am almost certain that within twenty-four hours I will have a dependable undercover agent infiltrated into Tit for Tat Taylor's Warriors. I will learn all the secrets of their tunnel and defense systems they have under their so called 'Free Zone.' Arrangements are being made to impeach and force that spade governor out of office. Our man goes in and the National Guard will crush the Warriors."

Collucci said, "Is how you planted the pigeon classified?"

Porta laughed and said, "Jimmy, if you're going to tip them off, it is. It wasn't difficult really. A black con just released from Joliet Penitentiary has a Warrior pal out here who had been his cellmate. I filed a detainer warrant for stick-up, murder against him on his release date. He agreed to help me bust up the Warriors. I arranged to have the beef withdrawn, with privilege to reinstate against him at any time, of course."

Collucci banged him on the shoulder and said, "Congratulations, Paul. And good luck!"

They shook hands.

Just before they parted, Collucci said, "Paul, your agent anybody I know?"

Porta said, "I doubt it. He's just an ordinary young spade whose street moniker is Rapping Roscoe. He's full of shit all right, but I've got him, as they say down in Texas, between a rock and a hard place."

They laughed together and Collucci stepped into the elevator.

And on the far Southside Rapping Roscoe rode in a battered black Pontiac with his ex-cellmate, Bumpy Lewis, and several other Warriors that Roscoe did not know were Warriors. They all were observing him closely for his fitness to become a Warrior.

CHAPTER SIX

The drama for Rapping Roscoe and the occupants of the battered black Pontiac started to unfold when Lotsa Black Hayes, the massive driver, glanced up at the rear-view mirror and said raggedly, "Ivory, we got two black rollers on our ass."

Ivory Jones, the squad leader, leaned forward toward Dew Drop Allen, the tiny white Warrior on the front seat beside the driver and said casually, "Drop, you know what to do and when if necessary."

Dew Drop nodded, and Ivory said, "Lotsa, do the thing now."

Lotsa Black stomped on the gas pedal. The finely tuned race-car engine booted the Pontiac forward with a roar. Rapping Roscoe, Lieutenant Porta's tool, turned jerkily and looked through the rear window at the fading headlamps of the blue Plymouth sedan.

Bumpy Lewis glanced at Roscoe and said, "Roscoe, be cool, my man. Ain't no reason now to keep it from you. You are with members of them bad muthafuckuhs, Warriors For Willie Poe. Them black rollers back there are lucky they ain't gonna get a chance to hit on us. No roller fuckin' with us is gonna get anything but offed."

Roscoe smiled weakly and mumbled, "I'm together, brother. You dudes are Warriors? Ain't that a bitch?"

A half-mile from the safety of the Zone the Pontiac suddenly started to lose and regain speed in alarming heavings and jerks.

Ivory Jones looked back at the pinpoint headlamps of the blue Plymouth and commanded, "Lotsa, take the next corner and cut into the first alley and kill your lights. Drop, get out the muscle."

Dew Drop leaned forward and rapidly punched at the car's radio pushbutton selectors, which if done in a precisely coded release pattern would pop up the top of the dashboard. This top was really the lid for a long shallow steel box which contained several pre-loaded Magnum pistols, a high-powered automatic rifle, a sawed-off shotgun, grenades and ammunition in the mini arsenal.

The lid did not pop up! Dew Drop twice again carefully punched the pushbuttons as Lotsa Black turned a corner and drove a half-block north down an alley and snuffed the Pontiac's lights and ailing engine.

The alley was dark and quiet except for the profane voice of an uptight stud in a distant flat.

Ivory Jones said harshly, "Drop, the guns, pass out the goddamn guns!"

Dew Drop stopped fumbling with the radio buttons. He turned his face toward the rear of the car and opened his mouth to speak. But no sound came out. His blue eyes stared through the rear window as if he was hypnotized.

He pointed and said in a hoarse whisper, "Ivory, the release gizmo, the switch to open the box must be out. I can't get to the guns, and I think I see them rollers coming down the alley with lights out."

Everybody in the Pontiac looked out the rear window. There was the dark hump of a car outlined against the glow of street lamps at the mouth of the alley.

Ivory flung open the heavy door next to him. He leaped to the alley floor and shouted, "Drop, get under the wheel and talk shit to them. Lotsa, get out and fade with me until we can maneuver from the rear and bust those roller's heads with a brick or something."

Lotsa Black had gotten one gigantic leg out of the Pontiac when the Pontiac and Ivory were blasted by a bright white light.

"Police!" a bass voice shouted. "Nigger, put your hands on the top of the car or get your head blown off."

Ivory spat in the direction of the voice and slowly placed his palms on the roof of the Pontiac. Roscoe's knee beat a frantic tattoo against Bumpy's thigh inside the Pontiac.

The tires on the blue Plymouth hissed like

tomcats against the gritty alley floor as the eye of the spotlight moved forward to stop two feet behind the Pontiac. Two hard-faced men sprang from the Plymouth. The slim one stood at the rear of the Pontiac. He switched and aimed a shotgun at Ivory Jones and the frozen figures inside the Pontiac.

Slim commanded Ivory, "Now you bad motherfucker, raise your arms high. Back up past this shotgun and put your hands on the top of the car at the rear."

Ivory followed the order, but spat again as he backed past the shotgun.

Thick Set went past Ivory to the driver's side with a thirty-eight snub-nose pointed at Lotsa Black's head and said, in a soft, almost sweet, voice, "All right, nigger, haul that fat ass out here slowly and stand beside that bastard at the rear with your hands on the top."

Lotsa Black slid his bulk slowly from the car seat. He took a step and a half toward the rear before he bellowed, whirled and lunged for the snub-nose. The thirty-eight exploded and a tiny bolt of orange lightning leaped from the muzzle. The Pontiac rocked as Lotsa Black smashed back against it and fell.

Ivory shouted, "You're gonna be iced, you faggot nigger, if you waste him. We're Warriors, motherfuckers."

Slim moved quickly and shoved the muzzle of his shotgun hard against Ivory's throat under the jawbone and pleaded in his loud voice, "Please! Please! Crack another word! Come on, you terrible bastard, do me a favor and open your jib again so your mammy can bury you without your head. Now let's march!"

Ivory went toward the front of the Pontiac, and its rigid occupants, with the shotgun rammed under his jawbone. He kneeled beside the front wheel with his palms on the fender.

Slim stepped back to cover Ivory and the interior of the Pontiac. He said, "Where did you hit Lard Ass?"

Thick Set laughed and said, "Through the right eye and out the top of his skull."

He pointed the thirty-eight at Dew Drop through the open door and said, "Get out and kneel beside this loud-mouth nigger."

Dew Drop got out and followed the order. Thick Set stood behind Dew Drop and Ivory. Slim moved to the open rear window of the Pontiac. He pointed the shotgun at Bumpy and Roscoe on the back seat.

Thick Set said, "Whitey Blue Eyes, are you a Warrior too?"

Dew Drop said loudly, "I sure am, and you can bet your mother's fucking life I'm—"

Dew Drop's reply was cut off as Thick Set took a step forward and fired two rapid shots. Roscoe and Bumpy saw the arms and hands of Dew Drop and Ivory slide lifelessly from the front fender.

Thick Set threw his head back and said gleefully, "What the hell, let's be tidy and go all the way."

Slim swung open the rear door and said, "You niggers hit the ground and go the clean way or sit right there and I'll blow you away nasty with this

73

shotgun."

Bumpy hurtled though the open door toward Slim and seized the barrel of the shotgun with both hands. Roscoe was paralyzed. His teeth chattered as if he was encased in ice. Bumpy struggled with Slim for the shotgun. Thick Set sprinted toward them casually, pressed the thirty-eight against the back of Bumpy's head and pulled the trigger. Bumpy sagged to the ground. Slim and Thick Set stuck their faces into the Pontiac. Vomit dribbled from Roscoe's mouth. His eyes walled toward the top of his head. He lay on the floor in a ball, whimpering piteously like a puppy with a crushed rear end.

Slim guffawed and said, "We should have a camera to get a shot of this bad Warrior crapping in his pants."

Thick Set reached in and jerked Roscoe to the alley floor. He pointed the muzzle of the thirty-eight at his temple.

Roscoe stared into the muzzle. His heels clicked together in a spasm of terror and he blubbered rapidly, "I ain't no Warrior, I swear I ain't. I'm one of you. Call Lieutenant Porta at Eleventh Street Station. He'll tell you I ain't lying."

Thick Set snorted and said, "Bullshit, you're no undercover cop. We'd know because we are members of Porta's special squad. What's your badge number?"

Roscoe waved his arms and pleaded, "I ain't got no badge number 'cause I didn't mean I was a real roller. I mean the Lieutenant is got me working to get inside the Warriors hide-out, to set them up and stuff like that. Please believe me, officers. I ain't stuffing on you. Call Lieutenant Porta at Eleventh Street. If he ain't there, I got his unlisted private number at home. I ain't jiving, officers. I ain't no Warrior."

Slim said, "Write it down."

He dug into his coat pocket and took out a small address book. He threw it on Roscoe's chest.

Thick Set flung a ballpoint beside it. Roscoe, in the glow of the spotlight, shakily scrawled a telephone number in the book. They pulled Roscoe to his feet. He leaned against the rear fender of the Pontiac. Then he shuddered and batted his eyes rapidly at a terrifying spectacle. Bumpy sprang up, grimly alive. He came toward Roscoe, followed by Dew Drop, Lotsa Black and Ivory Jones. They stood in a half-circle glaring at Roscoe.

Bumpy said coldly, "You a dirty nigger, Roscoe. We all Warriors, chump, and you gonna be executed!"

Roscoe's lips pounded together soundlessly. Slim tore a page from the address book and gave it to Ivory.

Roscoe croaked, "Ivory, that number ain't nothing but jive. I ain't never laid eyes on Lieutenant Porta."

Roscoe glanced resentfully at Dew Drop and said, "Ivory, I'm a black brother and you dudes shot me through hot grease. 'Cause I stuffed like I was working for the rollers, I gotta get wasted. Man, it ain't right and it ain't fair."

Bumpy shouted, "Lemme go, Lotsa! I wanta

bust his goosul pipe. I told that stupid motherfucker a hundred times before I sponsored him to cut me loose if he was wrong. Lemme go, Lotsa."

Ivory said firmly, "Cool it, Bumpy. I can understand your feelings about the brother. But you know, even if we knew for a fact that Roscoe is working with Porta, none of us here has the authority to waste him."

Finally Bumpy relaxed in Lotsa Black's arms and was allowed to step free. Ivory nodded. A fake cop handcuffed Roscoe's hands behind his back and shoved him onto the rear floor of the Pontiac. Ivory sat alone on the rear seat as the Pontiac, followed by the Plymouth, went down the alley with Bumpy seated between Dew Drop and Lotsa Black.

Roscoe looked up at Ivory's tight face when the Pontiac came out of the dark alley and said weakly, "I ain't been done right from the git go. What's gonna happen now?"

Ivory looked down at him for a long moment and then said coldly, "Guilty or not, you're a cunt sonuvabitch. I'm calling that telephone number when we get inside the Zone. If it fits Porta's pad, you get your big chance to meet our leader and rap for your life."

CHAPTER SEVEN

Collucci stared at the marble of light bouncing on the floor indicator panel as the elevator zoomed toward the Tonelli penthouse. He felt a twinge of paranoia. What if the meeting was really a cover for a Tonelli trap? What if Bellini, his only buffer against Tonelli's treachery, was absent? He suddenly felt stifled. He removed his overcoat.

The cage came to a halt and he stepped out onto the red entrance hall carpet. A brass chandelier shone like a cache of gold in the ceiling. He stepped into a large lounge. It was an around-the-clock station for Tonelli guards. But now the room was strangely unmanned.

Collucci froze in the silence. He felt the weight of the derringers dangling on the elastics down his arms. Just let him pick up an inflection between Cocio and Tonelli, a mere flicker of fatal electricity in a glance between them, he would leap like a lethal jack-in-the-box and dumdum the brains from their skulls.

He looked at the closed circuit TV monitors flickering on a control panel on a wall to the right. He saw the dome machine gunner reading a magazine. The two garage guards were flapping jaws and waving playing cards on the limousine's back seat. He moved his eyes across other tiny screens that revealed street activity around the building.

On a monitor flashing colorful action he watched a children's Christmas Party beneath a retractable plastic bubble on the terrace. Two dozen parents, including Consuella with Tonelli beside her holding her twins on his lap, sat with faces turned toward a makeshift stage watching children perform a play in Biblical costumes.

Collucci went down a brightly lit hallway. He went past a dozen and a half rooms and suites on both sides of the hall occupied by Tonelli guards and aides. He paused for a moment at the locked three-inch-thick steel door behind which lay Tonelli's private quarters.

He felt a twinge of hopelessness. He moved on and stepped down into the sunken living room. He thought, how tough can it get to put the bastard to sleep? He dropped himself down on a blue satin chair facing open glass doors. The terrace was glowing and pulsing with colorful Japanese lanterns and Christmas merriment.

The child actors took bows to the applause of their proud parents.

He lit a cigarette and casually eyed through the crowd for Papa Bellini. He didn't spot him. He swept his eyes through the terrace again. The twins leaped from Tonelli's lap. They scampered away toward a mound of presents and Santa Claus.

Tonelli glimpsed Collucci and his Barrymore-handsome face beamed. He rose from a sofa and left the terrace to greet Collucci. Collucci painfully managed to display his teeth as he went toward Tonelli.

Tonelli embraced him and said in Sicilian, "Son, my very best to you and your family for the holidays and always."

Collucci replied in Sicilian, "Thank you sir, and my best to you and yours."

Collucci stepped back gently out of Tonelli's embrace and said, "Please excuse my lateness."

Tonelli said, "With Olivia and Petey under the weather, you don't have to apologize. Besides, we cannot have *undienza* until Santa Claus Bellini finishes with the kids and shark Cocio trims the last sucker in the billiard room."

Tonelli said, "Excuse me, Jimmy," and moved to a nearby table and lifted an intercom receiver. He gave a brief order and cradled the instrument.

Tonelli said, "Let's have a smoke while we wait for the others."

Collucci followed him to the steel door. It was opened from the inside by Tonelli's eccentric and deadly chief bodyguard, lanky Carl "The Sphinx" Dinzio. He was heavily bearded and dressed as usual in a navy mohair suit. He wore heavy black sunglasses, and his black hair fell to his shoulders.

Collucci nodded as he went past Dinzio. Dinzio grunted. A corner of Collucci's eye snared a shiny device Dinzio manipulated in his palm. The steel door swung shut with a whooshing sound.

Tonelli draped an arm across Collucci's shoulders and took him down a shadowy corridor. Collucci felt a chill at the sound of Dinzio's catlike footsteps behind him.

CHAPTER EIGHT

The Warrior ruling council, in uniform, stood at attention in the stripped-bare, echoing cavern of the church reviewing the troops. The church was used as an all-purpose assembly area. Once a month a portable obstacle course was set up for punishing guerrilla maneuvers and toughening of the Warriors.

In the wintry night, the five hundred-man force of inter-racial Warriors was crisp and immaculate.

The barrels of the automatic rifles on their shoulders shone like a dull blue lake in the fierce glare of kleig lights. The solemn-faced columns had marched and maneuvered for the council with precise and vigorous grace.

The council gazed out at them proudly as they stood rigidly at attention.

T. used the reviewing stand microphone to dismiss the assembly. The council hurried from the church-arena for their return to the command bunker. They went into the basement of the parsonage attached to the church. T., his family, and fifteen of his inter-racial squad leaders lived with their wives in the once-palatial forty-room mansion.

The basement was crammed to the ceiling with abandoned refrigerators, stoves, and shattered furniture. T. opened a heavy door.

Here, if necessary, the Warriors' total force could retreat. Here they could indefinitely survive and pop in and out of the myriad camouflaged exits and entrances. The system and the Warrior training was designed to survive possible commando strikes by an enemy invading the Zone.

The council seated themselves at the table in the command bunker. Bama nodded toward the tiny image of the Pontiac on a TV monitor as it approached the perimeter of the Zone.

Tat Taylor's wife, Rachel, and teen-age daughter, Fluffy, in crisp white aprons served Christmas dinner to the trio seated at the bunker table. They and other Warrior women had served dinners to scores of inter-racial residents of the Zone since early afternoon.

Rachel said, "T., promise me you'll eat all your salad and the green vegetables. And don't leave yours, Bama and Smitty."

They nodded as they forked in steamy mounds of turkey and dressing. As Rachel and Fluffy turned to leave, Tat raised and pursed his greasy lips for their kisses.

George "Bama" Lewis, seventy-year-old ex-con man, with his jaws inflated with candied yams, jabbed his fork toward a large painting of slain council member Darrel "The Mole" Miller, in sandhog clothing, studying blueprints on a table. The Mole had been married to Willie Poe's sister, Reva. He had been the genius engineer responsible for the elaborate tunnel system beneath the Zone, and the free electricity and gas leeched from utilities' lines and pipes.

Bama said, "Too bad the Mole ain't here this Christmas to enjoy these yams."

Taylor stopped eating and looked at the painting hung on the earthen wall between shoring of steel rods and oak beams.

Taylor said, "Yeah, it's a heartache to hear his name. Everybody loved him except Porta and his killers."

Gigantic Lester "Kong" Smith snickered and said, "Sure, he was really together all right . . . for a paddy. But I hope you guys don't break down and bawl like a coupla bitches and spoil my dinner."

Bama snorted and said, "Smitty, I feel sorry for you. You're in bad trouble."

Kong frowned and said, "Old Man, why you cracking on me?"

Bama said quietly, "Because, son, Mole had forgotten he was white, and even when he's dead you can't."

Tat said. "The Mole is been wasted, by Porta's killers, close to two months. Soon we got to find a way to send Porta where Darrel is."

Kong said, "Porta's asshole could chew up railroad ties when he gets the wire his latest shot at us missed and Roscoe is executed."

Taylor stood and stretched his lean frame and

went to the water cooler in a corner. As the water gurgled into a paper cup he said. "Easy, Smitty, the young brother ain't been found no kinda guilty yet. And if he is, ain't no way now we know what kinda shitty game Porta ran on Roscoe. Maybe we will, and maybe we ain't gonna waste the brother if he's guilty. Smitty, *if* he's guilty."

Bama nodded toward the tiny image of the Pontiac on a TV monitor as it penetrated to the heart of the Zone. The Pontiac glided past other TV cameras. They were concealed in table lamps in the front windows of houses at all points of entry around the ten square blocks of the Zone. Driver Lotsa Black waved several times at sentries on foot and in unmarked cars.

Squad leader Ivory Jones, seated on the back seat, said, "Lotsa, pull over to that phonebooth next to that grocery store."

Lotsa Black coasted the Pontiac to a stop. Ivory got out and went into the booth.

Bumpy Lewis, on the front seat, said, "Roscoe, Ivory's calling that number. Shame on you nigger, if it jingles Porta."

Roscoe, huddled on the rear floorboards, shaking with fear, eased his head up and peered at grim-faced Ivory leaving the phonebooth. Roscoe smashed the heels of his handcuffed hands down on the door handle and leaped through the open door to the sidewalk. He scrambled to his feet and pumped his long legs madly down the sidewalk. Lotsa Black, Dew Drop, and Bumpy Lewis took up the chase. Ivory fired two pistol shots over Roscoe's head and three at his legs.

Ivory shouted, "Stop, Roscoe, or I'll kill you!"

Then as he raced out of pistol range the squad shouted, "Escaped prisoner!"

Roscoe had nearly reached the Zone perimeter when a rifle-carrying sentry ran into the street twenty yards ahead of Roscoe, put his rifle to his shoulder and shouted, "Halt!"

Roscoe veered onto the sidewalk. He zigzagged across a yard to escape between two houses. The M-16 chattered and flashed fire and Roscoe fell in the snow. The sentry and the squad ran to the scene and stood looking down at the ooze of brain and blood from the blasted-away back of Roscoe's head.

Ivory said, "He was Porta's nigger, all right . . . Porta's wife answered."

Bumpy said softly, "We lived next door to each other since we was crumb crushers. We stole together, laid foxes together, did five years in a cell together . . . why did he turn around for Porta?"

Then Bumpy sadly shook his head and said, "His mama ain't gonna never stop crying when I tell her he's wasted!"

The sentry put his hand on Bumpy's shoulder and said, "Man, I'm sorry. I had to do it."

Bumpy said, "I guess the nigger earned it."

Ivory turned and said to the sentry, "I'll send a wagon for him in a few minutes. Get your report ready for the council." The squad walked silently back to the Pontiac.

As Lotsa Black drove toward the parsonage, Ivory said, "Bumpy, I'm almost certain T. will want Roscoe buried here. It will be best for his mama and the Warriors if she never knows what happened to Roscoe."

Lotsa Black said, "I don't wanta guess what T. will do to us for losing Roscoe like we did?"

Two hours after Roscoe's death, Ivory Jones stood in the command bunker. He stood shaken by withering reprimand and demotion from squad leader by the council for his careless loss of his prisoner.

At the moment of Ivory's humiliation, Warrior Charming Mills and a band of masked dope jackers with pistols and shotguns battered in Pretty L. C.'s basement whore crib and shooting gallery beneath a condemned tenement in the Forty-eight Hundred block of Calumet Avenue.

Half pimp, half drug pusher, L. C. sat alone in purple shirtsleeves at a table filling glassine bags with heroin for his big retail trade. Charming Mills ripped from L. C.'s cute face the surgical mask worn against inhalation of the half-kilo mound of white powder before him.

L. C.'s teeth banged together in fear. A huge ring on a manicured pinky flamed and flashed his initials in diamonds and rubies like a swarm of pastel fireflies as he jerked wads of cash from his pockets. His yellow face was chalky as he held the money out in trembly hands. His Adam's apple yo-yoed in his throat as he tried to speak.

The gang, dressed in black jumpsuits, surrounded him with eyes glittering in their Halloween masks.

Finally L. C. said hoarsely, "Don't waste me!

86

Take this five grand. Here! Here! Take it, but please don't waste me!"

Charming Mills snatched the bills and stuffed them into his overcoat pocket.

He said in his soprano voice, "Slick ass, it's too late. You stopped selling our merchandise and got in the wind, and now you're in business for yourself. Whose dope is that you bagging?"

"It's Big Melvin's from New York," L. C. mumbled.

Charming stuck a finger into the white heap and put it against his tongue.

Charming said, "Melvin's got good dope. I want to meet him."

L. C. walled his big gray eyes and said, "He split back to the Apple. Please give me a chance. Please! I'll sell your stuff or pay two bills a day to deal Melvin's."

Buncha Grief, gargantuan cousin of Kong, stood behind L. C. with the snout of his forty-five automatic pressed against L. C.'s head.

He said, "Nigger, get up away from the table so your motherfucking blood won't ruin that smack. Get up, nigger, and kneel."

L. C. blubbered and tried to stand. He collapsed and rolled under the table. Buncha Grief stooped and thundered four slugs into his skull. Charming rolled the heroin up into the plastic tablecloth and shoved it and the wad of money inside into Buncha's jumpsuit.

He was leaving the basement when Charming glanced down at the thirty-grand ring on L. C.'s dead hand. He came back and worked it off the finger. He pushed it into a cigarette pack in his shirt pocket.

The five dope jackers walked casually to the pitch-black alley and removed their masks. Then three split off and went to their cars parked on the street at both ends of the alley. Buncha Grief and Mills went to Buncha's souped-up old Imperial.

As Buncha shot away he said, "Taking him off was sweet as nun pussy. Too bad, Charming, you ain't still pimping so maybe you could cop his slew of ho's. If I was a cute little yellow nigger like you, I'd cop his stable. My half-white mama and Kong's was two of the finest sister ho's in the streets. Ain't it a bitch they both got bigged by two black ugly tricks?"

Mills frowned. "I had class, Grief. I never had any filthy low-life junkie bitches when I was playing. The last and only stinking junkie whore that even touched me was when my old lady dumped my two-month-old ass into a trash bin."

A mile of silence away Buncha pulled to a stop, and they went into Buncha's gaudy first-floor apartment on Sixty-first Street.

Mills removed the black leather jumpsuit and dressed in blue suit and overcoat. L. C.'s bankroll counted out to fifty-five hundred. His dope weighed one pound three ounces. Buncha leaned forward on his black and gold checked sofa. He rolled up one of L. C.'s C-notes. He snorted up one of the sparkling rows of crystal cocaine off the black onyx coffee table.

Buncha turned to Mills and said. "Here man, take a blow. It's the last of that lady we heisted 'rom Double Head's old bitch, Wanda.''

Mills chewed his bottom lip and hesitantly took the rolled C-note from Buncha.

Buncha said, "You ain't got to worry this super bad lady will fuck up your skull in the ring tonight. Go on take a blow and get a first-set knockout over that no-punch chump."

Charming mumbled, "I'm not worried, even pissy loaded I'd hang him . . . But snorting coke is against T.'s rules."

Buncha grinned and winked and said, "I ain't gonna snitch on you, baby." He laughed his eyes moist as Mills slowly dipped his head and snorted up a row of coke.

Buncha said, "Nigger, are you for real? For that blow of coke, at worse T. would maybe bury his foot in your ass and toss you into that dungeon under the Zone. Do I have to run down to you what T. would do to you just for the L. C. set? Nigger, worry about serious things like what would Cous and me do to you if you dropped out of our thing."

Mills waved a hand and said, "Man, the bread is too sweet and regular to cut loose."

Buncha said, "Charming, you sure know what to say!"

Mills got to his feet and said, "Any message for Smitty besides the L. C. rundown?"

Buncha stood and walked Mills to the door.

Buncha's small eyes were bright maroon dancers in his gorilla face as he said, "Tell Cous I found out there is at least a quarter of a mil in Double Head's safe. It's Wanda's cocaine take and the numbers

89

skim from the dago's sixty-percent end. Tell Cous I said for a big one like this, he's gonna have to risk a meet with me soon, so we can polish the plan to take off that bread."

Mills' mouth gaped open and he shook his head.

He said, "It's a death trap, Buncha. There must be a dozen guards inside and others in disguise on the street outside the numbers bank. Even the police cruise by often when the runners are checking in. And that's the only time to get even a chump shot at that safe. And the baddest nigger in Chicago, Double Head himself, is always hiding somewhere with a machine gun."

Buncha held the door open and said, "Charming, squeeze your bowels together and listen. That punkin-head fat ass ain't so bad. For guts and rep, he's at the bottom of the list after T., Cous and then me. We'll ice his guards and blast into his pasteboard bank. I'll have him on his knees begging me like a broad not to waste him."

Mills grinned weakly, looked at his wristwatch and said, "I'm hitting the wind so I won't blow my title by default."

He went past Buncha to his Volkswagen a block away.

As Charming drove into the Zone, referee Tat was counting ten over a young Warrior heavyweight in the semi-main bout of the Christmas boxing show.

The arena was in the huge church. The three thousand inter-racial spectators sat on folding metal chairs. They cheered and applauded the winning underdog who banged his gloves together and leaped wildly into the air.

Taylor walked across the ring and whispered to the announcer, then climbed over the ropes and threaded his way through the excited throngs in the aisles. He went to one of the basement dressing rooms shared by Charming and his opponent.

Bama's naked skull glistened like an ebony pond as he kneaded the shoulders of Charming's challenger, stretched out on his belly atop a table. Kong, wearing a T-shirt stenciled "Charming Mills" on the back in pink letters, paced the concrete and violently chewed a wad of gum.

Taylor said, "Smitty, where the hell is your fighter?"

Kong scowled and said, "Somewhere either pulling his head outta a pussy or wiping off his dick. I'll wring his fucking neck and . . ."

At that moment Mills burst into the room with a radiant smile on his face. He shucked out of his overcoat and bent over.

He said, "Here it is, get in line and kick it good."

Taylor grinned and said, "Charming, go on and whip your tale on us."

Charming shot a look at Kong and said, "I muscled a gorilla off an innocent young sister from the big foot country on Sixty-first Street. We blew two hours before we found the alley and the raggedy van where her mama and ten brothers and sisters were padding."

Then he walled his doe eyes toward Taylor and cocked his curly head to one side and said, "Big T., you should have seen all of them crying and thanking God for sending me. They actually kissed the hem of my overcoat when I gave them money for kerosene and their first meal in two days. Good buddies, I was a Christmas miracle for them. I'll never forget their faces. How I turned them on! I felt like J. C. himself doing his encore thing."

The council and the challenger laughed as Kong booted Mills in the buttocks with his knee and snatched off his suit coat.

"C'mon outta your street clothes, you conning shit-colored bastard." Kong said as he lifted Mills and sat him on the end of the table.

Taylor and Kong started to undress him. Kong stooped to remove his shoes and Taylor started to unbutton his shirt.

Mills suddenly remembered the ring stashed in the cigarette package in his shirt pocket. He stiffened and leaped away from Taylor's hands to the floor. But not before L. C.'s diamonds and rubies flashed for an instant in Taylor's eyes.

Mills stared at Taylor's stone face for a long moment. He swung his right arm in a circle.

He said, "Damn! That was a helluva pain. I guess I pinched something when I punched out that gorilla."

Taylor laughed dryly through his teeth and said, "Charming, if he's up there, maybe God is chastising you for using his name in your jive and shuck."

Kong grabbed Charming's arm and took him to his locker in a corner across the room. Bama and his fighter left for the ring, followed by Taylor.

Kong glanced at the door closing behind Taylor

and said, "You shaky sonuvabitch. What went wrong?"

Mills handed the cigarette pack to Kong and said, "All news good. We stung for a pound three ounces of ass-kicking horse, and fifty-five hundred cash. Now gander L. C.'s ring I copped for you. I did that number with T. so he couldn't snatch that pack and grab a smoke like he does."

Kong stood gazing at the ring and shaking his head.

He looked at Mills sternly and said, "Nigger, why? Why? Why? Why would you lug our death into the Zone?"

Mills winced and said, "That's a twenty-five . . . maybe even thirty-gee hoop, and you miss the point?"

Kong slapped Mills hard on the side of his head. He seized Mills' face between his huge palms.

He pushed his fearsome face against Mills' and roared, "What point, you idiot muthuhfuckah?"

Mills trembled and, with his face still imprisoned, slipped out of his trousers and whispered, "Your first initial, Smitty . . . it's L . . . I thought remounting the C side with a S would be easy."

Kong flung Mills and he bounced off the lockers. As they left for the ring Kong shoved the ring to the bottom of the pack. He crushed it closed at the top and slipped it into one of the outside pockets of the canvas first aid bag he would use in Mills' corner.

Taylor went back to the dressing room when he saw Kong and Mills go to the ring. He searched all the clothing and the room for the ring. He got back to his ringside seat as the first round bell rang.

He noticed a bruise on Mills' cheek as he left the corner. He also noticed that Mills seemed unusually nervous. Taylor got up and went to stoop down beside Kong. Kong was glumly watching Mills' challenger flick stinging jabs into Mills' face without a return from Mills.

Taylor leaned and said into Kong's ear. "Smitty, your fighter ain't got his mind nowhere near the ring. What you say to going down the drain with him for another fifty, he don't win?"

Kong turned and studied Taylor's bland face for a long moment to cath a clue that Taylor's remark had a hook in it. The bell rang the ending of the first round.

Kong took several articles from the canvas bag and said as he and an assistant climbed through the ropes, "My fighter's got nothing on his mind but punching the dooky outta the other dude. I call the half a yard."

Taylor was about to get to his feet when he swept his eyes across the outside pockets of the canvas bag. He saw the bulge of the pack. He stared up at Kong busily attending Mills. He removed the ring and saw it was real. He returned the ring and the pack. He was in his seat across the ring when the bell rang for the second round.

Mills came out punching recklessly. He missed a whistling overhand right lead and received a crunching left hook to the jaw. Mills shuddered in the center of the ring before the back of his head crashed against the canvas with a sickening thud.

The referee took one look at his motionless

form, stooped and pulled back his eyelids. He waved it over as a knockout.

Bama and his assistant climbed into the ring. They worked on Mills for three minutes. Finally he came around and climbed through the ropes for the long and painful walk through a bedlam of boos.

Taylor stopped Bama and whispered, "Meet me quick as you can in the parsonage office."

T. had just finished his rundown to Bama about the L. C. ring when a media monitor in the bunker reached T. by telephone. He relayed the news of L. C.'s death and the police theory that L. C. had been robbed and slain by black gangsters for Chicago's white crime syndicate.

T. hung up the phone and said, "Bama, you called the shot! That ring Smitty and Charming is holding belonged to dope-pushing L. C."

Bama nodded. "He's dead?"

T. said, "Uh-huh, the rollers either conning, or been conned. They throwing out that black gangsters wasted L. C. for the dagos."

Bama chuckled, "No way. Anybody the dagos gave a contract to wouldn't fall in love with a stiff's flash."

"Then Bama, it's them black dope jackers," T. said. "And I'm gonna walk Charming's and Smitty's butts 'til they confess what kinda mess they fucking the Warriors and all our dreams up in!"

Bama, sitting in a chair beside the desk, leaned toward T., who drummed his fingertips on the phone base.

Bama patted the back of T.'s hand and said, "Now, son, I'm sad and hurting like you. I love Smitty and Mills like sons. But this is no time for anything except our smoothest control of the situation, and ourselves. Before we tip our hands we have to find out whether the mess they're in is in seed or blossom."

T. said, "You mean other Warriors. . . ?"

Bama said, "I mean that. And also, that since we sleep under the same roof with Smitty, we must not wake up him, or Mills, to our suspicions. Since Smitty's a council member, we could try him openly for any connection with drugs whatsoever."

T. shook his head and said. "We, and the Zone, would lose all the support and protection of the people."

Bama said, "No, we can't survive without the favor of all those white and black parents and decent citizens here and across the nation who believe in our sincerity. Police and soldiers would blitz and blast us out of the Zone the same day the public got solid evidence a Warrior leader was dirty with drugs and murder."

T. said, "I hope it ain't like it looks for Smitty and Mills. I been knowing them both long and good . . . I thought."

Bama said, "Let's feed Smitty and Mills with a long-handled spoon to set them up for a moment of truth. We'll run a powerful psychodrama on them in a private place the first chance we get. Maybe their innocence will let them pass it. If they flunk it, we quietly execute them on the spot.

We'll bury them and any Warrior accomplices."

T. nodded.

Bama got to his feet and said, "Remember, we must play the con that all's well and normal . . . And normally I go to bed around this time of night."

T. sat at the desk deep in thought.

Bama stopped at the door. "I said I'm turning in."

T. looked up and almost whispered, "Bama, I got a stout feeling Smitty ain't got no dealings in dope. And even in L. C.'s ring and killing, except Smitty got foolish trying to save his friend Mills from some kinda crooked hassle. Bama, Smitty ain't gone crazy. He ain't forgot them times I climbed in the devil's ass to save his life and saved him from a bum's bag."

"T . . . if he tests out guilty, maybe he soured and derailed because his debt got too big and painful to pay," Bama said over his shoulder and went down the hall.

CHAPTER NINE

T. flicked off the desk light and sat in the darkness. He spun the chair toward the window behind him and raised it several inches at the bottom. Great volumes of hurt and rage shook him as he dry-retched and sucked air. He leaned back into the chair.

His heavy lips shaped a grim line as he remembered a Fourth of July night forty-five years before. He was eight years old when he watched his mother, Pearl, heaving sobs as she took off his tennis shoe and hid the last few dollars left of his stepfather's paycheck.

Then, trembling, they huddled together at the front window. They stared at the ripply neon front of the Playhouse Saloon with sucker-trap blackjack and craps tables in the basement.

He could feel the snub barrel of Sarge's rusty Saturday Night Special against his knees. His mother had hidden it beneath the sofa cushion. He stroked fingertips tenderly across the lump on his mother's cheekbone.

He stared at the saloon door half a block away. He thought that he would kill Sarge if he came home cussing and abusing his mother again.

He said, "Mama, I hope Sarge get kilt shooting crap and don't never come back here no more."

Pearl kissed him and said, "Jessie, stop that kinda hoping. We all he's got and he's been my salvation man since Reverend Taylor passed away and we left Georgia."

He looked at her quizzically and said, "Mama, why you call my real daddy Reverend Taylor all the time?"

She laughed mirthlessly and said, " 'Cause he'd puff up like a hoptoad if I didn't. I guess even his mama wouldn't call him Eli to his face."

She laughed loudly. "Maybe he let that chippy Reba he set up in luxury and silk dresses, while I had no decent shoes even, call him Eli. Jessie, we owe Sarge a lot."

With a puzzled frown wrinkling his forehead he said, "But Mama, we don't owe that old crazy nigger no right to beat up on you, huh?"

"Jessie, I fell in the scuffle and hit my face myself on the kitchen table. Sarge ain't been real bad 'cept the past year. Now you think back real hard and see I'm right.

"I was broke, sick and still carrying you when Reverend Taylor passed. Sarge courted me with flowers and money once a week for months. He never touched me, until I made him kiss me.

"He'd just sit 'way 'cross the living room in that old green chair. He'd moon-eye me like I was a royal queen. He worked two jobs and loved you like his own when I birthed you."

"But Mama, he's crazy. We oughta ease away on his next payday. We oughta move to the Southside."

She shook her head and said, "He ain't . . . real crazy . . . I mean, he couldn't be a sweeter husband until he's drinking heavy or thinking he's back fighting in the Bulge Battle. I guess anybody's brains could scramble in all that blood and noise."

She caught her breath and her eyes widened at the sight of Sarge.

She said, "He's broke again . . . fooling the people again. Look at Mister Handsome marching home with his shoulders all reared back like some rich general."

"But Mama, look at his face in the light. He's in the war again! We oughta go next door to Rachel's mama's house and stay all night."

She said, "Jessie, don't be scared. He's gonna come in here and flop down into the land of nod. Jessie, don't butt in or anything and upset him. Keep quiet and leave him to Mama."

Sarge burst through the door. He stood weaving at attention with bloodshot eyes.

She said, "Sarge, stop looking at me so mean and I'll make you some fried chicken."

Sarge smiled crookedly and said in a quiet voice, "Paymaster, I ain't got the time. I'm gonna have a steak in Paree with a fine oo-la-la. The transports are loading right now. Don't fuck me around,

Paymaster. Give me all my money before I split your motherfucking head."

He went several steps to the sewing machine money stash. He jerked the drawers out and stomped them to pieces. He shoved the tattered officer's cap back off his face. He stood glaring at her and gritting his teeth.

She tried to smile, but her lips only trembled as she went toward him, her big eyes flashing fear in the Watusi head.

"Please, Sarge, I can't let you take our food and insurance money to them Playhouse slickers. Come on, Sweetie Daddy, let's have black coffee together and watch fireworks on the roof with Jessie."

He leaped at her with vacant eyes. He seized her outstretched arms and spun her. He locked her in a violent full nelson. She screamed as he hurled her to the floor.

He ground his knees into her spine and shouted in her ear, "Where's my money? Gimme! Gimme!"

Jessie came off the couch with the pistol held behind his back. He almost touched the ragged shrapnel scar behind Sarge's right ear and pulled the trigger. The gun clicked and Sarge stiffened and walled his eyes back at Jessie clicking again behind him.

Sarge whirled off Pearl. She raced toward the kitchen. He vised Jessie's throat with one hand and snatched the gun with the other. He smashed the butt down on Jessie's reddening head until his blows snuffed the lights in Jessie's eyes . . .

The police took Jessie to a hospital for scalp stitches and then to a juvenile holding station until a foster home could be found. Within two weeks Rachel's mother signed the papers to become his foster mother.

For weeks after his mother's funeral, nightmares woke him up dripping sweat. And he fell into deep silent depression whenever he thought of her. Three years later, when he was fifteen, he slipped into Rachel's bedroom and her strait-laced mother caught them petting and giggling on the side of the bed.

Two days after he was thrown out, he came out of an all-night Westside theater. On the sidewalk down the street he saw six tough-looking Italians leap from a jalopy. They had knives and ran to attack a powerfully built young black guy. He drew a switchblade and put his back against a building.

The black guy shouted at Jessie, "Man, you gonna let these dagos waste me?"

Jessie dashed to a sawhorse over a repair hole in the street. He stomped off a leg and gripping the two by four, rushed into the fray. A lean guy with odd yellowish eyes thrust for a heart shot. Instead he plunged his stiletto into the black guy's shoulder as he twisted away. Jessie brought the club down and saw the wrist of the hand holding the stiletto pop bone and blood. The lean guy screeched and spun to face Jessie. For an instant Jessie stared into his eyes, radiant with pain and anger. Jessie felt stinging slashes on his back. The lean guy rocketed a foot at his crotch. Jessie turned and felt toothache pain in his hip.

He stared into Jessie's eyes and said in a hoarse

whisper, "I'll remember you and I'll get you for this, nigger."

Jessie swung the club at his head. He heard the crunch and saw his jaw drop stupidly as bloody spittle leaked down his chin. He heard bones crack and break as he whirled and swung his club on the others. The gang fled. Jessie's and the giant's superficial stab wounds were oozing blood.

The giant said, "Man, I'm Kong."

Jessie said, "I'm Jessie. Why was they out to waste you?"

Kong answered, "Gang war, man, gang war. C'mon and let's get some patching."

They went to a jalopy and Kong drove away.

Kong said, "Them dagos is members of the Sicilian Knights. I'm the leader of the Black Devastators. That stringbean dago you busted up was Lupo Collucci, their leader."

Jessie said, "I guess I'll need a piece to stay on this side of town."

Kong grunted. "Jessie, you gonna need to be a Black Devastator. I'll shoot you right in. Make up your mind, brother. We need bad dudes like you to take over the Westside from Lupo."

Six months later Jessie had a steel plate in his skull from a bullet Lupo Collucci fired into his head in an ambush on Devastator turf in Douglas Park.

Kong had become dependent on Jessie's gems of strategy which gobbled up big chunks of Collucci's turf. Jessie's planning of creative burglaries and shakedowns of hustlers and dope pushers and their pads bulged the Devastator treasury.

Kong took a Collucci slug through a lung. When he got back to the turf, all the Devastators wanted Jessie to lead them.

Jessie's habit of taking prompt and reckless vengeance against any odds earned him the "Tit For Tat" moniker.

T. and Kong remained tight buddies. They and Kong's cousin, Buncha Grief, were ambushed one midnight on Sicilian Knights turf. They were gunned down by Lupo Collucci and his constant shadow and right hand, Angelo Serelli. Buncha Grief left the scene with a grazed skull.

After T.'s and Kong's wounds healed in the prison ward of county hospital, two crooked detectives put T. and Kong on show-up. Two of their shakedown victims had reported fake armed robberies. They fingered sixteen-year-old T. and Kong into Pontiac Reformatory until they were twenty-one years old.

They were put to work in the kitchen of the crowded prison. They lived in a four man cell. T. and Kong soon became the most feared cons in the tough joint.

Thirty days before T.'s release, Skinny Man Blake, a Devastator member, came in from the street. A half-dozen Devastators serving bits, including T. and Kong, led Blake to an uncrowded corner of the yard to get a rundown on recent street happenings in the free world.

They stripped off their shirts and lay on the grass in a semi-circle around Blake. Beneath the lush June sun they shimmered like seals lolling on a jade beach.

Blake said, "I guess you all hip to the trouble the Devastators was in when we lost T. and Kong. The club died a year ago from members OD'ing, bits in these joints, square-ups with wives and squealers, and the rest Lupo Collucci's Sicilians crippled or wasted."

T. said, "I'm gonna chase Lupo back up his mammy's ass when I hit the bricks next month."

Blake took a puff of his cigarette. "T., lemme pull your coat to the fact Collucci is poison you don't wanta take."

Blake walled his eyes fearfully and almost whispered, "The dude is a Mafia man."

Kong said, "Ain't that a bitch, T. ?"

T. said, "Yeah, we been standing still in a cage while the free world is speeding."

Blake said, "No shit, T., like when you and Kong got busted, there was maybe a dozen hustlers making a big buck. But now, on the Westside and the Southside, boo koo niggers, poor as Lazrus a coupla years ago, is living like kings."

Kong said, "How?"

"Offa dealing dope. Mafia dope," Blake said. "All of 'em got new Lincolns and Hogs. Their customers is everywhere, thick as bedbugs in a flop joint. They stealing and nodding and dying."

Blake paused while the captain of the yard, with brass buttons adazzle, passed swinging a leaded cane and beaming his sweet psychotic smile.

Blake continued. "Remember all the fat gut niggers that usta own the numbers and policy banks? Well all of them, except one, is got a new partner taking sixty percent off the top and the bankers gotta meet the nut outta their ends."

T. said, "When did the Mafia muscle in?"

Blake said, "Amos Lightfoot got a bit in Leavenworth for income tax a coupla years ago. Amos got diarrhea of the jib and woke up a dago hood from the Windy about the gold mine behind the nickel-and-dime policy game."

One of the original Devastators said, "Who is the policy dude shaking his dick at the Mafia?"

Blake said, "Willie Poe, outta the Apple. When the Mafia first moved in they killed Poe's son and dumped a banker into an alley with a mouth fulla balls. Willie Poe tried to organize the bankers. But they was all on their knees with shit for blood.

"Coupla months ago Poe shot and stomped two Mafia runners to death. Willie Poe is the only nigger in the history of the world that ever stuck his black ass out and told the Mafia to kiss it. He's the greatest and the baddest on the planet."

The whistle screamed that the yard period was over. T. lagged back with Blake as the cons moved off the yard into the cell houses.

T. said, "Blake, I ain't got my nose open and nothing like that. Understand me, for real, but about Rachel, she ain't answered my kites for six months. She died or what?"

Blake said, "T., you know I love you and I know you. Forget about her."

T. knifed his fingernails into Blake's arm and said, "Nigger, I'll tear your arm off if you dangle me about my woman."

Blake said, "You had to know. Well, a week

after she copped the Miss Black Chicago beauty title, Dandy Ike taught her hoss is boss. He turned her out on the 'boost.' They say she was like a magician stealing furs and C-note dresses from Marshall Fields and other ritzy Loop stores. They say she got busted and the judge sent her to Lex Hospital to kick the thing."

T. couldn't sleep for days. Until his release he murdered Dandy Ike dozens of way in bloody day fantasies and night dreams. They released him with a bus ticket to the Windy, a sawbuck and a roughly cut suit that hollered, "Penitentiary!"

He got off the Greyhound in Chicago's Loop. He went to the street. He blinked in the sunlight. He was shaken by the exploding bomb of traffic and the insane stampede of well-dressed people with white blank faces. He felt filthy, inferior and lost. A shabby alien covered with jail rot.

He rode streetcars to Rachel's house. He approached the house. He darted a glance at the horror house where Sarge and his mother had died.

Oh Mama! My sweet Mama!

He saw the name "Waters" was still on Rachel's mailbox. He rang the doorbell twice and the peep slot opened.

Rachel's mother said, "What is it?"

He said, "Mrs. Waters, it's me, Jessie Taylor. I lived with you once . . . my mama Pearl was wasted next door."

There was a long silence before she swung open the door. He stepped into the living room. On a large table he saw a mountain of ironed laundry she took in for a living.

She looked up at him and said, "My stars, you're twice bigger than when I made you hit the road. Pearl woulda looked at you twice before knowing you."

He sat on the sofa. She put her hands on her hips and gave him a level look.

She said, "Jessie, you just here out of the pen?"

He nodded.

She said, "You can't light here and eat me into the poorhouse."

He said, "Mrs. Waters, I heard what Ike did to Rachel and all, and I only wanta see her."

She wearily dropped down beside him.

She said, "Poor thing is still in the dope hospital down in Kentucky."

He said, "When she coming home?"

She said, "I fixed her a big peach cobbler and homemade ice cream two weeks ago and got disappointed. She called this morning and promised me she's coming two weeks from this Sunday coming for certain. But I ain't fixing a crumb 'til she walks through that door."

He said, "You seen Ike riding and sporting in the neighborhood lately?"

Her heavily veined hands made fists in her lap. "No indeed, and neither the police. They come by here every now and then asking about him. They want him about crippling a girl."

T. stood and said, "I'll see you, Mrs. Waters."

He walked to the door and opened it.

She followed him and said, "Jessie, you hungry?"

He said, "No thanks, I just ate."

He went to the sidewalk. He heard her footsteps behind him. He stopped and faced her. He smiled for the first time in months and he felt good. He didn't feel lost and puffed with tension any more. She put her hand on his arm.

A little out of breath, she said, "Jessie, you got a room?"

He said, "Yes ma'm, and a job on the Southside."

She squeezed his arm and beamed. "Jessie, you get back over here Sunday after next. I'm taking you and Rachel to join church."

He said, "We'll see, Mrs. Waters." He started to turn away.

She said, "You both need the Lord. Ain't nothing or nobody as powerful as him."

He said, "No ma'm." As he walked away, he said under his breath, "He is, if he's up there, Mrs. Waters. If he's up there."

He walked to Lake Street and took an El train for the Southside.

He exchanged winks with Easy Pockets, one of the original Devastators, getting on the train. Easy Pockets sat down beside a sleeping fat guy. The pickpocket unfurled a newspaper and cleaned out Fatso's pockets and his watch behind the paper curtain in just under a minute.

He got off at Sixty-first Street with T. They went into a bar under the El.

After usual long-time-no-sees, T. said, "Easy Pockets, you know what part of town Dandy Ike is pimping in?"

Easy Pockets tore his eyes away from a wallet

peeping from an unbuttoned hip pocket of a mule-faced guy playing stink finger behind a drunk broad leaning over the jukebox.

He said, "T., you're outta luck. He's got twelve ho's and boosters and pimping a zillion in Detroit."

T. said, "I hope you ain't passing on no unreliable shit, Easy, 'cause I got to hobo there."

Easy's foxy face screwed up in righteous suffering. "T., I saw him a week ago. He told me he was gonna tag your toe if you showed. We got our noses real dirty in the shithouse of a mack and ho bar in the valley on Saint Antoine."

T. got off his stool.

Easy said, "T., I know what you got in mind. Please don't go to Detroit and let him cross you outta your all in all. He ain't worth blowing your life. The nigger is rich as cream and farting in police faces. He's got boo koos of the best dope on the street. The hypes will line up a hundred deep to waste you for a small bag of that boss dope. He might oil one of his Hunt Street cops to bury you in Jackson Penitentiary doing it all."

T. smiled and said, "Easy, I ain't got my nose so wide open for living, or the free world, I'm gonna let a enemy slide free, even rich bad Ike, for putting the hurt to Rachel, my forever woman and heart."

Easy sat shaking his head as he watched T. walk to the street. That same evening T. slipped on secondhand coveralls and got a freight train for Detroit. He ate a supper of cheese and rye bread and slept all the way on straw in an empty banana car.

110

He got his suit pressed in the Valley, and soul food in the Faithful Family Restaurant. He stashed his coveralls in a condemned house. He stayed in the Adams Hotel. The second night in town he staked out in a stripped jalopy in a vacant lot. It was across the street from the pimp bar where Easy said Ike hung out.

T. watched a parade of peacocking pimps and their ho's coming and going in new fifty-one Caddie's and Lincolns. But Ike didn't show and a curious thing happened. The bar's outside lights went off at two A.M., but a loudmouthed crowd stayed inside.

Then he searched Hastings Street all the way to Sonny Wilson's Bar. He stalked John R. Street, and the Black Bottom District and every other ho haunt looking for Ike.

Steal him and kill him with these hands and feet, was the roaring litany inside T.'s skull.

The jalopy's rightful tenant had arrived with his bedtime bottle of grape as T. got back to it.

T. said from the sidewalk, "Where the hell is Dandy Ike tonight, brother?"

The derelict squinted and came to the sidewalk. He said, "Ike OD'ed and was deep sixed today. All the pimps and hos is holding the wake across the street."

T. sighed and walked wearily down the sidewalk. He got back to Chicago the next afternoon. He got shaved at a barber shop on Fifty-eighth Street across from Willie Poe's policy check-in station and twenty-four hour craps house in the basement.

An old hustler, with a hound-dog face and white

stubble on his face, climbed into the chair as T. climbed down and paid his bill. T. took a toothbrush and paste from his jacket on the rack. He waved them at his barber and nodded toward a face bowl. The barber nodded permission.

T. was brushing his teeth when the barber said, as he lathered the old hustler, "Decatur, it's a month since I seen you go into Willie's to whale the craps. You finally decided to save a fortune 'stead of win one?"

Decatur said, "Naw, I do all my crap shooting up on Sixty-first Street in Lucky Red's joint. Shit, I ain't for none of that action across the street. Anywhere in these streets they laying ten to five the dagos is gonna blow Willie's joint up and send him to the morgue."

T. came away from the bowl and was slipping into his coat when the hustler said, "There they are! Bama and Willie, the sweetest con team that ever shit between two pair of shoes."

T. walked to the window and looked at the Mutt and Jeff pair leaving a new black fifty-one Imperial.

T. said, "Which is Mr. Poe?"

Decatur said, "The black geechie with the wavy moss."

The barber said, "Yes indeedy, Willie Poe got his papa's inky skin. He got his French mama's features and silky hair. The combination is got the frails so creamy between the legs they can't walk for running to catch Willie Poe."

As T. walked toward the door, Decatur said, "O. C., I ain't got no sympathy for Willie."

The barber stopped straight-razoring Decatur's face to ask, "Why?"

T. stalled half out of the door.

Decatur said, " 'Cause, Bama and him was like foxes in a chicken coop. They been trimming marks since they was pissy punks 'til five years ago. Willie split off for the policy game. Ain't it a bitch that Willie the fox is gonna wind up a mark himself?"

T. stepped to the sidewalk. The street all the way to the el station a block away had been spooked of people. Nobody apparently wanted to be around when Willie Poe was sprayed with death.

The setting sun sprinkled Bama's shaved head with bloody light as he disappeared behind Willie Poe into the bar and grill front.

T. crossed the street and went into the bar. He stood blindly just inside the door in the murk. He was barely able to see several hunched shapes at a circular bar. He went across a cavern of dark carpet to a stool at the bar.

A harlequin face lunged at him, grinning. He said "Coke" to it and spotted a pair of vague shapes with fiery eye-whites rammed up against a wall in a booth that could have been Bama and Willie Poe.

He gargled his dry mouth with Coke. A flash of the harlequin's crotch-zinging legs reminded him of Rachel's gams. He visualized himself humping between the barmaid's sexy legs, blowing off the five-year pressure in his balls.

He was about to go over to the booth and introduce himself when a door beside the booth opened. He heard a clatter of adding machines. A guy in shirtsleeves and a shoulder-holstered forty-five automatic put a suitcase on the floor beside Willie.

Bama and Willie got up and came past T. He stood, started to speak. He took a step toward Willie, walking behind Bama who was carrying the money.

The barmaid leaned and seized his arm and said, "Are you crazy? Nobody touches Mr. Poe, or approaches his back."

T. turned away and went rapidly through the front door to the middle of the sidewalk and stopped. Willie was just closing the door on the passenger side. Bama was sliding under the wheel.

Willie stared impassively at T. as he said to Bama out of the side of his mouth, "You think he'll try for the scratch?"

Bama said, "Willie, you got glaucoma? Look at his eyes and give him an autograph. Or better still, interview him for this fucking chauffeur's gig. You know I'd like to team up with Bulldog Slim and play the East Coast for a month or so."

T. raised his voice without moving. "Mr. Poe, can I speak with you?"

Willie crooked an index finger. T. came to the side of the car as Bama unracked a machine gun from under the dash and placed it on the seat.

Willie said, "Say it fast, youngblood."

T. said, "I heard in the joint you having a big headache, dago-wise, and ain't got no troops. I'm Tit For Tat Taylor. I was the leader of five hundred Devastators on the Westside before I got busted."

T. patted his jacket. "Can I go to my raise and show you my proof?"

Willie stone-eyed him for a long moment before

114

he nodded. T. reached into his inside jacket pocket. He handed Willie a packet of articles and several headline items about the bloody wars between T.'s Devastators and Lupo Collucci's Sicilian Knights. Among the clippings were shots of Lupo Collucci, T. and Kong. Willie shuffled through them.

He gave them back and said, "Your publicity is great. But I got trouble kids can't handle."

T. said, "Excuse me, Mr. Poe, but I've outgrown kid gangs. I need a job and thought maybe you needed a bodyguard."

Willie said, "Nobody can bodyguard Willie Poe like Willie Poe."

Bama gunned the engine and put the Imperial in gear.

Willie said as they pulled away, "Taylor, I'll try to think of a gig for you. Meet me on this spot at ten in the morning."

T. grinned broadly and ran down the street along side the car.

He said, "Thank you, Mr. Poe. I hope you think of something."

Willie lit a cigar and put the machine gun on his lap. His sable eyes flickered into every passing car and every possible niche and hole of concealment for assassins as Bama rolled at a fast clip through the lavender light.

After a long silence, Willie said, "Well, goddamnit, Bama, what do you think of him?"

Bama smiled mischievously. "Who?"

Willie said, "He's a lot like Junior was."

Bama said, "Yeah . . . I know."

Willie said wistfully, "He's two, three years . . .

older . . . maybe an inch or so taller . . . but same treacherous black leopard body lingo. He's even got Junior's little-boy-lost vibes, like Junior, a sentimental sucker beneath that layer of brute avenger . . . so tough . . . so stubborn. Now, tell me, what do you think, Bama?"

Bama's cavedweller's face was serious.

He said gently, "Willie friend, you didn't finish. Taylor is vulnerable . . . and like Junior, so easy for the Mafia to trap and kill."

Willie nodded slowly in agreement.

He said, "You're right. Taylor's forgotten. We'll find a driver somewhere soon so you and Slim can go East."

Bama said, "You don't have to forget him, Willie. Hire him to drive us to find the location of that fabulous cabaret we want together. Willie, walk away from this war with the Mafia that you can't win. We got no roots, Willie. After twenty-five years of chasing suckers, and roustings into a hundred and fifty jails, I'm wondering, Willie, aren't we the suckers after all?

"The excitement of the con, the fat scores and glossy cunts struck us out Willie with our wives. Who the hell knows, but that better life the suckers are always bleating about might have some kind of valuable substance and meaning, and even a happy day now and then. Maybe the life we've been pissing on, we should've been getting."

Willie sat deep in thought until Bama reached their home on Michigan Avenue. Then Bama drove around the block several times to foil and spot any Mafia ambushers before driving into the garage adjoining the house.

They took a bath and got into their robes for a nightcap in the den. Bama frowned and shook his head but said nothing as he watched Willie place a record on the hi-fi turntable. Billie Holiday's "Gloomy Sunday" boomed out.

Willie swizzled the fruit in his old-fashioned with a sober face.

He said, "Bama, I've been thinking for some time about giving the sucker life a whirl. I'll dump the policy, the craps joint and the war with the dagos as soon as I make my point. That point is that I'm not a coward shit-heel like the other bankers the Mafia holds in such contempt."

Bama grunted. "And how soon is that, Willie? I hope the point you have to make don't refine down to a decimal point on a burial contract."

Willie leaned forward on the red suede-covered couch toward Bama behind the bar dropping ice cubes into his Cuba libre.

He said, "Bama, you know the toughest thing to get from Willie Poe is a promise, and that Willie Poe always keeps his promises."

Bama nodded. Willie went and stood at the bar. He clinked his glass against Bama's. "Bama, I promise that when you get back from the Apple, I'll step up or down, as it will turn out to be with the square life. We can get Sis and Darrel to help us locate and plan decor, name and things like that for our cabaret."

Bama smiled and clinked his glass against Willie's. "It's a promise I'll be very happy to hold you to, pal."

Willie went to his bedroom and was sitting on the side of the bed when Bama came to the doorway. He said, "You need a small insurance policy on that suitcase full of scratch Taylor's going to be driving around. Well, at least until you dump the policy wheel. Not that we really need it in his case. Remember, I touted the kid to you when he showed. But maybe . . . he's playing the con for us. And I don't have to remind you, nobody's immune to the right con."

Willie said, "You mean . . .?"

Bama said, "Yes, I mean test out his purity of heart with a little lie-detecting psychodrama!"

Willie frowned and said, "I don't like it. He's green and sensitive. If he's on the level, and I'm sure he is, he would chill on us and blow."

Bama said, "Jesus Christ, you're rusty, Willie."

Willie waved his glass. "Hold on, Bama, it's not rust, it's pure preoccupation with the wheel . . . and the motherfucking dagos."

"Sure Willie, I understand," Bama said. "Now, as I was about to say, we don't squeeze him ourselves. Gold Dust is playing in town. He can blueprint a take-off of the suitcase that would turn Willie Sutton bright green. It will be easy for Dust to cut into Taylor and lay the plan out for him and volunteer his help in execution for a reasonable percentage of the scratch."

Willie washed several powerful sleeping pills down to guarantee at least five hours' rest. Bama went to a window and peered into the twelve-foot-walled backyard at the prowling pack of giant German shepherds.

118

Willie looked thoughtful. "Bama, let's make sure the kid don't wake up we didn't trust him. Okay?"

Bama said, "Sure, Willie. Gold Dust is almost as sweet as you are when you're together. Let down and sleep well, pal."

It was the second morning of T.'s employment at fifty a week and room and board at Willie's house. T. was sitting at the unopened bar. He idly looked out the window. The street was alive with its crawl of sleepy-eyed derelicts. They blinked and gasped in the morning sunlight like iguanas.

Willie was in the rear booth going through some papers. A panel truck with "Snack Goodies" stenciled on its sides pulled to the curb in front of the bar.

Without taking his eyes off the swarthy driver who unlocked the rear door of the truck, T. said casually, "Uncle Willie, you expecting a snack truck this morning?"

Willie, without looking up, said, "Yeah Jessie, but watch that he don't dump his crushed pickups from the grocery next door on us."

T. watched the driver haul out, from the truck's rear door, an aluminum two-wheeled dolly-type cart. It was loaded with racks of cellophane-wrapped packages.

T., for an instant, shifted his eyes from the driver to the leggy barmaid. She had paused to shuck and jive on the sidewalk with a grocery clerk.

He shifted his eyes back to the truck. There was something about the way the driver's eyes flicked across the barroom window that brought T. to his feet. He snatched up the double-barrelled shotgun, ball bearing loaded.

The driver half turned his back. He reached into the truck. His hands blurred for an instant. He brought them out and started pushing the dull aluminum cart across the sidewalk. In that instant T.'s eyes trapped a reflected laser of metallic blue light and wondered why.

T. shot a look at Willie, still deeply concentrated on his paper work. T. crouched in the shadows at the side of the unlocked front door with shotgun in hand. The driver went past his grocery stop and wheeled to the bar's front door. He peered through the glass at Willie before easing the door open. He wheeled through it and the cart wheels rolled silently across the carpet.

Willie glanced up, and his eyes became enormous in the glow of a gooseneck lamp. He froze for a mini-instant before leaping to the floor. The assassin spat a Sicilian oath. He jerked a sub-machine gun off a hook at the back of the cart. He humped low and started around the circular bar toward the booth.

As T. sprinted from the shadows to within three feet of the assassin, a peanut shell popped beneath his foot. The assassin's face was strangely childish, eyes large and innocent appearing as he turned back toward the sound. He swung the machine gun around. T. lunged and stuck the exploding double barrels against the assassin's forehead.

The spastic trigger finger tightened on the machine gun and chattered a spew of slugs into the ceiling. The fiery blasts of ball bearings exploded the assassin's face and head asunder like a pricked balloon. A confetti of brain and gore splattered the back bar mirror.

The headless assassin flopped and knocked his feet against the bar for a moment. Then he lay still. T. stood staring down at the gore and shook. Willie dashed around the bar and snatched the shotgun.

T. turned dazedly and mumbled, "Uncle Willie, I feel funny . . . sick, couldn't help wasting him . . . he was . . ."

Willie quickly prodded and shoved him down into a distant booth.

Willie leaned over and whispered into T.'s ear, "One target is enough for the fucking wops. I blew that sonuvabitch's head off. Understand?"

T. nodded his head dumbly.

When the barmaid entered the door she screamed. She collapsed into the arms of one of the curious people attracted by the boom of the shotgun.

That night in Willie's house, the threesome sat in the den playing dirty hearts cards. T. played a card and Bama slammed down the Queen of Spades, black Meg herself.

T. said, "I played the wrong card again, and looks like ain't no way tonight I'm gonna keep my thinking on cards."

Bama and Willie looked into each other's eyes for an instant.

T. caught the exchange and said, "I ain't tender-hearted or nothing 'cause I drawed gallons of blood on the Westside, and even maybe killed one or two enemy at a long range in a big ruckus. But close-up pulling the trigger this morning smack-dab up in his face, I know I ain't never gonna forget him and his bloody stump neck."

Willie patted T.'s shoulder. "Jessie, don't worry about him. You didn't murder him . . ." Willie said quietly. "You killed him in self-defense. Everything is nailed down neatly. The district police commander guarantees there is no reason to worry about anything—official, he means."

Bama said, "Look, Jessie, this morning's shooting was the first time you were sure you killed another human being. You actually saw yourself blow his head away. Nobody except a foamy maniac could forget it just like that. I've got a hunch, son, that he will fade to a painless shadow in your mind sooner than you think."

T. said, "Hold on, Uncle Bama! I ain't feeling sorry and no pain for him, but for me that he was so crazy rushing in the bar to go, and it's me that give him his ticket. I just . . . well hope the fool ain't got one of them mama's that's gonna be grieving herself into no nuthouse, and even the grave."

Bama said, "Jessie, it's only midnight, play one more hand with us. Staying up a little longer may take the rocks out of your bed!"

T. grinned, "I don't wanta see old black Meg's mug enty more tonight. I'm gonna 'doss' like a baby soon as I check the dogs and work out on Bama's big bag after I run some."

T. turned and left the room.

CHAPTER TEN

Across town, top boss Louis Bellini sat in the living room of the Bellini mansion on Chicago's posh Gold Coast. The gold lame sleeve of his robe glittered in the moon-bathed room as he unconsciously combed long powerful fingers through his straight black hair littered with silver sproutings at the temples.

Bellini's deep-set black eyes stared out across the moon-bathed expanse of the estate's front yard. He focussed his attention on the road and on the guard in his cubicle at the front gate.

Suddenly headlights flared on the road. A dark sedan turned into the driveway leading to the gate. Bellini rose from his chair. He reached the intercom phone near the front door on the first ring from the cubicle.

Bellini lifted the receiver and passed his underboss, Joe Tonelli, and chauffeur through the gate. Bellini opened the front door and filled his chest with fresh summer air. He left the door ajar. Now he felt less weighted with tension when he sat down on the sofa.

He watched the chauffeur leap out to open the car door for Tonelli. He saw a flash of peach-colored pajamas beneath Tonelli's light topcoat and smiled thinly. Tonelli came into the living room and sat down beside Bellini. He had a harassed expression on his face.

Bellini let him stew for a long moment before he said, "Joe, I don't have to tell you why I wanted to speak with you at this late hour?"

Tonelli looked down at his burgundy bedroom slippers and said, "Mr. Bellini, it has to be about the death of Salvatore at the hands of Willie Poe this morning."

Bellini's soft voice had a slight edge of exasperation as he said in Sicilian, "No, I am not at this moment that much concerned with the death of Salvatore, except that it represents more failure. I am gravely concerned about the life of Willie Poe that still goes on to plague and threaten our business interests with the coloreds city-wide."

Tonelli's Adam's apple jiggled in his throat. He raised his eyes to Bellini's face, wearing its perpetual little half smile.

Tonelli said, "Mr. Bellini, excuse me, but you know we . . . I have done everything possible to solve the problem except the one thing you overruled last month."

Bellini's stern eyes muscled Tonelli's eyes back to another inspection of his bedroom slippers.

124

Bellini patted Tonelli's shoulder affectionately and said sweetly in Sicilian. "My friend, what's wrong inside your head? You got maybe big personal problems or secret troubles screwing up your head and our urgent business?"

Tonelli wiped his hand across his dewy brow. He shook his head.

Bellini smiled and went on. "Giuseppe, you've got me asking myself if I need a right arm who can't figure out why we can't offer fifty grand to coloreds to solve our problem."

Bellini stood and stared down at Tonelli. "Giuseppe, Poe's luck and guts, and your sloppy planning, have let this guy parlay himself into some kind of folk hero."

Bellini leaned his face down into Tonelli's upturned oval of chalk.

Bellini intoned, "He must go, Giuseppe, and we must send him before he becomes a living legend that our colored business partners will imitate. A lasting lesson of their bad Willie's folly will be taught the coloreds when he is dead with his mouth stuffed with his sex works and his black ass sliced off to the bone, *capisce?*"

Tonelli winced beneath Bellini's long and intense staring. Bellini knelt on the carpet before Tonelli and seized his face between his palms.

He said slowly, "My friend, I must have Willie Poe removed from my life. Two weeks, Giuseppe ... two weeks ... no more time, Giuseppe ... you have much to lose. *Capisce?*"

Bellini followed Tonelli to the door and said, "Who will you use?"

Tonelli smiled and said, "Frank Cocio has asked for Poe. He will take care of Poe assisted by my son-in-law, Jimmy Collucci."

Bellini bounced a gigantic hand off Tonelli's shoulder and nodded knowingly. "Ah! With the team of Collucci and Cocio, you will not further disappoint me."

Bellini paused thoughtfully and said, "I will not be unhappy if they hide a big salute inside his transportation as another way. . . ."

Tonelli beamed and said, "Never again, Mr. Bellini, will a nigger be permitted to become a Willie Poe."

CHAPTER ELEVEN

T. remembered the day before Bama went East to play con with Bulldog Slim, and a week before Rachel's release from the narc treatment center in Lexington. Bulldog, Bama and T. drove past a mixed couple going into a plush apartment building. Bama frantically blew the car horn.

The couple put suitcases down to wave. The thin, sharp-faced white man, in faded denim, was in stark contrast to his flashily dressed Amazonian companion.

Bulldog said, "Bama, that lady is some pretty, too pretty for a silk stud that's raggity as Yakima."

Bama chuckled and said, "That lady is Willie's sister, Reva, back from vacation. He's her husband. His skin is white, but he's as much nigger, in his heart, as we are. He wiped his ass with the social register. He split the white world with more money than Hollywood's got cocksuckers."

T. shook his head. "How did he get rich?"

Bama said, "Building better bridges and digging better tunnels all over the world. He's Darrel 'The Mole' Miller the Third."

At a stoplight, Bulldog said, "Lemme out here! Dig you on this corner later."

He leaped to the street and pumped his pipestem legs toward a sexy whore on the corner, grinning at him, as she ducked into a corner bar.

T. gazed back through the rear window. He shook his head. "That white joker for real? . . . Needs to at least blow a buck on a haircut for that lady's sake."

Bama said, "Reva digs him just the way he is, and she's all that matters to him."

They pulled up before Willie's bar and went inside. They joined Willie. He had his back rammed into the corner of his favorite rear booth. His eyes never left the front door. His hand was never far from the machine gun on the seat beside him.

Bama said, "Reva and Darrel are back."

Willie said, "I know, she was on the phone preaching to me a moment ago."

Willie pushed a miniature coffin to the center of the booth table. "It's some dago psyching that came special delivery a half hour ago," Willie said lightly as he raised the lid.

Bama and T. stared at the nude doll daubed crimson from its ragged throat to its crotch. The eyes and mouth in the black face were popped wide in terror.

Bama said, "Yeah, the cunning bastards hope to chill you into the palsy. When they try for you again you'll freeze and they'll have that fatal edge on you."

Willie said, "Shit, my ticker's pumping Prestone anti-freeze. Let the sneaky cocksuckers go on dreaming they can psych Willie Poe into a coffin."

Bama swung an arm toward the lone drunk at the bar and said, "Willie, why don't you bounce that barfly and take the ride with us to pick up Bulldog Slim?"

Willie jerked a thumb toward the numbers check-in station behind him. "I've got a policy wheel to run. And besides I close the bar early and the wops will think Willie Poe is folding up."

Bama said, "Well, why don't I leave Jessie to keep you company."

Willie snorted. "You mean keep me guarded, don't you, Bama?"

T. said, "Unc, I'm not leaving you in the joint alone."

Willie patted the machine gun and said evenly, "Jessie, you and Bama get out of my ass and leave Willie Poe to bodyguard Willie Poe."

Bama and T. exchanged a look between them and got to their feet. Hurt and angry, T. took off for the front door.

Willie called Bama back and said, "Goddamn! He's a sensitive jackass. Which reminds me, I told Gold Dust to nix that insurance con on Jessie for the scratch in the suitcase.... You're giving me a look reserved for marks. Bama, don't misunderstand why I nixed off Gold Dust."

Bama grinned and shrugged. "Oh no, I understand, Willie . . . I really understand," Bama said and started to turn away.

Willie stood up and said, "Go to hell, Bama."

He walked toward Bama and said, "Tell Jessie, Darrel is picking up me and the suitcase. Tell him he can sport his dick or wipe his ass with the double sawbuck in the glove compartment."

Bama grinned like a Cheshire. "Yes sir, cold-blooded Uncle Willie, I'll tell him."

Willie scowled and goosed Bama's rear end with the snout of the machine gun. Bama galloped for the door. Willie pursued and swung open the door. He said to Bama's back, "Hey, bubble butt, you want to bring Slim and Jessie to a get-together from ten on at Reva and Darrel's place?"

Bama turned, pointed at the machine gun and said, "Yes baby, if you promise not to bring your rattle to the party."

He went to the Imperial.

Willie waved at a squad of police cruising by and went into the bar. T. was behind the wheel with an injured expression on his face.

As T. bombed the car away, Bama said, "Damn, buddy, easy on the gas pedal. Willie invited us to a party Reva is throwing tonight. Her joint is gonna be lousy with round-butt foxes."

T. cut speed and said, "He gonna be there?"

"Who?" Bama asked.

"Uncle Willie," T. said with a frown.

Bama said, "Yeah, he'll be there. So what has that to do with boo koos of fine foxes?"

T. said, "Since he can't stand me in his face, I sure don't want him in mine."

Bama said, "You lop-eared mark! Willie don't

want you between him and that next dago on the turn. Sucker, you've hooked and hog-tied Willie. Which reminds me, old anti-freeze said tell you he's springing for the double saw in the glove damper so you can grease your Jones."

As T. cruised the Imperial into Gary, Indiana, he said, "Bama, I'm gonna deck out in one of them vines Unc bought me and have my first free world fun since I was a kid."

Bama said, "Always demand and feel you deserve the best you can yank out of the game, Jessie, before He calls it on account of darkness."

For two weeks Frank Cocio and young Jimmy Collucci had separately and together tailed Willie Poe around the clock. Collucci, wearing nondescript clothing, was staked out near the Fifty-eighth Street el station. He had been seated in a drab Ford sedan intently watching the front of Willie Poe's bar since T. had dropped off Willie that morning.

Reva Miller, lonesome and missing her husband, Darrel, away on business in Florida, had insisted against Willie's objection that she drive them to T.'s wedding reception at Rachel's home on the Westside.

Willie had told T. that morning that he would get to the reception on his own and that T. could use the Imperial to honeymoon at a resort in Michigan.

In the twilight Collucci saw Reva Miller's blue Caddie pull to a stop. He watched Willie Poe get in with his ever-present machine gun concealed in a tall leather hatbox. It was dark when Reva reached Rachel's home. The sidewalk was clogged with the overflow crowd of celebrants. Their parked, brightly streamered cars jammed the block.

Reva went down the block and parked around the corner. Collucci parked a hundred yards ahead and pondered taking off Willie Poe by himself. But he remembered the stern warnings of Tonelli and Cocio about going up solo against Willie and his machine gun.

Collucci went to a phone and within an hour Cocio arrived with a G. M. master key and a bomb. While Collucci stood as a lookout, Cocio placed the bomb under the front seat of the Caddie and ran a wire from it under the floor mat to the ignition.

At the reception, Willie gave the couple the key and deed to a Southside bungalow as a wedding gift. Willie and Reva kissed the happy couple and wished them well. T. threw his arms around Willie and Reva and walked them to the Caddie. T. stood by the side of the car as they got in.

Willie said through the open window, "Have fun, sport, but watch you don't throw your back out of joint."

T. laughed and said, "When I get old like you, Uncle Willie, I'll look out for my back."

T. waved and walked away toward the sidewalk. Reva waved and turned the key in the ignition. The blast slammed T. across the sidewalk and into some bushes where he lay dazed.

Finally he struggled to his feet and pushed through a ring of spectators to the odor of death and the bloody bits and pieces of Willie and Reva.

132

He was stony-faced and dry-eyed while Rachel walked him back to the house.

He locked himself in the cellar. Willie's death and T.'s piteous bellowing of sorrow and hurt chilled the guests and the party died. It was daylight before T. came up from the cellar encrusted with the coal dust that he had rolled in.

Willie's funeral was the biggest the Southside had ever seen. Willie and Reva's bronze caskets shimmered like slabs of gold as the pallbearers snailed from the church into the late summer sunlight.

Great crowds of the poor that Willie Poe had helped with a Christmas basket or a five-dollar bill pressed into the palm, wept and suffered that Willie Poe was dead.

And then the multitude raised their voices to a deafening din, chanting, *"Good-bye Willie Poe! Good-bye Willie Poe!"* until the hearse disappeared.

On the way to the cemetery in the family car behind the hearse Bama, T. and Darrel Miller sat silently huddled together in their sorrow and rage.

At the wake it was agreed that in their anger they should avoid taking reckless and ineffective action against their powerful enemy. In two months they would meet again, unhampered by unreasoning rage. Then they would sit down together and coldly plot how best to avenge the death of Willie Poe and Reva Miller.

Bama went back East to finish his last con tour. T. departed, determined to dredge up ex-members of the Black Devastators.

Darrel Miller locked himself away from the world and vowed to use his millions to avenge the murder of his beloved Reva. He gave birth to the concept of the "Free Zone" from which the Warriors for Willie Poe would battle the Mafia.

The Warriors bought the vacant church and, under the supervision of the Mole, started construction of the tunnel system beneath what would become the Free Zone. The Warriors would set up, in that Zone, an inter-racial rehabilitation clinic for "H" addicts. The clinic's high percentage of success would awe America.

CHAPTER TWELVE

T. sat very still at the window as he remembered one night a year after Willie Poe's death. He and Rachel had lain in the master bedroom of the parsonage, breathless and dewy after their wild lovemaking. She lay atop him, feeling him still hard inside her as they inhaled the honeysuckled breezes floating through the open window.

T. said, "What you thinking, Ra?"

She said, "About how much I love you. About how shocked and comical Mama looked when I let you just walk in after five years and carry me out to the car in your arms without first saying at least 'hello.'"

He laughed. "Wasn't nothing to shuck and jive about when I come to claim my forever woman."

She said, "Jessie, I hope we don't have to stay here forever."

He said, "Ra, why you say that?"

There was a roaring silence.

He said, "I'm living better than I ever did and even you, too. Ain't that right?"

She said, "Yes, Jessie, I know . . . but there's something about this whole setup that worries me."

"Why you worried, Ra?" he asked with a tiny edge of annoyance in his voice.

She said, "It's the tunnels . . . the guns . . . I get the feeling that we will someday have to pop into our holes like gophers to save our lives."

Silence again!

She pecked his lips. "I'm really worried the most about you, baby."

She felt him go limp inside her.

She heard him rumble from his chest, "I hope you ain't worried, Ra, like a lotta sisters figuring ain't no nigger smart enough and man enough to beat a white man in a death duel like we planning to whip on the Mafia. That why you worried, Ra?"

She oozed herself off his rod and rolled to his side.

She said flippantly, "Hell no, Jessie. My reason was I love you and want you alive. But since you're the baddest and the smartest there is, I won't worry any more, okay?"

He said, "Ra, you cracking shit on me I ain't laying still for. I may be the baddest, but you know ain't no way I can be the smartest with no big high school learning in books like you and your pimping dope fiend nigger dead and stinking in Detroit . . . but, Ra, I got too much smarts to let a mothuh pimp on me plus shoot poison dope in my body. Plus I heard them freakish dogs suck on a woman while she swallow their come."

She stiffened in shock. She fled to the side of the bed, whimpering and rocking with her head squeezed between her palms.

She sobbed, "You said he would be forgotten like pee down the toilet, remember? How could you break your promise . . . when you see me trying to be happy . . . staying well . . . wanting to forget?"

He stared at her heaving back and realized he was wrong. He felt remorse shake him. He scooped her into his arms and cradled her against his chest like a baby. His lips moved to say I'm sorry, but his hooligan pride choked him mute.

She said with a childish quaver, "Daddy, you sure you love me?"

He said, "Ra, I ain't got no doubt . . . I do, as long as you don't doubt I'm gonna be a man up 'gainst even the Mafia."

She said, "Could you do without me?"

He chuckled and said, "Ra, you ain't got to worry about dying, strong and healthy-looking as you are."

She propped her elbows on his chest and rested her face between her palms as she stared into his face.

She said, "Damn, Jessie! You're sure of me. I meant what would you do if I got up right now and left you forever."

He studied her face. Her eyes were glistening with guile, and his pride was hurt that she dared to test him. He visualized himself without her and felt a load of loss leaden his chest and spasm his scrotum. He realized he couldn't do without her. He recoiled from a vision of himself groveling and begging her with his eyes popping out not to leave him.

She thought, *your turn now against the wall*, and said, "Come on, Jessie, what would you do? Say?"

"Ra, I'd roll and cry like a crumb crusher, blocking the door so you couldn't get in the wind. I'd moan and groan, crap my pants like I had a thousand teeth and alla them rotten and aching."

She giggled, "Jessie, you jiving? You so stubborn you'd probably help me pack."

Then she traced his features with nippy kisses and said, "Daddy, you know I need you and love you too much to even ever want to get in the wind. Don't you?"

He nodded and sucked her tongue. She leaped astride him and impaled herself on his joint, heavy veined and fat with blood. She hooded her eyes and humped his weapon until she squealed and drooled saliva. Then in slow motion she looped the noose about the head of his organ.

Jessie gazed at her awesome butt reflected in a moonlit mirror. It was swaying and tossing with airy artistry as the noose leeched and grabbed. With a growl of joy he flung her beneath him. He eased himself into her and stroked her womb gate.

Later, after a nap, she said drowsily, "Why do beautiful dreams always have to run out so fast? . . . it was so real and wonderful. I wore a white mink coat that tickled my ankles when we went to the 'coming out' of one of our slew of lovely daughters

138

at a cotillion ball . . . you were so distinguished and handsome in white tie and matching sideburns . . . and we had a finer house than even those Braddock snobs that mama did laundry for . . . Oh Jessie baby, we were so happy!"

He said lazily, "Yeah Ra, you pretty and sweet and you dreaming sweet pretty dreams . . . real pretty."

She said, "You're pretty and sweet too, so what have you been dreaming lately?"

He said carefully, "Ra, I ain't had no pretty sleeping dreams since I dreamed in the penitentiary I was out here in the free world with you, and alla them was sweet and wet."

She laughed and belly-banged his crotch. "What kinda pretty dreams you having wide awake?"

He fidgeted and yawned. "Ain't but one all the time."

She pushed out her bottom lip. "Am I in it?"

He said, "Ain't that kind."

She beat tiny fists against his chest. "What kind! What kind!"

He sighed, "Ain't gonna tell you, Ra."

"Why can't you tell your wife?" she said and rolled off him and slapped wads of tissues between their legs.

He said, " 'Cause my wife might crack up and bust a gut."

He turned his back. "Sleep tight, Ra."

She said, "I won't laugh. Tell me, Jessie."

She razored a silver-lacquered fingernail down his spine to his buttocks. He shivered and howled and flipped to face her.

139

"Awright, Ra, the deal is, if you grin even, I'm gonna smack you cockeyed. A deal?"

"Damnit! Don't dangle me!" she said and swooped to scissor his nipple between her teeth. He flinched and pinched her honey-colored bottom.

He locked his eyes on her face and began. "Outta the box, you gotta know how the dream come to me through Uncle Willie. I growed to love him more than Bama even. Though I only knowed Uncle Willie a short spell, he's the foundation bricks of my dream.

"Before I knowed him I ain't doubted just a teeny mean look from a Mafia man woulda dreened pee down everybody's legs from the police to the president and me even. But no, no, not Uncle Willie, and 'cause I worshipped him I kilt one and lost my fear of Mafia men.

"After Unc was buried I rounded up more'n three hundred of the baddest niggers on the Westside to heist and shake down numbers banks and dope dealers for the geeters to buy artillery to waste all the Mafia men in Chicago for killing Uncle Willie.

"I guess except for Bama and them brains in his big shiny skull, and Darrel wasn't no slouch, you wouldn't have no husband here in the bed. They heard my plans and pulled my coat to how to use our power to fuck up the Mafia. How to get politicking protection by rounding up sympathy and blessings of the biggest baddest power there is. And they the people! All peoples, black, white and green, fear and hate the Mafia men and wish all a them was dead and stinking.

"So Ra, you see we building more 'n more tunnels and piling up guns. We training a army of commandos! It's all-out time by next Christmas to waste all the Mafia men in Chicago. Then we gonna waste them in New York, Detroit, Cleveland and everywhere cross country."

He raised and propped himself up against the headboard. His maroon eyes looked through Rachel.

He said, "Ra, after me and the Warriors waste the Mafia men cross country, I'm gonna . . . hear me good now, Ra! . . . me a convict street nigger nothin', is gonna be the greatest, famous nigger the world is knowed, and more'n Joe Louis even.

"Ra, the people gonna know Jessie Taylor livin' and dyin' and dead even, and even white folks eating, crapping or screwing, they gonna take time and feel sad when Jessie Taylor's leavin' and gone. Ra, that's my dream. What you think?"

She lay staring at his face through a long silence thinking, *How I thought I knew Jessie Taylor from way back . . . and I don't . . . but I love you.*

He frowned and said, "My dream, Ra, what you think?"

She said, "It's such a big one, Jessie . . . I . . ."

His face was fierce, "Too big for a nigger, huh Ra?"

"Hell no Jessie, I don't mean that," she said, deciding to placate him, certain she would convert him in time to her more practical dream.

"But hear this, Jessie Taylor, Rachel Taylor will see that you leave this world if you try to trade her

141

in on a fresher model when the glory days arrive. Let's go to sleep, Jessie, before the sun comes up."

He grinned and kissed the back of her neck when she rolled into his arms.

Just before they fell asleep she said, "Daddy darling, I'm so sorry we had a fight about past mess."

He said, "Ra, I'm sorry too, but sorry even more that dirty nigger Dandy Ike was kilt by his own hand when I got to Detroit looking him up."

And now in the parsonage office inside the Free Zone, T. saw the massive figure of Kong coming down the church walkway and his thoughts returned to the present and the possibility that Kong and Charming Mills were involved with the dope jacking gang who had murdered L. C.

T. remembered Bama's sound advice about staying cool and springing a psychodrama trap for Mills and Kong to prove them innocent or guilty. But T. was bursting inside to confront and quiz Kong at least in some oblique way and get the matter settled. T. heard Kong's heavy feet pass the office door and go down the hall toward his quarters.

T. was about to rise when he heard stealthy feet on the carpet behind him and felt soft hands clap across his eyes.

He touched them and said, "Fluffy," as he spun the chair around and faced his ten-year-old daughter.

She sat on his knee and fiddled with the blue wool collar of his shirt. "Mama sent me to get you to come to bed so she can sleep," she said. "Did I find you or what?"

He grinned and she slid to her feet as he rose from the chair.

"You found me, Fluffy, and tell Ra I'm coming."

They walked to the door embracing waists. He leaned and kissed her on the forehead and said, "Baby girl, reading late is got them pretty eyes red. You gonna go to sleep now for T. Dad?"

She smiled up at him. "If I get a big hug and a good-night kiss," she said with her bright tan pixie face upturned.

He hugged her fondly and kissed her tip-tilted nose. She pranced her long shapely legs down the hall a few paces and came back with enormous gray eyes sparkling intrigue.

She looked up into his eyes and said, "T. Dad, I'm not nervous and tender-hearted like Mama and you say I'm very good with a rifle. So promise me I can stay and fight with you if and when they come."

He looked at her for a long moment before he said gently, "Fluffy, you ain't never gonna shoot at no true target 'cause T. Dad gonna keep them too busy for them to come here."

He spanked her rump and she went down the hall beneath a row of cut-glass chandeliers that gleamed her black natural.

He waited until she disappeared and strode briskly down the hall toward Kong's door. He stood at the door fighting for control of his rising temper, with hand extended to knock.

He heard an insistent hissing sound behind him and spun around to face Bama across the hall outside his apartment. T. stood with mouth ajar watching Bama's index finger crooking in the air. T. sighed and crossed the hall with a sheepish look on his face.

Bama whispered, "Man, will you take your ass to the gym or between Rachel's legs and work that gorilla out of you before you blow our plan."

T. said, "Bama, you right. I gotta come to myself."

He turned away and went toward his apartment. He stopped and came back to Bama.

Bama said, "Well?"

T. said, "I wonder if Love Bone Larry's sister is in the phone book?"

Bama said, "Why?"

T. said, " 'Cause I'm gonna have her called to wire her straight about the dago being the one behind Love's wasting."

Bama nodded and T. leaned forward and said, "How'd you know I was gonna get on Kong's case?"

Bama grinned and said, "It was easy, nigger. Your monicker is Tit For Tat, ain't it?"

They laughed and T. went away shaking his head.

CHAPTER THIRTEEN

Tonelli, with his arm around Collucci's shoulder, had seated him at the conference table in the glare of a ceiling lamp. Collucci knew it was done to humiliate him.

Collucci had slipped on sunglasses and listened for many minutes to the programmed mouth of underboss Cocio spew a thinly veiled attack on him. His dark face was bland, but his eyes were slitted in hatred and contempt behind the black windows of his glasses.

Family *consigliere* Louis "Papa" Bellini was seated near the end of the table with Collucci. Bellini fidgeted and pressed his gnarled fingertips against his temples as if in pain.

Joe Tonelli was smugly neutral.

Cocio paused to sip from a glass of water. Collucci stared at his widow's peak slashing down the olive forehead toward his hooked nose and thought, *That little cocksucker sure looks the part for where I'm sending him.*

Frank Cocio set the glass down and locked his unblinking black eyes on Collucci's face. He said in Sicilian, "Giacomo, tell me does your ambition roar so loud inside your head it drowns out your hearing to the truth I spoke about the lousy drug business?"

Collucci lifted the corners of his mouth in a barely perceptible sneer, "Please sir, excuse me, but in defense of my ambition I am forced to . . . remind you that many years ago under your hand and teaching I became ambitious enough to lead a mob that snatched a thousand cars a year for you."

Collucci shrugged and said, "Excuse me again please for saying that since that time I was inspired to my present ambition by your example. I thought I heard you say the hard drugs have more value and profit in the smallest package than gold, and even money in most of its denominations. If my hearing is not good then I apologize."

Cocio said, "You heard me say that, but you could have assumed I was aware of the profits in narcotics. Are you denying that the blood and the trouble of the drug business outweigh the returns?"

Collucci shrugged. "Sir, how can I deny what Mr. Tonelli said earlier was decided by the National Commission?"

Cocio tented his fingertips beneath his pointed chin and stared balefully at Collucci. Cocio tapped the Love Bone Larry Flambert death account on the front page of the black *Daily Defender* on the table before him. "This is what I mean, narcotics and killings on the front page of this colored paper.

It's already hinting dope and Mafia and stoking the kind of heat that the Commission and everybody wants to avoid."

Collucci said, "We . . . the Commission can't be hurt because some spick broad and her jigaboo get knocked off."

Bellini said, "Francesco, aren't the white press and police buying the jealous spick theory?"

Cocio said, "Yes, Luigi, but maybe his sister or somebody will dig up a connection that some hungry bastard from one of the white dailies will run down to 'publishable substance.' "

Tonelli said, "We got real stand-up political friends from the big city and state governments all the way into the White House." Tonelli shrugged and lit a cigar. "As a member of the National Commission, I can assure that anybody who affects adversely any of our important friendships will be finished quickly."

Cocio said to Collucci, "The girl . . . was it necessary to . . . ?"

Collucci said, "Excuse me sir, but at his trial she heard too much. I ask you respectfully to trust my judgment and efficiency since you yourself guided me in the old days in matters of this kind."

Cocio said, "The old days are gone, and your romancing around with dope and blood must stop before you make the headlines." Cocio glanced at Tonelli and continued, "You want to be a fucking star, go to Hollywood. And you'll find more broads than even you can handle."

Collucci glared venomously at Cocio and thought, *The love-sick bastard wants the*

Commission to hit me so he can beg to suck Olivia's shit through a straw. So, snake, here's a kick in the ticker.

Collucci said, "I was through with the drug business the instant Mr. Tonelli told me the Commission's wishes." Collucci glanced at Tonelli and said to Cocio, "Excuse me sir, but you have perhaps insulted the father of Olivia Tonelli Collucci when you suggest my unfaithfulness. If you could but imagine yourself the husband of the magnificent Olivia, you would realize the impossibility of my unfaithfulness."

Cocio darted an embarrassed look at Tonelli and said, "Mr. Tonelli knows I meant no insult."

Tonelli smiled and pushed his palms in the air toward Cocio. "Francesco, I would advise my son-in-law to dally with broads here and there along the road." He shrugged. "After all, how otherwise can any guy fully appreciate a truly superior woman?"

Cocio studied a report of raids made on the organization-protected enterprises on the South and Westsides by Tat Taylor's Warriors.

Tonelli said, "Giacomo, your respect for the Commission pleases me very much."

Then Tonelli put his elbows on the table. He clasped his hands together and compassion flooded his face. "The dope is bad . . . very bad," Tonelli said.

Collucci stared at him in awe as he remembered Tonelli's long track record of cold-blooded non-feeling.

Tonelli went on with great pain on his face,

"The kids, Giacomo . . . I saw little colored kids in Harlem no older than Petey with a habit. I am saddened at the thought my beautiful twin girls could one day be poisoned with the dope. You, myself, all fathers, a wise man said, 'must realize their obligation of fatherhood to all children.' Think about it, Giacomo, and feel proud to drop the goddamn dope business."

Collucci smiled and nodded assent. A thrill of superiority and power shot through him to hear and see the softness and vulnerability of Tonelli crop out. For the first time at the table Collucci felt some of his tension drain away. He lit a cigarette and stared at Tonelli with a warm smile. He thought, *You senile old cunt, soon I will put you out of your misery.*

Bellini's heart galloped wildly. He had seen the imprint of the derringers when Collucci lit his cigarette. Bellini sat smiling his perpetual half-smile and scrutinizing Collucci's performance, determined to seize him if he moved to use them.

Cocio glanced up from the report of Warrior attacks and said to Collucci, "Taylor and his Warriors will soon attack this place if they are not stopped. You brag of learning from me how to handle urgent problems like Taylor. Those at this table know how I kept the coloreds in line.

"Mr. Tonelli before me also kept a lid of steel on them. Taylor goes on and on shoving his black ass in our faces. Every day he is allowed to live is an insult to your responsibility."

Cocio paused, his black eyes bright with triumph. Bellini, with eyes atwinkle, switched his attention to the smug face of Tonelli and back to Cocio.

Cocio waved his hand airily and said, "Giacomo Collucci, if you can handle only rabbits perhaps someone who can handle Taylor the lion should fill your position, eh? Perhaps you should exchange positions with the little tiger Momo Spino on the Westside and handle the soft craps and loan businesses."

Collucci carefully removed the dark glasses and locked his yellowish eyes on Cocio. Collucci shaped a smile as he languidly lit a cigarette and exhaled a blast of smoke. "Mr. Cocio, I agree Taylor is overdue . . . more than twenty years overdue," Collucci said. "For a month after we gave Willie Poe the big salute, I begged your permission, I even wept, so much did I want to put Taylor to sleep. But, do you remember your words, Mr. Cocio? You laughed when I showed you my crooked wrist and the scars Taylor gave me. You told me to write off my kid grudges. 'And anyway', you said, 'I have much more important work for you to do than getting the harmless flunkey of Willie Poe.' "

Collucci looked deliberately at Tonelli who darted an evil look to Cocio.

Collucci went on, "But Mr. Cocio, I will take all the responsibility for that mistake. Awkward as it would have been, I should have appealed above you for permission from Mr Tonelli, or if necessary, somehow to Mr. Bellini. Forgive me, friends, for poking into the unpleasant past, but it is better than confusion."

150

Cocio stared at Collucci with insensate hatred.

Collucci beamed his most charming smile and leaned forward. "I have Taylor set up . . . soon now he will be like an aching tooth extracted and we can all get together and celebrate over glasses of good vino."

There was a knock on the door.

Tonelli said, "Yes, Carlo."

Dinzio, the bodyguard, opened the door a bit and stuck his bearded head into the conference room. "The nurse wants a word with you, Mr. Tonelli," Dinzio said in heavy Sicilian. "Something about the twins."

Tonelli dipped his head and Dinzio admitted the nurse to Tonelli's presence.

The elderly Sicilian nurse stepped inside the room with a harassed face.

Tonelli said, "What is it, Louisa?"

She wrung her hands. "The twins, Mr. Tonelli . . . the twins, they are spoiled for only your singing of the Old Country lullabyes. I am hoarse as a goose and still they lie awake crying for you."

Tonelli smiled his pleasure and said, "Tell them I am coming faster than Batman and Robin."

Louisa closed the door and Tonelli shrugged and waved his palms helplessly in the air. "I myself spoiled them rotten, so what can I do?" he said, rising from his chair. He was followed by the others.

Collucci murmured pleasantries and started to shake hands all around. He had to literally hem in Cocio. He seized Cocio's hand, limp and hot with

151

anger. He smiled into Cocio's face and crushed the small hand in his powerful paw for a wincing instant.

Tonelli looked past Bellini as they exchanged last words to say to Collucci leaving the room, "Take my love to your family, Giacomo."

Collucci nodded and followed Dinzio and Cocio down the hallway toward the reinforced steel door. Dinzio manipulated the electronic device in his palm and the steel door, thick as a vault door, swung open.

Cocio turned down the corridor toward his ancient dwarf of a mother sitting in the living room. She was peevishly cutting her eyes at Cocio for his neglect of her during the long conference.

Collucci went down the corridor past the guards' lounge to the elevator. He pressed the "down" button. His Patek Phillippe winked two A.M. He felt a presence behind him. He turned slightly and snared Bellini in the corner of his eye. He turned and smiled into Bellini's face. He stared at Bellini's frozen face, waiting for it to thaw and blossom for him as always.

Collucci thought he caught a glacial glint in Bellini's eyes as he said in soft Sicilian, "Giacomo, you will take time to drop me off to pick up my car at the service station?"

Collucci said, "Yes Papa, be happy to."

The elevator door slid open and Collucci stepped aside and followed Bellini into the cage. He was surprised by Carl Dinzio getting on as the door was closing. As the cage zoomed down, Collucci wondered about Bellini's first and only coldness toward him in their thirty-year friendship.

He glanced at Bellini's face and Bellini's eyes avoided him. He shifted his back into a corner to face Dinzio and Bellini. His mind churned up the unthinkable thought that his fit of paranoia forced him to think. Had double-headed snakes Tonelli and Cocio somehow poisoned his old friend and mentor against him, and now on the elevator these two would put him to sleep?

Collucci stared at Bellini popping the knuckles on his monstrous hands, still powerful at age of eighty-five. Collucci stared at the monsters and remembered that strong rumor had it that Bellini, in his youth, had crushed thirty or forty throats fulfilling contracts in Sicily and in America.

Collucci watched Bellini's hands with one eye and the hands of Dinzio with his other eye. He loosely braced himself in the corner. He jiggled his arms so the derringers tickled the heels of his palms.

The elevator reached the basement. Collucci thought he caught Bellini giving him a peculiar look as he left the elevator. Collucci delayed stepping out of the cage for the instant it took for Dinzio to split off from Bellini.

Collucci drove Bellini through the tunnel to the street in silence.

Bellini said, "It's Del Campo's station."

Three blocks from the penthouse and with the blazing lights of the station in sight, Bellini said, "Giacomo, pull over and park for a few words with me."

Collucci parked and snuffed the car lights and

153

engine. All the while he locked Bellini's hands in the corner of an eye. Collucci fidgeted and listened to Bellini's chronic bronchitis scratching the long silence and thought, *Christ Papa! Dear friend don't turn around on me.*

Bellini said in Sicilian, "Giacomo, I am very sad for you."

Collucci laughed hollowly, "Why Papa?"

"You got troubles, big troubles . . ..Please let me help you, Giacomo."

Collucci said, "Papa, thanks for the offer but the biggest trouble I got is going to sleep with a slug in the head within the week and making everybody happy, especially Tonelli."

Bellini said, "Has the student lost so much respect for the teacher that he insults him with diversion?"

Collucci frowned. "I will always respect you for many reasons, my dearest friend."

Bellini said, "Do you also trust me?"

"As much as I respect you, I trust you. But why this quiz?" Collucci said.

They stared into each other's eyes.

Bellini said, "Then trust me, Giacomo, don't try to fool me. The trouble I speak of is not outside, it is inside your mind eating like a cancer."

Collucci said, "Read my mind. Go on. Let me also respect you for that."

"I saw the proof of your sickness at the table . . . You have lost all respect for the Honored Society I brought you into," Bellini said quietly.

Collucci turned the ignition key and the engine whispered to life.

Collucci said, "I'm sorry, Papa, but you're reading me all wrong. I'm tired and so are you. I'll take you to your car."

Bellini grunted.

Collucci wondered if Bellini had deserted him. "Papa dear, you still are my friend as always?"

Bellini shrugged, "Giacomo, what a pity that you must ask. I suspect I will be your friend when you are no longer my friend. Yes, I still love you, Giacomo, but . . ."

Collucci rolled into the service station beside Bellini's seventy-three Riviera. A grease-stained mechanic was just closing the hood.

Bellini turned the door handle and said, "There was a husband in Sicily long ago with a good but homely wife and a ravishing young sweetheart. All the villagers were certain the beauty owned the heart of the husband. Then one day he came upon his sweetheart astride his wife. She was about to plunge a dagger into the wife's heart. Without hesitation or a word the husband shot the sweetheart through the head. All the villagers were shocked and amazed to learn in this awful manner who really owned the heart of the husband."

Collucci's brow wrinkled. "Papa, why the hell tell me a parable that fits nothing that I can relate to? Good night Papa, good night," Collucci said wearily.

Bellini got out and went around the back of the car and leaned into Collucci's face as he was lighting a cigarette. Collucci, startled, recoiled.

Bellini shook his head and held Collucci's face gently between his palms and said, "Giacomo, please, you must heal your mind somehow and very soon! You worry me very much."

Bellini sighed deeply and his eyes became soft. "Dear friend, you must not forget that your Papa Bellini is married to the Honored Society," Bellini said.

He walked away to his own machine.

Collucci stared at Bellini's back for a long moment before heading home. He had retraced three blocks past the Tonelli penthouse when he saw Tonelli's bodyguard, Dinzio.

Collucci pulled to the curb and watched him talking to a tall brunette standing on the steps of a gray stone house. Dinzio gave her a gift-wrapped package and a peck on the lips.

Collucci felt high exhilaration as he pulled away for River Forest. His eyes sparkled as he sang to himself, *Dinzio's got a broad, and when I'm ready I got the key to hit Tonelli!*

CHAPTER FOURTEEN

At the moment that Collucci drove wearily into his River Forest driveway, Mayme Flambert left her apartment atop Mack Rivers' Voudoo Palace Cabaret.

The winds shrieked and flogged humpy snowdrifts. They resembled, beneath the funeral overcast, rows of tombstones. Christmas lights, in the darkened loneliness of shop windows, made Mayme's shadow gargantuan as she hunted a male animal for urgent Voudoo rites demanded by the death of her brother, Larry.

A dozen times during the hour and half that she hunted, dark shapes of cats and dogs eyed her with glowing fright and fled before her.

She went down State Street. After several blocks she stood before a fenced-in used auto lot. She cooed Haitian sweet talk at a Great Dane almost as large as a Shetland pony. He leaped and snarled.

She took a plastic-wrapped menstrual pad from a pocket of her fur coat and moved toward the slobbery beast. She thrust the pad against the fence. He sniffed hungrily at the meld of blood and vaginal slime.

His hind legs quivered and his crimson dingus eased out. He whined as he licked and gnawed at the corner of the pad through the fence. Finally he could no longer control his passion. He forgot duty and leaped over the fence. He followed her, snuffling his nose against her coat pocket. A block from her apartment his lust overwhelmed him. He knocked her down. He daggered air as he humped above her.

She led him up the stairs and into the apartment. He followed her to the closet that she used as a temple for her Voudoo ceremonies.

He balked at the threshold and growled. His great eyes were electric with intelligence as they followed her every movement. She realized he was trained to kill if attacked. She had to be sure she didn't miss when she shot for his heart with the butcher knife she scooped up.

She held the butcher knife behind her back. She realized that the butcher knife would be risky used on such a large beast. She lifted the lid of a small silver box containing a variety of deadly poisons. She slammed the lid down. She couldn't poison the Dane.

She squatted and inserted a finger deep inside herself. She rubbed the finger against his muzzle. He whimpered and licked his swollen organ frantically, but refused to enter the temple.

She stepped past him, concealing the butcher knife beneath her skirt against her thigh. She pretended to ignore him. He spun and sat on his rump with his tongue lolling out. He cocked his head from one side to the other as he gazed at her back.

Suddenly he lunged to his feet and galloped into the kitchen behind her. She lathered him with sweet talk as she turned away from the refrigerator holding a hunk of ham.

He snorted and leaped upon her. The butcher knife clattered into a corner. She crashed to the floor slightly stunned. He growled ferociously and ripped her skirt to tatters with his teeth.

He had pried her bare thighs apart with his paws and muzzle when her head cleared. She rolled to the butcher knife. He lunged and covered her like a blanket in the corner. He humped his wet organ against her thigh and lapped his sandpaper tongue against her neck and face. She lay on her left side with her hand touching the butcher knife beneath her. His hind feet slipped on the linoleum and he tumbled off her with a thud.

She got to her feet and scrambled to a counter top. Furious, he bared his fangs and gouged furrows into the counter with his front paws as he tried to pull himself up. She stared at the pulsing of his heart against his buff-colored hide. She grunted for velocity and backhanded the butcher knife deeply into the center of the pulsebeat. He shuddered and fell twitching to the floor, gouting blood. His mouth was agape sucking air.

Within a half-hour she had attended to her bruises and lacerations and was intently reading the entrails of the Dane for a lead to Bone's murderer. Suddenly she froze. A radiant smile lit her coal-black elfin face. She was certain she heard, faintly, the silky whisperings of the Loas.

"Attend the dead! Attend the dead! The murderer later! The murderer later!" she heard them instruct.

She looked at her wristwatch in the glow of the altar. She had given the undertaker a special fee. Yes, it was now late enough to slip into the mortuary morgue and properly release Larry's spirit.

She called to notify the undertaker she was on her way. She sat in her parked Mustang near the rear of the funeral home. Soon the garage door swung up. She carried a suitcase down the sidewalk. The undertaker led her past several limousines and a hearse. Then through a door. The mortuary morgue reeked of formaldehyde.

The undertaker went through a side door. The only light in the room was an overhead spot focused on the nude corpse of Bone. She went to the porcelain table and stared at the butchered remains.

With a strangled cry she flung herself on the bloated coldness and kissed his hands folded across his chest. She held her face against his for a long while. She sobbed uncontrollably for the first time in her life. She stroked the hideous wounds with her fingertips and chanted, through bared teeth, a Haitian vow of vengeance.

From the suitcase she took a small urn containing gunpowder. She lit and flung a match. There was a whooshing flash that would drive away her brother's enemies. She forced a pinch of arsenic powder between his stiffened lips. This to protect his eternal sleep from sorcerers who might

160

awaken him and press him into everlasting enslavement as a zombie.

Then she embraced him and shrilled her vow of vengeance until her voice was a whisper. She slipped out into the night and drove home heavy with sorrow.

She walked the floor until dawn thinking about Larry and herself as children. She remembered what a harsh lot it was to be the children of lowly peasants, half starving and half naked most of the time. But worst of all for her at least, was the utter facelessness, her tortuous feeling of non-being, as anonymous as the insects.

She was having coffee when the phone rang. She picked it up. A Warrior under instructions from Taylor persuaded her to ignore the police theory of Bone's death. He convinced her it had to be Southside enforcer Collucci who was responsible for Bone's murder. He assured her that the Warriors were very eager to kill Collucci. Mayme promised to give her life if necessary to achieve their mutual goal.

She went into her temple. She gave thanksgiving to her friends, the all-powerful and wise Loas, for revealing Collucci as the murderer of her brother.

CHAPTER FIFTEEN

The day had come to put Tit For Tat Taylor to sleep. Collucci was alone behind the locked door of his study. One wall of the study was a bookcase crammed with works from Shakespeare to Schopenhauer. High up near the ceiling was an extremely well-thumbed volume of illustrated examples of human sex organ deformities and trans-sexuality. The urgency of removing Tat Taylor had given him no time to open a book in weeks. Not even his favorite.

Now he concentrated on matters that related to the everlasting sleep of Joe Tonelli.

Collucci stood before a mirror, bearded and mustached in the image of Dinzio the Sphinx. He mimicked into a tape recorder microphone the mumbly voice of the Sphinx. Collucci listened for the dozenth time to the playback and smiled his satisfaction.

Listening intently, he was unaware that Angelo had pulled the limousine into the driveway. Angelo got out and opened the rear door for Olivia and for Bellini, invited to Olivia's celebrated lasagna on the cook's day off.

Olivia and Bellini went into the entrance hall. They removed their coats before seating themselves in the living room. After brief chitchat, Olivia went to the kitchen to prepare her specialty.

Bellini listened to the odd sound of Collucci's muffled rehearsal. He rose and went across a hallway toward the door of the study. He halted abruptly several feet away. He was surprised and shocked to hear what was unmistakably the voice of Tonelli's most trusted bodyguard, miles from his responsibility.

Bellini's further curiosity was impelled by the memory of Collucci's hide-out derringers at the Tonelli conference. Bellini put his ear against the door to hear the repetitious droning. Bellini went quickly back to the living room and pondered the mystery.

Collucci switched off the recorder. He stripped off and secreted the Dinzio beard, Old Country mustache and tape. Collucci went into the living room and greeted Bellini with a wide smile and a warm embrace.

Bellini said, "Giacomo, how about letting me pick your pocket for a couple of sawbucks before lunch?"

Collucci bowed extravagantly and flung his palms out toward the study. Every play of the cards was a misadventure for Bellini. He was preoccupied with the mystery of Dinzio's voice.

At lunch Collucci watched Bellini pick at his favorite dish and said, "Papa, have you found a new great love that steals your appetite?"

Bellini shook his head and said softly, "No,

Giacomo, not after my Angelita." He paused and looked squarely into Collucci's eyes. "Perhaps even our simple pleasures eventually desert us like false friends near the end."

Collucci grunted and said as he rose from the table, "Papa, a guy can say hello to you lately and you're going to bend his ear with a buck and half worth of crackerbarrel philosophy."

Olivia and Bellini looked at each other as Collucci stomped from the dining room.

Olivia said, "What on earth . . . ?"

Bellini leaned toward her and squeezed her hand. "Don't be upset, my dear. I was not offended," Bellini said as he rose from the table.

He stood beside her chair looking down into her upturned face, bright with concern.

He patted her shoulder and said, "I am very sorry I could not eat more of your delicious food. I will devour even the plate next time."

She rose and followed him to the entrance hall coat rack.

She said, "Have one more cup of coffee before I ring Angelo."

He shook his head and slipped into his overcoat with her help. "Angelo said his wife is ailing, let him nurse her," he said. "Besides I need the walk to the cab stand."

She kissed his cheek and said as he opened the door, "I apologize for Jimmy . . . he . . . well, one of his playmates has probably picked up her marbles and he'll be up tight for a hot week or so."

Immediately she regretted revealing her bitterness.

Bellini said, "I am afraid his problem is not that simple."

She said, "Papa Bell, do you know something . . . something about him, some danger or trouble I should know about?"

Bellini embraced her waist. He looked down into her anxious eyes and lied. "I don't really know anything that you should worry about. Persuade him to take you away for a while to some new, quiet place. Perhaps he can reacquaint himself with you and realize his good fortune. It will be a blessing for his health to escape the pressures of his business and ambition."

She said, "If there was something bad . . . unpleasant, you wouldn't spare me? You would have faith in my strength?"

He said, "You are a Tonelli and I would trust you with my life."

He cupped his monstrous hands. "Since I held you like this at your christening, the Bellinis and Tonellis have co-mingled their blood and trusts, and for five hundred years before that. Need I remind you my Angelita was sister to your father's mother?"

She shook her head and said, "I too would trust you with my life, Papa Bell."

She brushed his cheek with her lips as he turned and stepped away. She pushed the door shut. She sensed a presence behind her as she looked through the front window at Bellini striding down the walk. His silky mane of hair was like a platinum skullcap in the sunlight. She turned her head to glance at Collucci's tight face standing behind her looking past her at Bellini.

Bellini halted on the sidewalk as Petey's private school bus pulled up. Petey got off the bus and ran into Bellini's outstretched hands.

She said without turning her eyes from the window, "Jimmy, you were an ass and you should apologize to Papa Bell."

Collucci grunted and said, "When he apologizes for his senility. Already he's reading minds. Next he'll have his exclusive hot line to Mars or somewhere out there. Olivia, you stop calling me names . . . talking to me like that, or I'll swat some tone into that old bouncy butt of yours."

She turned and gave him a treacherous hooded look. She hissed, "Wretched bastard!"

She turned to greet Petey with a warm bright smile.

Collucci went to the kitchen back door and put his hand on the doorknob. He turned and went to the dining room. He swept a vase of fresh flowers off the buffet. He went to the breakfast nook. He scooped up a bowl of fruit and went out the back door to Angelo's apartment.

Angelo opened the door and Collucci stepped into the neatly arranged living room, brightly decorated in turquoise and red. He placed flowers and fruit on the coffee table next to Angelo's butterball wife napping on the couch. Her olive face was pale and moist with flu.

Angelo said, "Maria will be cheered."

Collucci nodded and pointed to his wristwatch.

Angelo said, "Five minutes."

Collucci shut the door and went up the stone

steps leading to Lollo "The Surgeon" Stilotti's second story apartment. Collucci drummed his knuckles on the door. The door opened and Stilotti's half-naked bulk almost filled the door frame. Collucci glanced past him at Stilotti's possum-faced blonde. Her forty-eight boobs spilled onto a tray as she munched lunch in bed.

Collucci whispered, "Lollo, I need you . . . in five minutes."

Stilotti looked petulant and stroked stubble on his jaw.

Collucci intoned, "Five minutes," and went down the steps.

Olivia was in the master bedroom repairing a broken fingernail when Collucci went to get his black melton overcoat. Olivia gazed at him and thought how well it went with the dove-gray Brooks Brothers suit he was wearing.

Perversely, she went and plucked a dot of lint off his coat sleeve and said, "Ah! At least there's a bit of business she won't perform for me."

He said, "Madame Paranoia, clean your fucking crystal ball and see it's your father's lousy business again. Just for laughs I ought to take you along." He whirled out of the room.

She hurled at his back, "I apologize if I'm wrong this time, Rubber Dick!"

Collucci scowled and hurried to the limo for the trip to kill Taylor at Rachel's uncle's funeral.

Angelo was behind the wheel. Collucci signaled him to remain. Collucci climbed into the Caddie. Collucci and Angelo laughed to see Stilotti with his collar and tie askew lumber down the driveway and trip on an untied shoelace. Stilotti crashed, bounced and landed on his rear end. He struggled mightily to rise and then sat there, his outrage and embarrassment twitching his pink face.

Angelo went and helped him to his feet. Stilotti hoisted himself into the front seat. Angelo backed the Caddie through the electronically opened gate of steel bars.

When they got to Phil's white stucco house in suburban Cicero, Stilotti, Phil's first cousin, went to the door. Phil's oldest son admitted him. Stilotti fought to keep his face straight as he sat in the living room watching Phil's Amazon wife, Ella, draping and pinning material on Phil's gaunt frame.

Phil darted a look at Stilotti as he shucked himself free of the cloth. "I'm the only one in the house close to her height," Phil said as he straightened his checkered bow tie. Phil hunched his shoulders. "So, I'm the dummy for the dress she's making for when Junior gets his degree in pharmacology next week."

Stilotti glanced at his watch and rose from the sofa. He grinned and said, "Filippo, with some silicone up front—" Stilotti's hands made a pinching gesture. *"Marone!"*

They laughed. Phil led the way through the house and out the back door to his workbench in the garage. He took an encased 257 Wetherby magnum rifle off a shelf and slipped it free of its case before passing it to Stilotti, who hefted it and examined it with satisfaction.

"A lotta rifle."

Phil said, "Yeah, with the 180-grain slugs the

ɔoss is gonna get high speed and the accuracy that
ʒoes with it."

Stilotti said, "Sanitary?"

Phil said, "Yeah, a hundred and ten percent
ıntraceable!"

Stilotti gestured toward the large Buick sedan in
he garage. "That's the transportation?"

Phil said, "Uh-huh, and also a Dodge already
tashed in a drop with clean plates."

They got in the Buick. Phil drove to the street.
Angelo and Collucci followed a block behind as the
Buick cruised toward the far Southside. Phil pulled
o the curb at a light honk of the Caddie's horn.
Collucci and Stilotti switched places in the cars.
Angelo drove the Caddie to the Dodge sitting in a
wo-car garage behind a fire-gutted house. Angelo
and Stilotti transferred to the Dodge. Several miles
ater Phil turned into an alley and drove past a row
ɔf condemned tenements.

"Mr. Collucci, you know I'd be happy to do the
ob on this dinge," Phil said seriously.

Collucci said, "Phil, you do it, I'll feel only half
ʒood. For most of my life I've wanted to put him
o sleep. Today is my day to feel all good!"

Collucci chuckled, "And besides, Phil, even with
a scope, at four hundred yards, maybe you'd be
slightly unsure going for the noggin. You're damn
ʒood, Phil, but not for this one."

Phil shrugged and braked behind a corner
enement. They got out. They stepped toward the
abandoned building. They noticed Angelo and
Stilotti walking down the alley toward them. The
Dodge was parked in the backyard of a condemned

house.

Collucci and Phil went up a scabrous stairway through the stench of ancient urine to a rubble-strewn apartment on the fourth floor.

Collucci stood wide-legged and flexed his gloved fingers like a gunfighter before a showdown in the Old West. He sat down on a tattered sofa covered with newspaper that Phil had positioned the day before.

Phil's gloved hands set the rifle up on a revolving tripod. Phil suctioned-cupped it to a steel milk crate several feet from the window sill. Then he wiped the whole installation thoroughly with his handkerchief.

Collucci sighted through the scope across four hundred yards of urban clearance. The church and milling people were blurred under an overcast of dark sky.

Collucci said, "Without this starlight scope, I'd have to postpone my pleasure."

He zeroed in on the head of one of the mourners streaming from the church. Collucci glanced at his wristwatch and said, "Taylor should be coming out!"

Phil said over his shoulder as he hastened toward the door, "Get a bull's-eye! I'll get the hell out of here and take care of things downstairs."

Before the noise of Phil's shoe soles grating on the gritty stairway had faded away, Collucci saw the pallbearers come from the church and start down the stone steps with the casket. From Collucci's perch they were like black beetles in the dull light.

Collucci felt his heart boom as he caught sight of a trio of cars containing Warrior bodyguards pull to the curb behind the family car. A dozen Warriors leaped from their cars and descended upon the hearse and lead family car. He peered eagerly through the scope. He swept it back and forth across the pallbearers as they descended the steps.

In the alley, Phil set the Buick's engine athrob. Angelo, armed with a sawed-off shotgun, peered from the blistered carcass of a jalopy on its side twenty yards behind the Buick. Stilotti, near the exit end of the alley, lurked in the ruins of a tenement cradling a machine gun.

The Warrior guards had formed a double line facing one another on the sidewalk. The funeral director opened the door of the lead limo. He assisted to the sidewalk Rachel's mother and Rachel, followed by Fluffy and Taylor, the target!

Collucci trapped and savored the Watusi head in the spy glass. His amusement shaped an odd smile. He was reminded how his organ somehow felt electrified by the sting of kinky bush when he pistoned his lust into black women. His finger masturbated the trigger.

Fluffy was going down the church steps when her shoe heel caught in a crack and she was twisted off balance.

Collucci squeezed the trigger and T. heard the crack of the Wetherby at the exquisitely synched instant of his move to reach forward to support Fluffy.

T. heard the shriek of the bullet and stared hypnotically at the wisps of smoke curling from

171

the tunnel through Fluffy's natural hairdo. In one motion, he swept her off the steps and into his arms as he dropped to the pavement. A ball of bile rolled up T.'s throat when he saw the dwarfish funeral director collapse. He flung his hands to his lidless head as if to contain the ooze of brain matter dribbling down like a troublesome forelock into his dead eyes.

People shouted and scuttled for cover. For Collucci's radiant eye, the sweet illusion was bull's-eye! A thrill sparkled him when T. crashed to the pavement.

T. rolled Fluffy and himself to the shield of cars at the curb. Collucci gouged a half-dozen slugs into the pavement in pursuit.

Phil heard the second shot and realized Collucci had missed. Collucci sat stunned and drained by failure. His nostrils quivered in the stink of emotion sweat. He was unaware that a sharp-eyed Warrior had spotted a flash of muzzle from the room darkened by the overcast and soot-encrusted windows.

Phil plunged up the stairway into the room and shouted, "Mr. Collucci! Please for love of the Holy Mother come the hell out of here!"

Collucci nodded dazedly and got to his feet. He went almost casually down the stairs. Phil was livid with strain behind the wheel. He bombed the Buick down the alley with Collucci half inside. Angelo's eyes glowed excitement on the back seat. Stilotti hauled himself into the rear of the Buick.

A half-block away a carload of Warriors roared toward the Buick. They slammed it with pistol fire as it turned out of the alley to double back to the Dodge drop.

Just as Phil sprinted the Buick around a corner, the back window disintegrated. The Surgeon's bulk hurtled off the back seat into the back of Collucci's seat and banged him against the padded dash. Angelo dived for the floorboards. He lay open-mouthed staring at the drippy hole in the back of Stilotti's head.

Angelo shook his head and said quietly, "Lollo is a goner."

Phil turned his eyes toward Collucci for an instant and glared accusation.

Collucci whirled and yelled, "Stay down, Angelo!"

Collucci drew his heavy magnum pistol from a shoulder holster and thundered slugs into the radiator and block of the pursuing Chevrolet.

The Warrior car shivered like a poleaxed steer and wobbled to a stop. All the way back to the Dodge, there was only silence and the stench of Lollo's terminal B.M.

Grunting and sweating, they finally managed to remove the Surgeon's four hundred pounds of blubber from the Buick. Phil tenderly wrapped a plastic litter bag and the bottom of Lollo's overcoat around his leaky head before they hoisted him into the Dodge trunk.

They climbed into the Dodge. Phil darted evil eyes at Collucci, who caught it. He lounged loosely on the back seat with his eyes apparently closed. He spied through slits at Phil's stony face in the rear-view mirror on the dashboard. Collucci pondered why he had missed when he was certain he had fired on target with the first shot.

Without widening his eyes, Collucci said casually, "Phil, it's a fucking shame about Lollo. You know I've, like yourself, cared about him since we were all punks on the Westside. I'm sorry to say we have to deny Lollo a big proper funeral."

Collucci watched Phil's jaw muscles work in the long silence before Phil said bitterly, "Is it because he was just a soldato that we can dump him in a hole like a bag of garbage?"

Collucci said, "Don't crack that shit on me. We already got enough goddamn pressure on us from the bosses to get Taylor. Phil, Lollo deserves a hundred-grand funeral, but the dead can't feel slighted.

"Phil, you're so upset you can't see how stupid it would be to lay ourselves and the Organization open to the police and newspapers just to get a burial permit and some flowers for Lollo."

Angelo said, "Jesus, I hate it about Lollo. He gave me a trillion laughs. And the kicks we usta dig up! I remember the time we muscled a mud kicker when we was oh ten . . . twelve and got our first blowjob together. He passed out when he popped. It's too bad, just too bad about Lollo."

Phil said, "Yeah, maybe it's too bad for Lollo because Mr. Collucci didn't let me do the job on Taylor."

Collucci had the cruel thought that Stilotti had been eating himself into an early grave anyway.

Collucci said, "Phil, stop dreaming you can outshoot me, or out anything me. The lucky cocksucker stumbled forward or bent over to tie a shoelace or something at the same time I squeezed off the first round."

Phil grunted sourly.

Angelo said, "Nobody's luck stays peaches and cream forever. He'll poke his dome into the next one."

Collucci said, "I don't want anybody to know exactly what happened. I'll put together a report for the bosses that won't give them an ass ache. *Capisce?*"

Angelo nodded his shaggy head and said, "Sure, Mister Collucci, I got it."

Phil remained silent and his jaw muscles rippled defiance.

Collucci, white hot at the insult, leaned toward him to jab his index finger into his shoulder to force his reply. He sprawled back onto the seat instead. In that same instant he decided that Phil should be put to sleep as a hazard.

Angelo glanced back at Collucci's face and knew Phil was finished. He sighed and put himself on alert for Collucci's moves.

Oh this stupid mother! Collucci thought. *He sucks my ass for most of his life. So with my blessing he's a capidecina, the boss of ten soldati! And now the lousy cocksucker insults me, his capiregime. Today he sees me a little off form, a little off base and he decides I'm ready to switch ends.*

He makes it clear to me himself that he's too big a risk to afford . . . He's leaving nice kids, nice house, and Ella's great legs and cute ass . . . All the

175

*guilt and responsibility for that is his. He's stupid
like the others. He deserves killing like the others.*

Phil, apparently shaken by the doomsday vibes,
turned and peered at Collucci and said, "I'm a
thousand percent with any way you handle
things . . . all right, Mr. Collucci?"

Then meekly, "You're not salty, Mr. Collucci?"

Collucci managed a smile and his cat eyes lulled
Phil with warm yellow light. He remembered Phil
owed him a bundle.

He said, "Salty? Phil, you think I'm sucker
enough to fall out with a guy into me for seventeen
grand?"

They laughed. Collucci sneaked the magnum
from its holster to his pocket.

He thought, *Angelo should do it to Phil so I can
be sure he doesn't have sentimental hang-ups. I've
always liked Phil . . . But what the hell, the guy's
mouth could get diarrhea and give the bosses the
angle to sour my support and bury me.*

Darkness was quickly falling when they pulled
alongside the Caddie. They got out and Collucci
lunged and seized the back of Phil's overcoat
collar. He jerked it down to pinion Phil's arms to
his sides at the elbow like a straitjacket.

Collucci yanked. The willowy Phil crashed to
the concrete. He lay on his back gasping, half
stunned. Collucci dropped a heavy foot against
Phil's forehead and looped a finger around the
trigger of the magnum in his overcoat pocket.

He pointed it at Angelo and studied his eyes for
a long searching moment before he dipped his
head. Angelo drew his forty-five and squatted at

Phil's side. He pressed the snout of the silencer between Phil's popping eyes.

Collucci said, "Spare him the pain and slop. A clean one through the pump."

Phil walled his eyes up piteously at Collucci and his brow popped sweat bubbles.

His gray lips flapped mutely before he whispered, "Why? . . . why am I losing my life?"

Collucci said in soft Sicilian, "Because I was hurt to lose your respect, Filippo. You should not have forgotten you are just a lieutenant. I must spare myself the greater hurt to lose your loyalty . . . Money . . . everything will be provided for Ella and the kids."

Angelo watched Collucci's face harden as he stepped back and almost imperceptibly winked his right eye. The forty-five bucked in Angelo's fist. Phil's back arched like a taut bow for an instant. His tiny feet kicked lazily like a swimmer afloat before he lay still.

They gently lifted him into the trunk beside Stilotti. Collucci drove the Caddie a half-mile behind Angelo. They unloaded the bodies in the garage behind Collucci's Sweet Dream.

Collucci used the roadhouse phone to call the same undertaking team of Marty and Freddie Rizzo that had planted the corpses of Love Bone and his Mexican sweetie.

Collucci tipped Marty, in code, that there were bodies to be buried in the mob cemetery.

"For Christ sake! Pick up your old man. He's got a snoot full and he's spoiling Tony's wedding," Collucci said.

177

Marty said, "Yeah, thanks."

Then he said something in code that pleased Collucci a great deal. Marty had discovered a time and place to hit Cocio!

They left the Sweet Dream and stopped for the late papers after Angelo dumped the Dodge. Collucci sat up in the front seat reading by dash light an account of the sniping death of the funeral director.

There was mention of the police discovery of the sniper's roost and the tripoded rifle. Collucci smiled grimly. There was only brief mention of Taylor, as a black militant who could have been the target, but he had denied it.

There was nothing about the shooting when Phil barreled out of the alley. Taylor had obviously sent out the word that had gagged the pro-Taylor witnesses. There could only be one reason for this, Collucci reasoned. Taylor intended to strike back, hard and soon.

Collucci said, "Angelo, you better head for the penthouse so I can make the report to Tonelli I just put together."

There was silence for some time as Angelo drove Collucci home after the report to Tonelli.

Finally Angelo said, "Excuse me, Jimmy, for sticking my big mouth in . . . but was everything peaches and cream up there?"

Collucci laughed, "What else, Angelo? The story I fed them was so obvious and simple. It was tough luck that Phil and Stilotti bungled the job on Taylor. It was worse for them to be obviously captured and disposed of by the Warriors. I, we know nothing of what happened except what the papers and the police surmise. So, relax, old friend, everything, like you say, is peaches and cream."

When Angelo pulled into the Collucci driveway, Collucci said, "Kill the engine, there are several important things you must attend to."

Angelo turned and faced his boss, moon face serious.

Collucci said, "First thing tomorrow, get Marty and Freddie into Lollo's rooms with the responsibility to guard the grounds. I want you to pull out three of the men on security at my Big Dipper gambling joint upstate.

"Get the armored Lincoln out of storage and tuned up. Put those three on shifts around the clock cruising my block. Tell them I'm doubling their salaries."

Angelo said, "I got it . . . but the extra commotion . . . the neighbors . . . the chief of police?"

Collucci said, "Fuck the neighbors! They beef to that old buck-grabbing bastard and he'll tell them I've brought in private security to block a kidnap threat to Petey."

Collucci decided to test Angelo for any possible changes in his attitude or slavish subservience that the day's bloody happenings could have brought about.

"Too bad Phil and Lollo had to go. We will miss them, won't we?" Collucci said.

Angelo said, "Lollo a lot." He frowned and hunched his bullish shoulders. "But Phil, maybe a little . . . the way he was feeling about Lollo and blaming you and all, his big mouth woulda finally spilled for the bosses."

Collucci smiled and threw Angelo a luscious curve. "Angelo, I am convinced that nobody has ever had a finer stand-up friend than you have been to me for all these years. I have perhaps been selfish to keep you so close to me. And now I want to reward you."

Collucci paused and scrutinized Angelo's face. "I want you to replace Phil."

Angelo's mouth gaped open, half in surprise and half in alarm that Collucci could be ordering him out of his treasured groove as closest friend and confidant.

He shrilled his protest, "Jimmy, please! Who the hell would take care of you and understand you if I took Phil's spot?"

Collucci smiled and banged him on the shoulder. "Nobody! You sweet lug head sonuvabitch. Nobody!"

Collucci moved toward the door and Angelo leaped out and opened it. Collucci stepped out. They embraced for a long moment in the frosty starlight.

Collucci turned away and went toward the mansion thinking how certain he was of Angelo's friendship and loyalty . . . *well, at least for now anyway.* Weary, Collucci thought as he let himself into the mansion, *Goddamn! . . . going for that cocksucker . . . and missing . . . was one helluva drain. . . .*

CHAPTER SIXTEEN

Around midnight on the second evening after Collucci's failure to put Taylor to sleep, Taylor, trembling in fury and desperate for revenge, paced the parsonage office. He smashed his fist again and again into a blood-red palm. His mind whirled with plans to exterminate his mortal enemy, and all the Chicago Mafiosi. He was certain he had enough weapons and a sufficient number of fanatical Warriors like himself for an all-out war against the Mafia.

Bama stood for a moment in the chill January night looking at the tigerish silhouette pacing in the glow of the desk lamp across the window shade. He entered the building and knocked lightly on the door. Taylor opened it.

Bama said, "You got a cigarette?"

Taylor went to the desk and flung a pack of Salems into Bama's cupped hands and himself into the chair behind the desk. Bama sat down beside the desk. He tossed the pack on the desk and picked up a lighter. They looked into each other's bloodshot eyes in the burst of fire as Bama lit his cigarette and leaned to light Taylor's.

Bama said harshly, "Jessie, you don't know who did . . ."

Taylor frowned and the creak of his chair was loud in the quiet as he leaned back and studied Bama's face. "Bama, my head ain't in no shape to juggle shit balls, so don't throw me none."

Bama said, "I'm glad you said that yourself about that mulish head of yours . . . Jessie, you can't kick off an all-out war against the dagos tomorrow!"

Taylor's long fingers worked together in his hair like nesting vipers behind his head. "There ain't nobody with his asshole pointing to the ground can stop Jessie Taylor from doing nothing he makes up his mind to do," he said.

"Bama, I've called for a full assembly in the morning. I'm gonna send the death squads out night and day. We got the addresses and hangouts of ninety percent of the Mafia men in Chicago. Bama, just like they usta do in Nam, the Warriors gonna search out and waste until there ain't no more Mafia men."

Bama said, "But why now, Jessie? We've only half completed that same groundwork outside Chicago. Jessie, our necessary advantage of surprise would be lost forever. We'd blow our chance to simultaneously strike the dangerous New York families and the other families in big cities across the country as we've planned for so long. We'd have the Mafia and whole police departments alerted and waiting to massacre us. The Warriors are commandos, guerrillas who can only win against our powerful enemies if secrecy and surprise are not denied them!"

Taylor said, "They almost wasted my heart."

182

Bama said, "But Fluffy, bless her heart, wasn't hurt. So, why the hell blow our cool and the master plan?"

Bama paused and shook his head. "Jessie, I just can't understand how you see this whole thing."

Taylor said, "'Cause Fluffy ain't your daughter . . . and Bama, you forgot they wasted poor Henderson, the undertaker."

Bama said, "Oh shit, Jessie, I love Fluffy, and I haven't forgotten Henderson. But you've forgotten or overlooked the one reason beyond all the others why Jessie Taylor has to stop Jessie Taylor from starting all-out war in the morning."

Taylor glared at him for a long moment before he said, "All right, Solomon, my skull ain't closed."

Bama said, "You agree that our best political friend is in the governor's mansion up in Springfield?"

T. nodded yes.

"You know that corrupt Mafia whores among the police brass want our black asses dead and stinking? Don't you also know that the Cook County machine is plotting around the clock to frame and impeach the governor out of office and shove some racist cocksucker in?"

Taylor nodded.

Bama said gently, "Then, will you agree, son, that in an all-out war their man, as governor, would find a technicality, an excuse to send the National Guard against us. Soldiers who would be the brothers, husbands and others close to the best and only allies we have in the state . . . the people!

Jessie, do we want to fight and kill pawns? Soldiers? Be tricked into failure and the grave? Do you understand why we have to wait until we have the capacity to strike a lightning, fatal blow nation-wide? Jessie, it would be fatal for the Warriors to lose our cool and blow our stand-up supporters, black and white across the nation." Bama darted his eyes heavenward. "And wouldn't we blow His support too if we failed to waste them all and their evil, through our own selfishly evil misplanning?"

Taylor got to his feet, gnawing thoughtfully at his bottom lip.

He said quietly, "Yeah Bama, if He's up there . . . You sure bend and reach high to make a point."

He patted Bama's shoulder and thought what a rotten shame it was that poor dead Mama dear, from the git go, down in Georgia couldn't have hooked up with a guy like Bama.

Old shiny dome sure 'nough always yanked his coattails to save him when blind rage racked him up, he thought, as he looked down fondly on Bama's bald skull. He wouldn't send the death squads now.

But he was gonna kill Collucci quick as he could. No matter if Bama and J.C. himself even, on their knees, begged him to let Collucci slide awhile.

Bama said, "Well, Jessie, do I call off tomorrow's assembly?"

Taylor said, "No, Bama, 'cause while I ain't gonna use the death squads right away, I'm gonna need volunteers for something I ain't got worked out yet!"

Bama said, "Jessie, why the hell . . . are you planning to get him on his turf like in your kid rumbles?"

Taylor said, "I'll lay it out for the council at the bunker table in the morning, like the Warrior rules say."

Bama shook his head. "You solo or go without the proper muscle now, and the odds will be a zillion to one for a morgue slab."

Taylor flipped off the desk lamp and they left the office. As they went down the hallway toward their quarters, Taylor said, "Bama, I appreciate you pulling my coat to them traps. But you ain't stopped Jessie Taylor from doing nothing. 'Cause Jessie Taylor's mind wasn't nowhere near made up."

Rachel was staring at the ceiling when Taylor slid into bed beside her. They lay there listening to each other's breathing for a long while. Taylor's leg touched Rachel's and he felt her stiffen for an instant.

He scooted up to a sitting position. As he swung his legs and feet over the edge of the bed to the floor, he said, "Ra, ain't no way I'm staying in this bed if I feel like saying excuse me when I touch you by accident even."

She crawled across the bed and he felt the warmth of her bosom and thighs as she knelt against his back. She threw her arms about his neck to restrain him.

He struggled feebly and said, "Lemme go on in the spare room, Ra, 'cause since the funeral you been playing games and showing your natural ass."

She pressed her cheek against the back of his neck and said, "Do you still love me, Jessie?"

He struggled harder and heaved a heavy sigh of irritation. "Like I always did, Ra, and forever even. Ra . . . now lemme go," he said as he reached to unlock her arms.

She moved and sat beside him. She looked up at him daringly, yet fearfully, as perhaps would a cunning child beaming bright-eyed naivete before uttering a preposterous request.

"Then, Jessie, instead of whatever angry thing you planned to say to the assembly tomorrow, tell them you're taking your family away for a few months . . . to give us our first vacation . . . a change for a little bit away from this place, this tension."

Then she burst a torrent of words, "Bama and Smitty could do all right until we got back. Maybe we wouldn't want to come back from some big city in the South. They say life down there now can be pretty sweet for black people with something on the ball.

"Martial arts are all the thing. You're an expert in all of them. We could have a chain of schools in no time. I'll bet that when Fluffy 'comes out,' the Jessie Taylors would be ranked with the black muck-de-mucks down south. Please Jessie, for us, tell them your family's nerves are shot and we have to be taken away for a while. Please, Jessie!"

He got to his feet and looked down at her with bleakly distant eyes. Her eyes were tragic feline slits, looking up and through him.

She said, "Killing them . . . him comes first with you?"

He nodded.

Then she said in a bitter monotone of despair, "No big happy house for me . . . no 'coming out' cotillion ball for Fluffy . . . and Jessie, you'll die before your sideburns match a white tie."

He frowned in puzzlement, for he had lost sight of her dream in the blinding dazzle of his own. Before he could ask what she meant, she worked her hands violently in the air like talons.

Her contralto voice was squeaky with hysteria. "Don't you dare, Jessie! I'll tear your eyes out of your head if you do! Don't ask me to explain."

He stood mesmerized and hurt to the quick by the hatred in her eyes.

He said softly, "Ra, I can't get in the wind when the people need me the worst . . . We'll get away after I finish what I got to do."

He put his hands on her shoulders and she clawed them away. He picked up his pillow and walked away.

She stood with her face twisted hideously, and said stridently to his back, "Goddamn the people! Put the people in your empty bed, Jessie Taylor! Stick your dick in the people, Jessie Taylor! If you don't announce tomorrow that you're taking us out of here, I'm leaving you."

He came back and, towering over her, said in his lazy drawl, "Ra, you knowed me in grammar school. And ain't nobody then and now, my mama even, could make me do a goddamn thing I ain't wanted to do. Ra, I ain't gonna hold still for

187

no pressure bullshit. I got used to loving you and Fluffy—" He paused and swallowed. "I guess I gotta get used to making it alone . . . I been alone before and ain't died."

His jaw was steely and his eyes sparkled lasers of determination through her. "Ra, I'm swearing on God himself . . . if He's up there . . . and Mama dear's grave, I'm gonna ship that dago to the maggots . . . and later the rest of the Mafia men running the misery game on the people. Ra, I gotta do my job 'fore luxuries of my mind or body. Your leaving ain't gonna kill me or drive me crazy . . . so you and Fluffy even, my heart, must be luxuries I can make it without. So Ra, now you sho' nuff know where I'm coming from."

Her eyes flamed and her cracked lips twisted grotesquely as she said in a deadly voice, "I hate you, Jessie, and this place for every second of my life I've lost and suffered here . . . I hope the dagos torture and burn you alive here."

He turned sadly away and went to the spare room across the hall next to Fluffy's, and locked the door. He listened to Rachel's sobbing and had a helluva time falling into lumpy sleep.

Next morning while shaving and brushing his teeth he avoided his haggard, red-eyed image in the mirror. He picked at his eggs and grits at breakfast and averted his eyes a dozen times from Rachel's piercing stare. Finally leaving his coffee untouched, he got to his feet.

Rachel said, "You going after them?"

Taylor stared down at the scorched furrow in

Fluffy's natural.

He said carefully, "I'm gonna go to a meeting with Bama and Kong."

Fluffy looked up at him wide-eyed and said, "T. Dad, take me with you when you go to get even."

He leaned and kissed Fluffy's forehead. He stepped around the table and Rachel turned her cheek when he tried to kiss her lips. Rachel rose and followed him as he walked away to the back door. He held the door open and half turned.

She said, "Jessie, you understand I meant everything I said last night?"

He said, "Uh huh, Ra. And understand this nigger is gonna make that dago drop some bloody turds 'cause Mr. Henderson's innocent brains was blowed out, and Fluffy was mighty nigh wasted. Ra, they got you more scared and weak than even Fluffy," he taunted her as he stepped outside.

Rachel said to his back, "Watch me, Jessie Taylor! I'll be strong enough to leave you in this shithole!"

She slammed the door and stormed back to reprimand Fluffy for butting in with her juvenile bravado.

Taylor walked into the command bunker and exchanged solemn nods with Bama and Lester "Kong" Smith at the pine conference table. Taylor went to the coffeepot bubbling and rattling its lid on a hotplate in a corner. He poured himself a cup and fell heavily into a chair facing them. He watched them over the cup rim as he blew on and sipped the coffee.

Kong grinned weakly, "C'mon, Jessie, don't

dangle us."

Taylor, face hardened as he stared at Kong and thought about Kong's apparent involvement with Charming Mills in the dope jacker's murder of pusher L.C. and Mills' possession of L.C.'s thirty-grand diamond ring.

"Dummy up, Smitty, I don't need no priming from you," Taylor said harshly.

Kong shrugged elaborately and wondered why Taylor was so hostile toward him of late. Bama sent T. an eye signal.

Taylor, reading the warning in Bama's eyes not to tip off their suspicion of Kong, said, "Man, I'm sorry I throwed out that salt . . . but with them dagos and all the other shit happening, I just ain't myself."

Kong felt surprise and suspicion to hear Taylor's apology. For Kong had never before heard or heard of Taylor apologizing to anybody for anything he had done or said.

Why really did Jessie kiss his ass like that? He stared at Taylor with a bland face, but he now realized how much he feared and hated Taylor. Perhaps from the beginning he had hated him for taking over leadership of his kid gang. Hated him, because for all the long years he had hurt and been humiliated, standing always as an inferior in Taylor's all-powerful shadow.

Kong laughed and said, "You sure as hell ain't yourself, brother. I been knowing you a thousand years, and I ain't never heard you be sorry for nothing you ever said to any motherfucker."

Bama said smoothly, "Smitty, it looks like some

190

of my gentle manly class and grace is at last rubbing off on the big-foot savage from Georgia."

They flashed teeth for one another in a chorus of flat laughter.

Taylor looked at Bama and said, "My mind is made up about that dago we know was up there on the trigger or sent a trigger man up there. I'm gonna ask for a squad to volunteer for a secret mission."

Kong said, "You mean you gonna try to find and nail him with one squad? An hour after the first dago spotted you over there, you and the squad would be wasted."

Taylor said, "I ain't gonna underrate him like I did when he sent me to get my skull patched with this steel plate. I'm gonna snatch his head, nigger. I'm gonna shop our turf for Collucci. I think if mean Mack Rivers ain't strawbossing the thieving tricky niggers dealing numbers and dope, that spaghetti-gut enforcer got to stick his ass out for me to blow it off. Collucci got to collect the Mafia's usual bread from over here."

Bama said, "Jessie, I wish you'd wait until we move against the others . . . but I know your mind is made up on him. It won't be easy even to bag Rivers. He's slick and slippery as owl shit, and he's got a mob of treacherous niggers backing him up . . . How soon?"

Taylor shrugged, looked at his wristwatch and stood up. "Soon as I can check out his routine and plot the snatch . . . No more'n a week and maybe sooner I hope."

They emerged inside the church. Taylor moved

to the microphone and gazed out at the Warriors proudly as they stood at attention.

At the parsonage, Rachel and Fluffy heard his request for volunteers over a speaker in the living room. Rachel went swiftly to the bedroom and started emptying drawers onto the bed. Fluffy came into the bedroom and burst into wild tears.

The mass of men moved toward Taylor as one at his request for volunteers. He selected the members of the squad that had run the psychodrama test that Rapping Roscoe, Lieutenant Porta's tool and intended infiltrator, had failed.

Shortly after, in the command bunker, Taylor briefed the squad and reinstated joyous Ivory Jones to squad leader. Ivory Jones, massive Lotsa Black Hayes, driver of the squad's battered-looking but supercharged Pontiac, Dew Drop Allen, the tiny much-loved white Warrior, and Bumpy Lewis, the unwitting sponsor of Roscoe, the dead spy, left the bunker radiant with the challenge of the mission.

Rachel and Fluffy were loading the last of their possessions into the banged-up family Ford outside the parsonage when Taylor walked up. Rachel, fighting tears, waved good-bye and flung herself under the wheel before she broke down. Fluffy lingered on the sidewalk sobbing in Taylor's arms and begging him to force Rachel to stay.

Rachel yelled hoarsely, "I'll leave you, Fluffy, so help me, if you don't come on this instant."

Taylor tenderly led Fluffy to the car and opened the door. Fluffy kissed him and held on until Rachel seized her arm and pulled her into the car.

Taylor shut the door and leaned in and said softly, "Ra, since we ain't got no doubt you my forever woman, ain't no doubt, is it, you ain't gone for long."

She whipped her face away to hide the gush of tears and thundered the Ford away for her mother's Westside house.

Taylor's face was drawn and ashen with emotion as he stumbled against Bama.

Bama said, "Easy, pal, I know how it hurts from raw experience, but soon it won't pain except every now and then."

Taylor turned his wild face and glared down at Bama. "Goddamn you, Bama! Jessie Taylor don't need none of your granny ass nursing."

Bama said, "Nigger, don't be mad with me. I ain't left you . . . yet . . . and damn my stupid soul, odds are I never will. You ain't been drunk since the party at Mole's place when you were a kid. Now you got a star excuse to get flying drunk and I got enough whiskey to fly us to the moon."

Taylor grinned, and arm in arm they went across the sidewalk. Taylor ducked into his quarters to his intercom system. He dispatched patrols and guards to protect Rachel and Fluffy around the clock.

And across the hall a curvy black beauty, who had climbed through Kong's bedroom window against Warrior rules, lay in his bed watching him impatiently as he snorted cocaine and wrestled with a momentous decision. Should he tip off Mack Rivers that Taylor was planning to use him to hit Collucci?

CHAPTER SEVENTEEN

On an early evening a week after Taylor had selected the squad to help him in the extermination of Collucci, the Collucci mansion rang with music and merriment. The occasion was a gala ball given to honor the husbands of the League of Women for a Greater River Forest. Club president Olivia Collucci was proud. And she felt rekindled affection as she noticed her husband's urbane and charming social intercourse with their elegant guests.

Finally the last guest had departed. Collucci removed his tuxedo for a change into street clothes. He glanced into the closet door mirror and found Olivia's eyes gazing raptly at him. He smiled oddly at her through the mirror.

She came and pressed herself against his back and embraced his hips. He moved free and shivered a little. She nibbled at the patch of goosebumps on his back. He reached a hand back under her panties. She spread her legs as he gently massaged his knuckles against her vulva. She squeezed his organ, bloated with blood. He turned his head and alternately sucked her tongue and lips. He turned and sucked and licked an erected nipple. Her legs trembled as she pulled away and said breathlessly, with great eyes shining, "Can your business wait?"

He stared into her pleading eyes in the mirror and shook his head. He said, "No, beautiful, it will be sweeter for us unhurried."

She pouted her bottom lip and bashfully pointed at his crotch like a vulgar child. "You will save him for me and bring him back soon?"

He grinned and crooned in Sicilian, "Where else could this bum find a goddess waiting for him?"

He walked into the closet. He flipped on the light. He stood looking thoughtfully at suits and coats of cashmere, vicuna and other lush materials. The garments were shades of charcoal, fawn and indigo blue, his favorites. Black garments were also in abundance. He wore these to church and on those solemn occasions when he dignified himself to magistrate or perform executions.

He lifted a blue suit from the rack, but his eyes were snared by a slate-hued suit. He had known, looking into the mirror at the tailor's first fitting, that he would never wear it. He'd remembered blowing a bloody hole into Bobo Libbrizzi's slate-hued jacket. He winced, remembering Cocio's lies and the pressures that had tricked him into his first execution.

Olivia stared at his face, so strangely disturbed with hatred and pain. "Jimmy!" she exclaimed. "Are you all right?"

He grinned, free of the trance, and lied

wide-eyed. "Sure, I'm fine now, Sugar Tit. Just a bitch-kitty charley horse in the foot."

She pulled him to the bed. He sat smiling on the side of the bed. She squatted before him, massaging the foot he lowered into her lap.

Collucci got dressed. Olivia followed him to the front door. They heard Angelo gun the Caddie in the driveway. He opened the door. She clung to him.

She said, "Am I acting silly?"

He said, "No . . . Why?"

She disengaged. "I feel silly . . . you know like I could love you hard again."

Then tremulously, eyes shining up, "Is it safe?"

Her transient helplessness reminded him of her little-girl charm and sweet vulnerability in the dizzying beginning. He felt a rare tenderness for her as he kissed the tip of her nose. "You're in no trouble, it's just the bubbly jazzing you around," he said as he ducked away from her delicate fist flailing at him.

He smiled back at her and went to drop onto the Caddie's rear seat. Angelo drove toward Collucci's meeting with his secret ally, Westside captain Cono Spino.

Collucci remembered that Phil and his cousin Lollo had been dead and buried for ten days in the mob's secret cemetery. Angelo had only mentioned them once. Collucci was curious. Why not? He made a note to find out. Collucci mulled the subject matter to be considered by Spino and himself.

Angelo said, "Excuse me butting in my big

mouth, Mr . . . Jimmy. I keep remembering this guy Spino was nothing but a stick man in a craps joint when Mr. Tonelli, with Mr. Cocio pushing it, picked him up. In ten years he's a big shot. A *capiregime*, like you, leading his own *borgata* . . . maybe he ain't solid . . . maybe he owes Mr. Cocio too much."

Collucci laughed, "Angelo, you got it all screwed up. Spino gets to keep twenty percent of all net of gambling with cards, craps and bookmaking and the numbers on the Westside."

Collucci paused and shrugged. "Spino is very displeased with twenty percent and very anxious to be my underboss. His bright future depends on the bosses' removal . . . Spino can be trusted."

Collucci noticed concern still creasing Angelo's face as the Caddie picked its way through neon thickets on the far Westside.

Collucci thought aloud. "Spino's *soldati* and my own combined are four hundred, four fifty to sixty . . . only seventy *soldati* loyal to the bosses. So, cheer up, old friend of mine."

Angelo grinned. "Yeah, I guess you got the edge on the bosses."

Collucci said, "And another secret edge Spino and myself have imported from Sicily."

Angelo's mouth started to open, but Collucci frowned and said, "Angelo, we need our eyes instead of our mouths. I think we passed Spino's setup, back there a coupla hundred yards."

Angelo U-turned and retraced. He turned into a wide driveway and the headlamps illuminated a sign: *Holy Mother Home for the Elderly* atop a ten-foot gate of grilled steel.

A guard wearing double forty-fives around his sweatered waist put aside a magazine inside his cubicle. A revolving TV monitor scrutinized the Caddie and its occupants as he spoke briefly on a phone. He pressed a button that swung the gate open.

Angelo drove into the twenty acres, walled in by twenty feet of concrete. Angelo drove, for what seemed like an hour to him, through a long black tunnel of wind-flogged trees, swaying and groaning in the howling loneliness.

Then suddenly the Caddie entered a circular acre of light, seemingly bright as noon. In the center of it sprawled a two-story building of casket-gray stone. Angelo drove down a graveled driveway and pulled the Caddie to a stop before several stone steps.

As they went up the steps, the front door opened. The runt Spino, impeccable in double-breasted blue mohair, greeted them with warm Sicilian words of welcome and embraces.

Angelo removed his overcoat and dropped down into an overstuffed chair in the foyer. He riffled an old copy of *Playboy* to the centerfold. Spino led Collucci down a glossy hallway leading to the office.

Spino stopped and gestured toward a door. Collucci peered through a rectangle of glass at a score of illegal aliens from Sicily. Some lounged on sofas watching TV shoot-'em-ups, while others sat and stood kibitzing around players at pool, card and domino tables.

Collucci said as he moved away, "They all clean?"

Spino nodded. "Like the ones before them. No criminal beefs whatever. And like the others before, they have special skills, useful in the family's bakeries, restaurants, meat markets. One of those you saw is a whiz at counterfeiting money, passports and stock certificates to dump as collateral for big loans."

Spino turned into a walnut-paneled office. He flipped a wall switch. A three-tiered chandelier burst a crystal firebomb. Spino was dwarfed as he seated himself behind the massive desk.

Collucci exhaled smoke and said, "They are in good spirits now . . . but I wonder after they slave awhile for coolie pay . . . ?"

Spino jiggled his doll head. His wide mouth shaped his deceptively sweet Howdy Doody smile, "They know a phone call to immigration will dump them back into their shitholes in Sicily. And they understand that the Honored Society can shrink the whole fucking world to the size of a coffin for informers."

Collucci said, "They came Mexico way?"

"No," Spino said. "These came in from Windsor by motorboat to Detroit."

Spino picked up a stiletto letter opener from the desk top. "But many others will be coming both ways soon. They will be needed to replace the *soldati* who sour when we retire those two old bastards."

Collucci said, "Tonelli's head has rotted between his broad's thighs. Now he weeps like a cunt

199

because punks in Harlem shoot smack. And Cono, I'll lay ten to five, sissy Cocio's mama still spanks his ass if he gets sassy."

They laughed.

Then Spino's eyes glittered with excitement as Collucci said, "Cono, I am sure that while you have not been doubtful, you have been concerned about my promise over a year ago to get a foolproof source of pure drugs."

Collucci paused for an instant. "I intend to be completely open with you in all matters as I am certain you will be with me. I have arranged a meeting in Rome in the near future with a powerful government clique to secure the control and licensing of a pharmacological firm which will manufacture tons of merchandise for the drug end of our partnership. At this moment I invite you to share in it equally.

"Our emigrant coolies will also be the mules to lug the kilos. So you see, partner, what a perfect setup we're putting together?"

Spino did a pleased jack-in-the-box from his chair.

He came around the desk to pump Collucci's hand, exclaiming, *"Exquisita! Exquisita!"*

Spino tiptoed and slid away, from the mantel top, a superb copy of *The Last Supper*. Collucci gazed through a two-way mirror at a half-dozen nude couples, drinking and laughing in the amber glow.

They were dreamy-eyed as they sat on a gold satin couch, and on the mammoth silk cushions strewn on the snowy carpet of the sunken living

200

room. The flashing smiles of the men did not, however, warm their frozen dark eyes, nor mask the cruelty and menace etched on their swarthy faces.

Spino answered Collucci's unspoken question. "They are survivors of the Bomato Family . . . as you know Sicily's most skillful contract assassins for two generations. Their talents will be necessary for that last difficult stage of our plan."

Collucci hesitated before he nodded. "But, I thought those not wiped out by the Carbinieri massacre in Palermo years ago were given sentences to hold them for several lifetimes."

Spino grinned. "True. But for enough lira to tempt a saint . . ." Spino threw tiny hands into the air, and sighed helplessness.

"The ex-warden's disgrace was perhaps not a bad bargain at the price."

They chuckled. Collucci pushed *The Last Supper* back in place to cover the spy mirror.

As they walked down the hallway toward the front door Spino said, "I keep them happy here while they wait for work and payoffs bigger than they got in Sicily. They eat like wardens here, have ritzy suites, the cream of cunts from my cathouses up north and the best vino from the Old Country . . . and I've convinced them the high walls and the guards are only to protect them."

They laughed heartily at that one.

Collucci's index finger made a circle near the side of his head, "We must carefully decide about the terrible ones . . . when their last jobs . . . the old cocksuckers of the Commission have been retired."

Spino jerked his thumb toward the back of the building. "We will use the terrible Bomatos for the jobs on Cocio, Tonelli and the jigaboo?"

Collucci buttoned his blue cashmere overcoat. "Yes, on Cocio. He will be set up very soon. I will notify you as to time and place. Taylor and Tonelli will be all my pleasure."

Collucci shook Spino's hand. He opened the door to step out, and a blast of icy wind teared his eyes.

Spino touched Collucci's arm. "Guns on Cocio?"

Collucci's yellowish eyes hardened. "No! A snake must be hacked to pieces and his head crushed to mush . . . afterwards doll him up in bra and panties like a faggot for the police and newspapers."

Spino looked deep into Collucci's eyes and said softly, "Will your old friend, Bellini, be on our team?"

Collucci stood as a statue for a long moment before he said harshly, "He will or leave the game."

As Collucci stepped through the doorway, Spino's words of caution were almost blotted out by the raucous wind. "Take care, Giacomo! We must not arouse the smallest suspicions of Tonelli and the Commission."

Collucci smiled bleakly. "Cono, who wants to shrink the fucking world?"

Spino shut the door and Collucci felt euphoric as he went down the steps to the car and sat up front with Angelo.

202

CHAPTER EIGHTEEN

Angelo moved the Caddie through the section of the Westside that years before had been the turf of Collucci's Sicilian Knights. Collucci turned on the radio and spun the dial to the recorded voice of Beverly Sills singing *Aida's* title role.

Collucci looked at one A.M. on his watch. He stretched out his legs and pulled the brim of his gray hat over his eyes to shield against the lances of oncoming headlights.

He was microscoping his meeting with Spino for any overlooked signs of possible impurities of Spino's heart, when he felt the Caddie pull over and stop. He slid his hat back and sat erect as Angelo pointed past him to a wire-fenced junkyard covering almost a city block of what had once been a colony of well-to-do Italian-Americans. He looked and wondered why the hell Angelo was fascinated by the graveyard of wrecks.

Then Collucci remembered even as Angelo said, "A lot of that usta be your father-in-law's estate."

Angelo pulled the Caddie away.

Collucci said, "How the hell . . . ? Tonelli himself would have passed it."

Angelo grinned. "Me and Lollo made a helluva score in that old pink house caving in over there one night. The owners were fucking around at the King Crip's first Coronation in the White House."

They smiled.

Collucci silenced Sills. He pulled his hat brim over his eyes to muzzle Angelo. He relaxed to the whispery pianissimo of the tires as Angelo drove masterfully through the night.

Collucci lounged, slit-eyeing and recognizing the wind-mauled streets, bleak and deserted, except for the phantoms his memory conjured up. His mind started to feast on his early pain and suffering at the hands of Cocio and Tonelli. Collucci remembered his last day in the hospital after the fracas with Tonelli's *soldati*.

The afternoon of his release he went directly from the hospital to Cocio's apartment. He had checked out of the hospital an hour before the Tonelli limousine was expected to take him to his car, garaged on Tonelli's estate. He walked the half-mile to Cocio's place in the July heat to collect his thoughts and test his strength.

Cocio opened the door. He was showing out a teenage "hard face" wiggling an adult rear end and rouged to the gills. She rolled hot eyes up at Collucci and brushed her epic chest against him.

She yapped, "Cheapskate, gimme another fin for a real snazzy pair of baby dolls or never call me again."

Cocio shoved her hard. He showed Collucci his teeth as Collucci stepped into the living room and sat on a sofa beside Cocio. Collucci felt the sofa's horsehair stuffing prickle through his sweaty linen trousers. Under Cocio's stare he shifted himself nervously.

Cocio said, with a sly smile, "Jimmy Collucci, the whiz. First day in the streets and you're here to tell me to read in the evening papers how you made your bones. Eh? Knife or gun?"

Collucci looked him in the eye. "Mr. Cocio, I'm here so you can name somebody else I can make bones on."

Cocio threw his head back and laughed. "Mr. Bellini oughta be here to glim his hotshot prize, crawfishing on his bones."

Collucci's face hardened. "You gonna give me another guy?"

Cocio frowned and the tip of the blue-black widow's peak undulated on his forehead. "No dice. It's gotta be Librizzi."

Collucci shook his head stubbornly.

Cocio stood up and glared down into Collucci's face. "Are you saying no to Mr. Bellini's wishes?"

Collucci stood up, towering above the bantam. "I'm saying I'll get Mr. Bellini's okay to make bones on some other guy instead."

Cocio horselaughed and said, "Wake up! You're just my strawboss for a gang of punk car snatchers. You're not in. Even if you was, you could get a quicker *undienza* with F.D.R. than you could bend Mr. Bellini's ear. Even I can't bring him a problem except I go through Mr. Tonelli."

Collucci felt trapped as he stared at Cocio.

He mumbled, "Why Bobo?"

Cocio said harshly, "I got legit reasons, but I

don't have to give you no fucking reason."

Cocio smiled and lowered his voice, "Maybe Mr. Bellini saw those guys you busted up and overrated your guts. I oughta tell him what you showed him was maybe some freakish miracle, considering your old man had less balls than a broad."

Collucci reeled as if fist-clouted at the mention of his father's widely publicized cowardice.

Cocio tensed before Collucci's wild face. He stepped back to get drawing space for the forty-five automatic holstered beneath his dressing robe.

Finally words leaped from Collucci's tight throat, "Mr. Cocio, no disrespect, but no bullshit, if you ever mention that crummy cunt to me again, one of us will die. I ain't nothing like him. I got the guts to take a crack at anybody, any time. I even got the guts to race your piece at this distance. You believe me?"

They stared into each other's eyes until Cocio shrugged and decided to shoot an angle.

He said softly, "Sure I believe you'd try . . ."

Cocio took a pack of cigarettes from his robe pocket and held it out to Collucci.

They lit up and Cocio said, "Forget Librizzi. I'll have Ya Ya knock off that finking bastard."

Collucci saw the danger to his pride and image if Ya Ya Frazzio, his arch-rival, did a job on a fink he had turned down. But most unbearable for him would be the implication of cowardice. And could Ya Ya and Cocio afford to let him live with so great a feeling for the victim?

Collucci moved close to Cocio to study his face

as he said, "Who to?"

Not one muscle in Cocio's face was awry as he lied, "He's gonna gab to a secret Grand Jury poking around for a connection between kid gangs and organized crime . . . the finger came from big brass downtown . . . no doubt about Librizzi at all."

Collucci said, "I've known the guy almost all my life and nobody can tell me he's gonna walk in and empty his head just like that."

Cocio said, "The source said he was caught cold in Stickney wheeling a hot El Dorado two weeks ago. The jury is gonna get the beef and his parole violation squashed after he flaps his mouth."

Collucci said quietly, "I'll do it."

Cocio said, "It must be done quickly. He might get called tomorrow."

Then Cocio added, "You can get a clean rod?"

Collucci nodded.

"You gotta watch you don't tip him by some kinda changes in your face and acting. Remember, no witnesses, and you will do a sweet job on him if you got the rod rammed up under the hump on the back of his noggin when you blast. *Capisce?*"

Collucci nodded solemnly.

Cocio's eyes were radiant with victory as he added, "I chose you, not just to make your bones, but because it will be very easy for you . . . he trusts you. Eh?"

Collucci said, "He trusts me."

Cocio followed Collucci to the door and extended his hand. Collucci hesitated for a mini-instant. During the handshake Cocio said, "Everybody that's got business, friendship or whatever between them is gotta bitch at each other sometime. So let's forget today's hassle. Eh?"

Collucci said, "It's forgotten," and stepped outside.

Cocio thoughtfully stroked his earlobe and followed. Collucci stopped and turned to face him.

Cocio said, "Say, he only lives a block from the dump. You can con him out there and strip him. Pile a lotta crap on him . . . the zillion of rats will finish him to the bones. Maybe he won't be identified if ever found."

Collucci dipped his head and went down the sun-baked walk. He picked up his Buick and went home for a bath and some rest.

That night directly after dinner with Olivia at the Tonelli mansion, Collucci went back to his apartment to plan and prepare himself for the job on Librizzi. He sat at a window in his darkened living room peering through binoculars at Angelo, Lollo and Phil and their girls eating and laughing it up at the combination deli-poolroom hangout across the street.

It was early, only ten P.M. by his watch. A minute later Bobo's girl, beauteously blonde Carlotta Fugatti, made the scene driving a used blue La Salle coupe Bobo had given her. She sat alone at a window table on the deli side sipping gin-spiked Coke.

Collucci had finished planning. He sat drinking stout red vino like water, and stoking up a poisonous fury inside himself. Maybe he could catch Bobo at home. He was reaching for the phone when it rang.

Collucci was shaken for an instant by Bobo's voice saying he'd meet Collucci at the hangout and share some dynamite grass he'd scored for.

Collucci said, "Bo, some guy threw a coupla slugs at me. I got a tip it may be Ya Ya after the both of us. Walk out to the east end of the dump and make sure nobody follows you. I'll meet you in fifteen minutes."

Collucci listened intently as Bobo said, "Yeah, Jimmy. I'll be there. Oh, what about Carlotta? She's gonna meet me at the hangout."

Collucci said, "We don't wanta tip off any moves if Ya Ya is around, so don't call her. I'll send one of the broads across the hall over there with any message you got."

Bobo said, "Swell. Tell her to blow the joint and I'll call her at home later."

Collucci put Carlotta in the binoculars for five minutes to check if Bobo was conning. Carlotta wasn't called to the phone.

Collucci stuck a thirty-two automatic under his waistband at the small of his back and wore a summer shirt outside his belt.

On his way to put Bobo to sleep Collucci felt a pang of regret at the sight of Bobo's ten younger brothers and sisters singing and laughing on their stoop as they waited for their mother to come home from her eight-to-twelve shift. Two blocks later he felt really low as he passed the listing frame house that had rung with the screams of his mother and sister.

A half-mile away, the stink of the dump poisoned the summer air. He parked the Buick on a side street, two blocks from the dump. A hundred yards from it, he felt nauseous in his belly pit at the squealy thunder of the rats. His flesh crawled as he stood at the edge of the rat pit and heard the rustling roar of their teeth and bodies as they scampered and scavenged through the sea of rot.

He turned at the sound of footsteps, rocking on his heels from the vino. Bobo stood there decked out in a slate-hued gabardine. He wore his dimpled smile, and his eyes were enormous and innocent in the glow of the full moon.

They said, "Hi," together.

Collucci thought, *Nobody should have to croak the fucking Mona Lisa.*

The burning tip of the stick of pot Bobo passed him reminded Collucci of the fiery agate he'd swindled Bobo out of when they were five years old, in trade for a cracked barber-pole agate he'd glued together.

As he filled his lungs with the biting smoke, he remembered Mrs. Librizzi broom-beating them that same fall their mothers enrolled them in kindergarten. Mrs. Librizzi had caught them rubbing their organs together in her basement.

He passed the joint back and studied Bobo's face as he said, "I think we better fix Ya Ya tonight before he tries a double-cross . . . did you bring your piece?"

Bobo grinned. He drew a nickel-plated snub-nose that sparkled in his palm.

He said, "My other close friend," before he

210

returned it to his hip pocket.

Bobo turned his head to glanced behind himself. "I looked for your short . . ."

When Bobo turned his head, Collucci scooted himself a few inches closer to Bobo without lifting his feet. He needed to brew up a murderous storm inside himself to do a job on Bobo.

Collucci wiggled his head as he said, "It's parked over there . . . maybe you need glasses, Bo?"

Bobo stood in a long silence and wondered if he'd really heard a strange raw note in Collucci's voice and also why Collucci wanted to meet right here at the stinking dump.

Bobo said, "I got double twenty peepers, but the both of us could get galloping T.B. inhaling all this crap."

Collucci said, "You . . . we can't live forever, Bo."

Bobo said, "We can try . . . you think Carlotta got salty 'cause I couldn't show?"

Collucci's bottom lip curled. "Bo, you need glasses for your mind too, if you don't know that broad wouldn't quit you if you crapped on her chest. She don't wanta go back to that dry cleaners."

Bobo comforted himself that Collucci's peculiar mood was due to the weed.

He said nervously, "This batch of tea is pretty good stuff, huh Jimmy?"

As Bobo held out the glowing butt toward him, Collucci said, "That alfalfa don't even buzz me."

Bobo drew on the butt and said, "I been thinking . . ."

Collucci said, "No shit!"

Bobo exhaled. "Yeah, I been thinking the guy was loony that told you Ya Ya was ready for a showdown. Ya Ya ain't got more than a deuce of troops that he could count on, on his side . . . the guy is too cagey to risk his ass in a sling when he don't stand a Chinaman's chance."

Collucci studied Bobo's face as he said, "Dummy up and listen Bo. Ya Ya is gonna give secret evidence on me to the nailers and take over . . . Mr. Cocio got it from downtown."

Collucci stared with lidded eyes while Bo chewed his bottom lip in puzzlement. Ya Ya couldn't be so stupid he would try for Collucci's spot with a secret finger. Everybody in the car ring knew Mr. Cocio had a wide-open pipeline to downtown.

Bobo shook his head stubbornly, "Jimmy, I can see Ya Ya double-crossing, but much smoother than that."

Bobo got a whiff of Collucci's breath as he weaved a little closer.

Bobo said, "Jimmy, let's go to my joint and finish talking, and I can call Carlotta."

Collucci's voice was shrill and slurred a little as he said, "When is the last time you called your old lady? Don't you know your old lady slaving for forty a week is more important than some pushover broad . . . don't you know that, asshole?"

Bobo backed up from Collucci's twisted face and burning eyes.

He mumbled, "C'mon now, Jimmy, gimme a break with the needle, huh? Carlotta ain't just some broad I'm banging. We're gonna get hitched next month after her divorce is in the bag."

Collucci said violently, "You poor sap, that old stale floozie would marry a jigaboo if he was making big dough."

Bobo recoiled and said, "Jesus Christ, Jimmy! Drop Carlotta, huh? I know for a fact she ain't been banged by a lot of guys . . . She's only twenty-six."

Collucci snickered and said, "If all the pricks shoved into her was stuck outside her, she'd look like a fucking porcupine."

Bobo's eyes batted nervously, but he said with heat, "Lay off her, Jimmy."

With long fingers dangling like some ancient gunslinger, Collucci said, "Make me, chump! You got a piece . . . make me!"

Bobo said, "You gone nuts? I'm clearing the hell out of here."

He retreated several steps backward with a thumb hooked into the corner of the side pocket holding his nickel-plated piece.

Collucci said, "Defend yourself, chump," as he eased on the balls of his feet toward him.

Collucci's smile was full, his yellowish eyes compelling, like the reach-out-and-touch moon.

Bobo was like a wild-eyed bird trancing before a rattler.

Three feet away, Collucci sneered, "Whatsa matter, you lose your voice with your guts?"

Bobo said jaggedly, "I ain't . . . Lemme go, Jimmy . . . I can't talk to you."

Collucci said, "Pretend I'm the secret Grand

Jury, stoolie cocksucker!"

The utter shock on Bobo's face at the accusation was translated by Collucci as lead-pipe cinch guilt.

At the instant that Collucci lunged, Bobo darted his hand into his pocket for his piece. He tripped as he stepped back for drawing space. He crashed flat on his back. Collucci stomped the gun out of his hand. He lay there staring up at Collucci leveling his thirty-two automatic at his head.

Bobo pleaded, "Please Jimmy! Don't! Somebody put a bum finger on me!"

Collucci frowned in his anger with himself because his finger, his goddamn trigger finger, was paralyzed . . . couldn't pull to blast out the fink's brains.

Suddenly in one agile motion, Bobo jackknifed a leg and blurred a heel cleat against Collucci's kneecap, and rolled toward his piece.

The staccato bombing of Collucci's automatic shuddered the air and silenced the rat pit as he collapsed to his knees.

Bobo, unhurt except for a rill of blood across his cheek, pointed his shiny gun at Collucci's belly.

The automatic spewed bolts of orange lightning and Bobo was dead with a neat triangle of holes in his forehead. Then he blasted holes in Bobo's slate jacket over his heart.

Collucci struggled to his feet and stripped the body of credentials, watch and ring. Bobo's clothing he would burn in his apartment building furnace.

Limping to spare his throbby knee, he dragged the corpse to the brink of the rat pit. He rolled it over and stood breathing heavily. He listened to the awful commotion of the rats as they descended to feast.

He walked to his car and battered down his guilt and remorse by blaming Bobo for his own death.

He tried to croak me. The lousy bastard was responsible for his finking and dying. He was stupid and guilty, so he had to go. So Collucci coined the con for his conscience.

Several days later, as the discovered remains of Bobo Librizzi were lowered into the grave, Collucci saw Cocio comforting Carlotta as she theatrically wailed grief. A week later, Collucci saw Carlotta dolled up and driving a new La Salle sedan. He tailed her to a posh bar in a Loop hotel. Several cocktails later he watched them take the elevator for the obvious purpose.

Collucci sat there across the street in his car for over an hour. He was stuporous with remorse and rage that he had put Bobo to sleep just because Cocio had had a hard-on for the slut Carlotta. He decided to stalk Cocio for that moment when he could kill him and avenge Bobo's death.

After Collucci and Olivia were married with full church ceremony, the freshly weds were honored at a party on the Tonelli estate that even a Caesar might not have quickly forgotten. Collucci noticed that Cocio's ferret eyes were bright with envy and hatred.

In the center of the quarter-scale Colosseum, the guests feasted on prime cuts of barbequed beef, lobsters, clams, sausages, cheeses, huge black olives and the hearts of the artichokes. There were finally French and Italian pastries and frozen desserts, sculpted and lavishly decorated. They guzzled gallons of beer and Scotch whisky. French champagne leaped and frothed from crystal fountains that splattered rainbow lights and gleamed the papier-mache columns like purest alabaster. The wedding cake stood in the center of the feast. It was a five-foot replica of the Vatican, with bride, groom and priest dolls assembled on top.

Mobster leaders and their lackeys, from six states, laughed and danced with their women to the band's Old Country music that resonated the night.

Then the center of the arena was cleared of the banquet. Burly Mafiosi, in gladiator costumes, wrestled and clanged shields with bludgeons and swords in realistic bouts for the revelers.

Collucci stood tall beside his spectacular bride, gowned in peach satin, as the long lines of Mafiosi passed with kisses for Olivia, and for him congratulations and envelopes fat with paper money.

After a two-week honeymoon in Mexico, Collucci and Olivia moved into Joe Tonelli's wedding gift, the River Forest mansion, luxuriously furnished and clear, except for taxes. That same week he was summoned to become a chauffeur for top boss Bellini.

Soon after shopping trips and camping trip in the lush Wisconsin wilds, Collucci crept into the hearts of Frank and Angelita Bellini as a real son would have done. Collucci, for his part, was very proud and admiring when, with Bellini beside him on the front seat, and cars of bodyguards behind them, they visited Little Italy on the Westside.

Housewives, leaning and chattering gossip from tenement windows, the cute-butt broads, the ditch diggers, the thieves, the kids stickballing in the lumpy streets, snow-crested old men cackling to each other's hoary lies and jokes, pasta-bloated shopkeepers and leather-lunged pushcart hucksters all would freeze in awe at the sight of Bellini's entourage.

They would whisper to one another, "It's him! It's Papa Bellini!"

All eyes would follow as he alighted from his limousine and went into Scatattis, the restaurant of a boyhood chum. He sat calmly at a table with his face unreadable.

The people with problems and in dilemmas bowed and scraped before his bodyguards for permission to enter his presence. Then before him, they trembled as they asked to be forgiven for violating his privacy.

Old friends and acquaintances going back to the old days in Sicily hugged him and kissed his hands and face. A clubfooted ancient needed condemnation of a duplex rescinded. A weeping mother needed a decent lawyer for her son accused of killing a bank guard.

A cement worker pleads that Papa Bellini force a crooked contractor to pay him a month's back wages so he will not have to kill him. He has thirteen children and if he goes to prison their bellies will shrivel up and ache with hunger.

A wrinkled landlord hobbles forth on crutches and wired jaw. He sobbingly mumbles for the eviction and chastisement of a hoodlum tenant who refuses to pay a cent of rent.

Papa Bellini almost always listened in silent sympathy until each had spoken the last word of his plea.

Then he would command one of his aides to "Handle this" or "Look into this."

The people had great trust in him because they knew he would make himself and his clout, political and otherwise, available to them several times a week to solve their problems and resolve their dilemmas. A multitude were in his debt and yet no one knew when, if ever, he would demand payment.

Collucci, on many occasions, after he drove Bellini home for the day, would prowl for a chance to kill Cocio. He had decided to visit Cocio on some pretext and blast him at home with the risk a neighbor would possibly see him coming or leaving.

He sat in the living room about to draw his piece and put one through Cocio's head as he tied a shoelace when a woman came from a back bedroom and stared at him.

Cocio straightened up and said, "Meet my mama come from Sicily just this morning."

The next year the team of Cocio and Collucci gave bad Willie Poe his booming salute into oblivion. Shortly after, with determined politicking by underboss Tonelli, Cocio was given the choice plum of Southside Enforcer.

The demands of husband and Mafioso upon

Collucci's time and energies reduced his raging urgency to put Cocio into his grave to cold everlasting hatred and first-chance vow.

Collucci moved up quickly as Bellini's protege to a lieutenant in charge of a squad responsible for the gambling and vice take from a large hunk of the far Westside.

Bellini summoned Collucci to his house, when Collucci was in his early thirties, one early evening. It was the day after the funeral of Bellini's wife, Angelita.

After dinner Bellini gazed across the table at Collucci before he said in quiet Silician, "Giacomo, I would be very happy if you managed our affairs with the coloreds."

Collucci was stunned. *Capodecina!* Enforcer!

Then he thought, what about Cocio? Had he committed some executable offense? He felt giddy at the possibility that the old man could be hinting that he put Cocio to sleep.

Bellini smiled as he read Collucci's face and said, "Tonelli has been passed the big responsibility and wants Cocio for his underboss."

Collucci's suspicion of Tonelli and concern for Bellini whitened his face as he leaned forward. "Papa, are you in trouble?"

Bellini frowned at the disrespectful implication that Tonelli was capable of treachery. "Hell no, Giacomo," Bellini said evenly. "And keep that garbage out of your head."

Collucci said, "Then I don't understand why, Papa? You are not young . . . but you are not sick."

Bellini pressed a bell for coffee, and lit mammoth cigars for himself and Collucci.

Bellini exhaled blue smog and said, "Giacomo, because I feel that down deep in your insides, you are in heat for that treacherous witch, power, you are puzzled that I don't stay between her thighs. Now I will have the time to really enjoy the short, precious time left with my Angelita, fine music and my painting."

Bellini half turned to gaze at his favorite oil painting hung above the Chippendale buffet behind him. Bellini had captured his teenage ethereal Angelita emerging from a holocaust of blue lake, aflame with Sicilian sun. Neoned rays of gold beamed from coils of honey hair atop her elfish face, tinted the patina of priceless porcelain.

Bellini sighed. "We were virgins when we found each other. We . . . I will be as pure at the end as we were in the beginning.

"You must administrate the coloreds with iron muscle?" Bellini's index finger made a circular motion at the side of his head as he said, "Because the coloreds know none of them will ever really be allowed past the window in this country's candy store, they have big mental problems . . . problems that will make many of them pigs for dope. Also, they will be happy to get a chance to strike gold playing the numbers and policy with their nickels and dimes."

Bellini blew a gust of Havana aroma toward the high ceiling and looked into Collucci's eyes.

"Consider a suggestion?" Bellini asked.

Collucci smiled. "Sure would, Papa."

Bellini's face was solemn as he leaned forward. "Now is the time to slam down the steel lid . . . before the hatching of so many Willie Poes makes it suicide for white faces to go in and kill them all."

Bellini stroked his chin thoughtfully. "To protect our enterprises and to keep the lid on, you must have a dependable colored spy system . . . You will also need a mob of coloreds to guarantee the speedy death of all coloreds with a serious itch for our take and power. We must avoid newspaper stories embarrassing to our stand-up police and political friends. We must not punish with our own hands any except those coloreds that we have given responsibility to, who double-cross us."

Collucci said, "Papa, I like the way you see it for them. I must get a line on one of them qualified to help me put it all together . . . perhaps Mr. Cocio can steer me right."

Bellini gravely shook his head, "He had lousy relations with the coloreds. He never found out what they are, how they think . . . he never tried . . . they shuffled for him and walled their stepin-fetchit eyes from the tops of their heads for him. He never had a Chinaman's chance to find out what it is really like with them. You need a colored who knows the whole score over there to help you organize."

Bellini puffed on his cigar as he threw his head back for a moment and closed his eyes in concentration.

Finally he looked across the table and said, "There are several, but on proved performance and reliability my vote goes to old Mack Rivers if you can pull him in. Willie Poe tried, and couldn't get the time of day. Causes, colored or white, don't move Mack Rivers . . . just the long green, and the power, and the lacy fluffs that go with it.

"Rivers has been in touch with the streets over there since the Twenties. I dug him up for Big Al, to protect our trucks and the alky we peddled to the coloreds. He's got a gambling joint in the Forties on State Street that the heisters never touch. They are afraid because of his reputation with a rod and his street savvy."

Collucci said, "He sounds like what I need over there."

Bellini laughed, "Mack Rivers knows when the bedbugs screw on the Southside."

At Collucci's leaving, Bellini stood at the door and said, "Good luck, Giacomo, and remember your Papa Bellini let go before the witch of power could hustle a price on my life, or drag my rear end with cancer that can come from the power pressure."

They embraced and Collucci got behind the wheel of his limousine to drive himself directly to find and lure Mack Rivers.

His bodyguard Lollo Stilotti and chauffeur and closest friend Angelo Serelli played out a hand of draw poker for a big pot on the back seat.

Bellini scowled through the door glass at Collucci's chumminess with his underlings, and his loose security.

Collucci reeled in Mack Rivers from his drab craps joint on a gaudy hook.

Collucci said, "I'm inviting you to become the biggest and richest hustler on the Southside . . . with Mack Rivers flashing on the marquee of a plush cabaret . . . and your own numbers bank . . . clear and free. You start when I take them over . . . Understand?"

Rivers nodded.

Collucci stood up and extended his hand, "Mack, you accept my invitation?"

Mack Rivers stood. He showed his naked blue gums. He leaned his long bony frame across the table and shook Collucci's hand. "Mr. Collucci, does Mack Rivers want to lay Lena Horne?"

Mack Rivers' Green Pastures became the plushest quicksand for suckers in Southside history. Rivers peacocked joyfully in rainbow suits as he bossed the spies and assassins he recruited so that Collucci could slam down the steel lid that Bellini demanded.

The Green Pastures name for the cabaret lasted until the arrival of Larry "Love Bone" Flambert's sister Mayme from Haiti. Then it became the Voudoo Palace.

CHAPTER NINETEEN

And now Collucci came out of reverie on his way from the meeting with Spino. He noticed that Angelo, driving on Roosevelt Road, was approaching Halstead Street.

He suddenly said, "Turn south on Halstead and go to the Palace."

Angelo made the turn and darted a look of apprehension at Collucci that they were risking the Southside alone.

Collucci caught it and said, "You're jittery as a cunt. Fuck Taylor and his jigaboos . . . you got that, Angelo?"

Angelo grunted, "Uh-huh," and stomped the gas pedal.

Twelve minutes later, he parked in the no parking zone in front of the cabaret. A grinning tank draped in dazzling purple hurried across the sidewalk and opened the car door for Collucci. Then the doorman opened the padded front door covered with orchid leather. Angelo followed Collucci into the mirrored bar section.

Collucci felt a twanging sensation at the root of his testicles as he gazed at Mayme's reflected image.

The dollish dancer's pinch-bottle curves gleamed like sealskin in a blue spot. She quivered her black cherry melon tips in synch with a funky drumbeat, and her G-stringed dimpled rear end tossed airily in the pool of light.

Angelo remembered he had tricked Bone to slaughter. He averted his eyes from the sight of Love Bone's face recreated in living ebonic color.

He whispered hoarsely, "Jimmy, I got a feeling I better wait in the car so nobody fucks with it . . . and I can keep an eye on the street."

Collucci gave Angelo an intense look before nodding him away.

Mack Rivers saw Collucci and he leaped from his supper of chitlins in the dining area at the rear of the barroom. His death's head beamed as he shimmered toward Collucci wearing a pink satin suit that hung on his cadaverous frame like a shroud.

They greeted each other and shook hands.

Mack Rivers looked about the crowded bar. He bared the diamond inset at the front of his gold upper choppers and said, "Mr. C., if you don't want your table, I'll pull one of these chumps off a stool so you can have a taste . . . or you can have one with me at the back."

Collucci said, "I'll have one at my table and catch the finale."

After checking Collucci's hat and coat, the headwaiter seated Collucci, with an unopened fifth of Courvoisier, at his permanently reserved table at ringside.

Rivers winked at two gunmen seated at the bar

to cover Collucci and slewfooted back to his soul supper.

Collucci watched as the dozen men and women members of the show crept on stage, costumed as African leopard cultists. Their bright eyes gave the cat masks eerie life as they felined toward Mayme with claws arcing whitely in the gloom.

Mayme belly danced furiously as the drummer went berserk. She jackknifed her legs and bared her teeth in mock orgasm as the creatures made spitting erotic sounds and descended upon her. She flopped her hair like a blue-black curtain across her face and glared hatred through it at Collucci.

As she lay supine, with satiny thighs agape and chest heaving, the cats, daubed bloodily with paint, hissed and clawed above her in a spot. She oozed sensuously from the tangle to her feet.

The sextet broke into an Haitian death dirge as the victims of sexual greed twitched in a gory heap. Mayme looked back over her shoulder with glowing black eyes every several steps as she bumped and humped through a curtained doorway.

She went down a short hallway to her dressing room. She phoned Taylor to tip off Collucci's presence. She stood before a dressing table mirror blotting perspiration from her body with a Turkish towel.

She was certain Collucci would come to hit on her for sex as he had done a half-dozen times in the past. Now she would pretend to open herself to him, play on him to set him up for Taylor.

She slipped off the shoulder-length mane of hair. She hung it on the side of the mirror where it gleamed blue-black like the carcass of a raven. She dabbed tissues at the pox of sweat on her brow. She blotted her skull, shining and stripped naked and black as an eightball by a childhood scalp disease.

A thin line of surgical scars ran from her temples inside her dead hairline around and down past her ears to the sides of her neck. Ten years before, when she had been the toast of Paris, she had taken her fifty-year-old face to a European wizard of plastic surgery.

He had made incisions and then employed retractors to pull the flabby skin taut across her high cheekboned face and neck. He secured it all with sutures in her scalp before he snipped off the excess, leaving her a face and neck ageless and velvety free of wrinkles and wattles.

She heard Collucci's knock as she was about to slip into a robe. She smiled wickedly at herself in the mirror. She slipped the wig on. She half reached for the robe, but instead moved voluptuously to the door in only the G-string of sequins.

She would hold him for Taylor, she thought as she asked who.

He said, "Jimmy Collucci."

She heard the urgency in his testicles, and called him a murdering motherfucker in French-Haitian patois under her breath.

She looked up at him with dark eyes wide and vivid with girlish heat, and Voudoo con, to be in the presence of such an ungodly handsome charmer. For the mini-instant his eyes were trapped by the bulge of fat bush against the G-string, her eyes glared lunatic hatred.

She noticed his erection as he said, "I had to come back here to tell you, you've got to be the sexiest dancer, pound for pound, anywhere."

She opened the door wide and stepped aside and her black cherry bow of a mouth pouted. "It sounds like a fight game compliment . . . but thank you anyway, Mr. Collucci."

She smiled to see his eyes narrow just the slightest as he searched her face for a clue in her boxing reference that she suspected him of Love Bone's murder.

He said, "Mayme, have I got to ask a dozen times before you'll call me Jimmy . . . ? Baby, don't run that modesty game on me. You know even a blind man, working with just your voice and vibes, couldn't feel a fight game connection."

She sat down at the mirror. She dabbed on cleansing cream and watched him sit on the arm of an overstuffed chair behind her. His smug expression, she was sure, blossomed from the soul shit he was proud to put together and toss at her.

She tissued off the cream around her eyes as she thought, *Well here's some hot grease for your hard-on.*

She said softly, "Jimmy, your flowers for Larry were lovely . . . the most extravagant of all . . . that day at the chapel."

She watched his eyes harden and his mouth toughen in the silence. He dropped his eyes to the carpet for an instant. She watched him take a deep breath and put his wary eyes in the mirror again with a pious grimace.

"I was fond of Bone," he said. "I miss him."

He lit a cigarette and suddenly the room keened with the presence of the Loas, the Voudoo Spirits. There was something about the cast of his face in the lighter flame that stroked her memory. She remembered an insane witch doctor in Haiti long ago. She had presided at his trial and death by fire for the mutilation murder of several female children.

She smiled into the mirror as she thought, *Too bad it can't be the fire for you.*

To slow him down she said, "How is your family?" as he rose from the chair and stood.

He said, "I suppose your asking about my family means you're dangling me again."

She stiffened at the look on his face. He came and pressed himself against the back of her chair.

She fought for control and said in a voice ragged with hatred, "I've never encouraged you, Jimmy, so how can I dangle you?"

He smiled to hear the break in her voice and he erected fully with the thought that he had cornered and was exciting the hot nigger bitch, and she had been in heat for him all along.

"Don't shuck me, baby doll. You did everything but put it on my table a few minutes ago. I swat teasers' rear ends raw," he said as he nuzzled her peeking earlobe.

He gazed at the blue jet swell of crossed thighs. He greedily inhaled the raw meld of Paris perfume spiced with vaginal slime that she smeared on herself. He caped the dressing gown across her shoulders.

She glanced down at the scissors on the table top. She visualized his neck gouting gore. For an instant her hands shook uncontrollably with the urge to strike over her shoulder and stab the scissors to the hilt, up into the soft spot under his ear.

She saw by her watch only ten minutes had passed since her call. Taylor needed another thirty-five.

She stared at the dazzle of scissors and willed herself into light trance to make him believe she was relaxed.

She said with sugar on it, "I need more time. I'm afraid to be sweet on you . . . suppose I got really hung up on you and then you . . . ?"

He freed his long hard organ from his trousers, and vised his powerful hands on her shoulders. He leaned down and pressed his cheek against her face. He stared into her eyes in the mirror as he rolled the muscles at the sides of her neck in a crushing massage.

He said in a deadly whisper, "You can't feed me that ingenue shit any more. Our time has come to fuck . . . and what the hell, I can make you queen of the Southside if you take it deep and pretty for Jimmy Collucci."

She said, "I can't tonight. I've got the girlie whirlies."

He tightened his hands around the base of her throat.

"The what?" he said.

She enjoyed an interior guffaw that she hadn't

menstruated in two decades as she said, "Another month has whirled away again, and I'm wounded again . . . until day after tomorrow."

He said, "You're full of shit," as he lifted his bloated organ and stroked it across the top of her shoulder.

Her face ashened with rage at the violation. She scooped up the jar of cleansing cream and cracked it violently down on her shoulderblade as he leaped back an instant in time. She did a jack-in-the-box and her chair toppled to the floor between them like a crashing counterpoint to the blare of the band's final dance number.

"You crazy jigaboo! You think Jimmy Collucci has to tear his asshole loose to lay a spook?" he screamed in a whisper.

She curled her lip and pointed to his exposed organ and taunted, "Look, trick, take your pitiful white pecker out of my face and stick it in that dago cunt you put on that throne in River Forest!"

He moved toward her.

She backed against the table and her eardrums vibrated with the gabble of the Loas. *"Fly the scissors! Fly the scissors!"*

He said, "I'll kill you! I'll fuck you or kill you!"

Her hand blurred through the air, and he saw a laser of silver fire streaking for the center of his right eye. A spastic muscle in his neck jerked his head a fraction. He felt a gentle zephyr against his eyelash at almost the same instant that he felt the scissors gouge a stinging rill across the tip of his ear.

He lunged and his fist skidded off her heavily

creamed jaw. She went down and lay stunned on the carpet. He dragged her to a small adjoining room and threw her onto a daybed. He shucked out of his clothes and patted a handkerchief against the dribbles of blood at his ear tip.

Mayme stole a glance at her wristwatch. Twenty more minutes! Mayme looked up at him with slumberous eyes. He stooped and placed the luger on the carpet beside the bed. He lay down beside her. She was rigid with rage. She quivered as she fought the impulse to leap over him and try for the luger. He pried at her thighs. He heard the grit of her teeth in defiance. He backhanded the side of her face.

The Voudoo spirits chorused so piercingly she clapped her hands over her ears. *"Trance away! Trap away! Trance away!"*

She went into trance. She relaxed and opened her benumbed cave to his steely stabbing.

With a groan he jabbed his tongue into her half opened mouth. He seized hers and sucked brutally as if to tear her tongue from its roots. His scrotum sparkled excruciatingly as he exploded seed to spawn a million Mafiosi.

But even as his joy spewed, it soured in the realization of her powerful pull, of the danger, her threat to his self-image of power, of complete control, his immunity to sexual entrapment.

This freak would have to go away, right away, out of his sight and temptation, he thought as he spat and scrubbed his mouth with a corner of sheet. She would go away, or he would put her away in the mob's cemetery on the rise behind his

Sweet Dream Roadhouse.

He scooped up the luger as he rolled off the bed and got to his feet. He looked down and was fascinated at her dreamy eyes that seemed to be staring through him, and at the odd smile lifting the corners of her mouth. He shook her. She lay still as death. He slapped his palm against her cheek. She trembled a bit and came to.

She rubbed the back of her hand across her eyes to cover the glance at her wristwatch. She had done it! Taylor would be out there waiting for him!

His voice was harsh. "Mayme, I . . . what the hell is your real name?"

She said, "It's always been Mayme Flambert."

He stuck the snout of the luger between her eyes and said shakily, "Nigger, I won't be seeing you again."

She said, "I know . . . I can't say I'm sorry."

He pecked her forehead with the luger barrel. "I mean I don't want you in my sight! I mean leave the city quick as you can haul out your freakish black ass. Understand?"

She nodded.

He went to the washbasin across the room and watched her in the mirror as he soaped the inside of his mouth and washed himself. She lay motionless while he dressed. The instant that he left, she raced up a rear stairway to her apartment front window to see his death.

CHAPTER TWENTY

Collucci stopped to have one for the road and light chitchat with Mack Rivers at the bar.

At that moment Bama was losing his argument with Taylor not to go alone for Collucci. Kong stood in the parsonage living room watching poker-faced. Taylor stood unsteadily on legs weakened by a two-day bout with flu.

For the dozenth time he demanded from Bama the keys to the Warriors' supercharged old Pontiac sedan.

"I ain't saying it no more. Gimme the keys, Bama," Taylor said as he waved a flashlight and brushed by Bama in the doorway. "I ain't forgot how to hot wire a ride," Taylor flung over his shoulder.

Bama shook his head and followed him down the hallway to the door to the street. Kong went to the phone in his apartment to tip Mack Rivers. Bama tugged at Taylor's overcoat sleeve as he went through the door. Taylor ignored him, but stopped in the middle of the sidewalk and turned.

Bama threw him the ring of keys and said, "Star natal fool, you still got the flu. At least take the squad with you."

Taylor unlocked the Pontiac at the curb and said before he got in, "Ain't got no time now, grand-maw Bama, to roust up no squad and two of 'em got galloping flu." Then he grinned and said, "I might chastise you when I get back for shuckin' and jivin' away all them minutes. 'Sides, it looks like ain't but him and one more dago."

He started the engine. He punched the proper pattern on the radio's selector buttons to pop up the top of the dashboard. It was the steel box containing an arsenal. He took out a sawed-off shotgun, automatic rifle and several handguns, and placed them on the seat beside him. He pushed the dashboard lid down and locked it shut with a quick tattoo on the radio selectors. He rocketed the Pontiac away.

At that moment, Mack Rivers came away from the phone at the end of the bar. His black face was gray.

He stood gesticulating mutely before Collucci before he blurted, "Mr. C., we got to put out all the lights and steel bar that front door! Taylor is coming to waste you . . . and he ain't stuck on me."

Collucci felt a tiny flutter of fear behind his navel. He was suddenly irritated and angry that Mack Rivers' fearful face had triggered the one emotion he was most ashamed of, and afraid of feeling himself.

He said harshly, "Mack, you cunt! Get yourself

together!"

Rivers said, "But Mr. C., that chump is crazy!"

Collucci buttoned up his overcoat.

"He alone?" he said softly.

Rivers said, "Yeah . . . but . . ."

Collucci said, "Mack, when I was just a pissy punk, I got the reputation that any ass that comes solo against me gets the bloody shit stomped out of it."

Collucci turned away toward the front door.

Mack Rivers snapped his fingers for a half-dozen of his gunmen seated around a nearby table lapping up an on-the-house setup of Jim Beam. They looked at Rivers.

He jerked his head toward Collucci at the door. "Back up Mr. C. with Taylor. Some of you get in them gangways from the corner down, and some of you just shuck and jive like squares on both sides of the stem out front."

Collucci whipped himself around and his teeth flashed in his dark face. "Mack, why, why can't I get it across that I don't need anybody out there to help me put a tag on Taylor's toe tonight?"

Rivers shook his head and heaved a sigh. He called Lieutenant Paul Porta's office at Eleventh Street headquarters. Within minutes, Porta's office radioed him the Taylor info as he cruised with his squad a half-mile away from the Voudoo Palace.

The gunmen picked up their glasses and went, with Rivers, to peek at the street through front window drapes.

Collucci stopped in the middle of the sidewalk and struck his lighter to a cigarette. While he lit up, his eyes swept both sides of the block. They locked on a silhouette inside an oncoming car halted by a stoplight at the intersection to his left.

It's him! Collucci thought as he plucked the luger from his overcoat pocket and gripped it flat against his thigh.

Taylor spotted Collucci and stiffened inside the Pontiac.

Collucci walked to the curb near the front bumper of the bulletproof limo.

Angelo slid across the seat and lowered the glass. He stuck his head out toward the sidewalk and said, "Everything peaches and cream?"

Collucci said, "Yeah, Taylor is on the turn . . . stay inside and start the machine."

From the corner of his eye he watched Taylor ease the Pontiac across the intersection and pull to the curb at the end of the block and snuff the Pontiac's lights. He saw Taylor's silhouette vanish. He was certain Taylor was racing toward him behind the cover of parked cars.

Let the cocksucker come, he thought as he telescoped himself behind the limo's grille and peered around a headlamp at Taylor's form bent over in a running crouch, bumping car sides as he lurched down the street on legs rubbery with flu.

Collucci smiled as he gazed at Taylor's feeble gait. He thought, *I'll move up the sidewalk and blow him away when he goes past my cover.*

As he turned to streak for a point of ambush, he noticed a knot of black people had formed behind him and others were at windows and standing in doorways staring at him.

He thought, *What if one of them is a Warrior sympathizer with a gun? Or what if one of them shouts a warning to Taylor that I'm waiting for him?*

He slipped quickly into the limo and said, "Pull out, Angelo, and do no more than fifteen straight ahead."

Angelo pulled away from the curb, and Collucci saw Taylor straighten up and stop fifty yards away for a moment, with sawed-off shotgun dangling in his hands. Taylor turned and scuttled back toward the Pontiac.

Collucci turned from the rear window and said, "The cocksucker moves like he's busted up or something . . . just keep going west."

Angelo said, "I got the M16 out of the trunk. Want it ? . . . maybe you can put a round or two in his noggin."

Collucci said, "Too much traffic . . ."

An instant later he saw Taylor suddenly bomb the Pontiac forward.

Collucci said, "Kick the piss out of this crate!"

Angelo stomped the gas pedal and the limo shot forward and regained its block distance from the roaring Pontiac. Collucci slid aside a silver dollar-sized steel cover on a porthole beneath the rear window of three-inch-thick glass. He leaned across the front seat and got the M16 rifle off the floor-board.

Three blocks east of Taylor, Mayme Flambert was packing her portable possessions as if expecting a visitation from a horde of enemy Voudoo demons. She had just moments before seen Porta's squadron of gangbusters racing after the Pontiac. She knew the odds were now riding with Collucci, and she was red-hot with death.

Inside the limo Collucci said, "Cut left fast into that alley over there and kill the lights."

Angelo swung into the maw and slammed through the littered alley at fifty miles per hour for a hundred and fifty yards without lights.

Taylor brought the Pontiac into the alley mouth on two wheels and torpedoed it toward the limo's dark shape.

Collucci let go a burst from the M16 that shattered the Pontiac's radiator and the windshield just as Taylor screeched the brakes and almost in the same motion flung himself to the alley floor, rolling and firing his automatic rifle at the flashes of flame jetting from the muzzle of Collucci's M16.

At that same instant Porta and his squad careened into the alley and Taylor was bathed in spotlight before he rolled under the Pontiac.

Porta bellowed over a bullhorn, "Jessie Taylor, this is Lieutenant Porta of the gang squad. Roll out with your hands clean."

Taylor rolled beneath the front bumper. He decided he'd spring up and, using the Pontiac's hulk to cover his back from Porta, rush Collucci with a fire storm of automatic rifle. He was past thinking about himself now. He just wanted Collucci dead.

As he slid his legs out to take his feet for the attack, Collucci leveled down on Taylor's shadow and a burst of twenty bullets ripped and mangled Taylor from thighs to ankles. The impact blew him into the middle of the alley floor. His kneecaps were blown away, and he lay blacked out with pain and shock.

Porta put the spot on Taylor's motionless form, and in the glow saw Collucci marching down the alley toward Taylor gripping the M16 with both hands.

Porta leaped from the police car and shouted, "Mr. Collucci! Halt! That bandit is our business!"

Collucci marched grimly on, zombie-like, his eyes bulgy and bright.

A woman screamed from a tenement window overlooking the alley, "For the luvva Jesus Christ! Somebody stop him!"

Porta leaned into the police car and said, "This may be delicate. I better handle it."

He turned and double-timed his heavy legs down the alley toward Taylor.

Collucci reached Taylor and rammed the snout of the M16 against the center of his forehead. Taylor's eyes fluttered open and hardened as Collucci's looming figure came into focus.

Taylor said haltingly, "You spaghetti-gut motherfucking pussy . . . you too yella to pull the trigger even?"

Collucci jerked his finger violently against the trigger at the instant that Porta kicked the exploding rifle off target. The burst riddled the Pontiac's side as Porta struggled with Collucci for the M16.

"Let me finish that cocksucker, Paul . . . let me finish him, Paul," Collucci pleaded.

Collucci stumbled over Taylor and fell backward to the alley floor. Porta twisted the rifle free. He helped Collucci to his feet. At that same moment

Porta heard the feet of his men against the gritty alley floor, and he caught a glint of Collucci's pocketknife blade as he squatted and opened it to slash Taylor's throat. Porta swung the barrel of the M16 against Collucci's chest.

Porta's voice was low. "It took me thirty years to get that office downtown. Jimmy, I won't let you coup-de-grace even a nigger before five young bastards with assholes itching to move up in the department, any way that turns up."

Porta turned a flashlight on Taylor's now unconscious face and his gaping wounds spurting blood with his every heartbeat.

Porta whispered, "Jimmy, this shine will be D.O.A. at County . . ."

The squad pounded on scene and stood gazing down at Taylor.

Porta said, "Yablonski, get back to the car and call a wagon out here."

But the screaming woman in the tenement window had long ago called the Wabash Avenue Police Station to report a man downed by gunfire.

Yablonski, the cop, backed the police car out of the alley to allow the yowling ambulance to barrel down the alley to Taylor.

Both of the black paramedics recognized Taylor instantly. One of them had a relative who was a Warrior. They fed plasma into him immediately. During the short ride to Provident Hospital's emergency intensive care facility, Taylor was given the most gentle handling. At the hospital he was prepared for immediate surgery and tranfusions of blood.

Porta walked back with Collucci to the limo, gouged and dented by Taylor's rifle. Angelo's moon face was solemn as he moved a flashlight beam across Collucci's rumpled clothing, looking for wounds, and hand-brushing grit off the back of Collucci's overcoat.

Collucci said, "What hospital, Paul?"

Porta shrugged. "Not to County, that's a cinch. Those two spades are his fans. They would probably spring out of their own pockets to get him into the nearest and the best . . . Provident is my guess. You got no problems. The guy can't make it . . . and Tonelli and City Hall want him planted."

Collucci got into the limo beside Angelo and lit a cigarette. He blew out a gust of smoke and said, "Paul, if that cocksucker makes it, I'm going to find a way to finish him in there."

Porta blew through the air in exasperation and said, "At best he'll be a helpless cripple. I'm telling you to celebrate." He turned away.

Angelo moved the limo away.

After frequent glances at his boss's inscrutable face, Angelo broke the long silence as he tooled the limo toward River Forest. "Jimmy, is everything peaches . . . ?"

The sudden expression of extreme annoyance on Collucci's face cut off Angelo.

Collucci said sharply, "Cut the gab! All right? I'm kicking around some angles."

Then he turned and sat staring through the windshield. He laid out for himself the negatives threatening his giddy dream, the risks and pitfalls, his upcoming complex and dangerous kidnap of

Dinzio, Tonelli's bodyguard.

His jaw writhed in excitement as he visualized himself moving past the hawkeye gauntlet of garage guards, past the machine gunner in the dome above the elevator to the penthouse. He watched himself as Dinzio, stepping out into the lounge command post moiling with Tonelli's torturers and assassins. He smiled, and an ecstatic shiver shook him, as he saw himself press Dinzio's electronic device in his palm that swung open the vault door to Tonelli's inner sanctum.

His jaw lumped. The most deadly obstacle would be mass sleep for the other National Commission's ancient cocksuckers.

He was led into laying out for himself the positives favoring his dream of succession as monarch of the kingdom of Chicago . . . and after that . . . ? *Capo di Tutti Capi! Boss of All Bosses!*

Porta was right. He had finished Taylor. Even if Taylor made it, his bullets had blown away Taylor's image as a leader. He would be pathetic with his hooligan pride trapped in a wheelchair. Scratch Taylor!

Scratch Cocio within mere days! Suddenly as Angelo pulled into the mansion's driveway, heady jolts of power and euphoria trembled him.

He stepped out of the car and said across the seat, "Angelo, have a good night's sleep . . . everything is peaches and cream."

CHAPTER TWENTY-ONE

Ida Schmidt opened the door of her Gold Coast apartment to let out a stout cheapskate wearing a vicuna overcoat. Standing there in the soft shadowing hallway light, and smiling her economical fifty-buck smile, the one that didn't show her imperfect teeth, Ida Schmidt was more than a fair ringer for the young Olivia Tonelli Collucci.

She moved beneath the living room chandelier and brassy Roman candles streaked from her mane of blonde hair. But purer ones showered from Olivia's golden fleece.

She went to the bathroom. She stripped off her nightgown and stood before the washbasin. She put one foot on the commode cover. She dabbed a soapy washcloth at armpits and crotch. Then she brightened her make-up for Cocio, who was Larry Fillmore to her, she let him think.

Her face close up in the mirror was stained with whiskey blotch. The feet and fists of her pimp, who OD'ed the week she met Cocio, had rashed her face with scars.

As she blotted her lipstick, she remembered that Cocio had been so excited by his first sight of her, he slammed on the brakes. Hazarding life and limb, he leaped from his car and sprinted through the heavy traffic.

She was properly indignant to force apology for the crudeness of his sidewalk approach to a lady. Then she let him con her into his car. She was glad she had let him muscle into her life. She had to admit old Larry Fillmore had the weirdest hang-ups of all her johns. But he was the best, buck-wise, she thought as she went into the bedroom with her trademark sway of sexy hips and butt double dimpled.

She took a nun's habit, stained with semen, from the closet and quickly returned it. For to-night's date she remembered she had been told to wear the bridal gown. Her nose crinkled at the rank odor of the semen-encrusted gown. She wiggled into it. It was an expensive replica of the peach peau de soie gown Olivia had worn at her wedding and at the reception on the Tonelli estate that night her beauty broke the rhythm of Cocio's heart.

Ida adored herself for a moment in the dresser mirror, cocooned in the new blue mink maxi Cocio had orgasmed her with on her thirtieth birthday.

She gazed at a group picture on the dresser of herself at fifteen with her ma and pa and brothers and sisters, towheaded and tattered on the stoop of the cedar chopper's shack down in Walberg, Texas. *Holy Toledo, I was pretty that year the trucker brought me here*, she thought as she turned away.

She felt suddenly very tired as she locked her door and headed for the elevators. Halos of frozen fire glittered on her fingers as she pressed the "down" button. She jerked her eyes from her haggard reflection in the elevator door glass.

A twinge of pain razored her hip and her right leg buckled and went dead for a long moment.

I've got to be the loneliest, ass-draggingest hooker in Chicago, she thought as she rode down to the garage.

Two of Spino's terrible Bomato assassins from Sicily watched for the highway approach just outside Chicago of Cocio's Jag. They peered from the office of one of Cocio's chain of motels, darkened except for a pale desk-lamp light.

They did not expect or fear discovery. They trusted the renowned casing skill of Collucci's undertakers, Marty and Freddie Rizzo.

They learned from the undertakers that Cocio always closed down the motel for his dates with Ida. He gave his employees a day and night off, with a bonus and instructions to stay off the motel grounds. On those occasions Cocio needed absolute privacy with Ida to act out, suffer and enjoy his love-hate fantasies about Olivia Collucci.

The fox-and-bull team of Bomatos tensed and grinned at each other as they ducked down into the office murk.

Cocio's Jag pulled off the highway into the motel driveway. He coasted to the steel gates of the ten-foot chain-link fence. He didn't notice, as he turned his key in the lock on the gate chain, the metal-painted putty on a sawed-through link of the chain. But then neither had he spotted the Bomatos' sedan hidden in a stand of trees down the road.

He pulled the chain through to swing open the double gates. He pulled the Jag inside the fence and sat smoking a cigarette as he watched the highway in the rear-view mirror. On his second puff he spotted Ida's silver El Dorado approaching. She drove inside the fence and Cocio relocked the gates. Ida followed the Jag to the end of the most distant row of rooms.

The Bomatos watched Cocio insert his key and unlock the unit that he had completely mirrored from ceiling to wall-to-wall polar bear carpeting.

Ida stepped inside. Immediately she flung her coat on the bed and stood near the door with emotion twisting her face. She was prepping for the familiar scenario with Cocio.

Cocio sat inside the Jag smoking nervously. He was eager to have his fantasies about Olivia become real for him in the scenario.

Inside the office, the sharp-faced Bomato waved his brother to the plastic garbage bag they brought along. They stripped off their clothes. They opened the bag and put on rubber boots and glossy pegleg jumpsuits. They were of a rubbery plastic that had the dull sheen of the rubber aprons worn by the butcherknife masters of the heart shot down in the stockyards.

The Bull took the master key from a board above the desk and dropped it into his jumper breast pocket. He sat down beside his brother.

They watched Cocio go inside. They lit up strong black cigars to enjoy while waiting for the couple to settle in.

Cocio stepped through the door and frowned annoyance to see Ida.

He said, "You goddamn slut. Why have you come here on your wedding night?"

She clutched at him with an agonized face as he shucked out of his clothes. His forty-five automatic fell silently to the fur rug from his overcoat pocket.

She pleaded, "Please forgive me! It was a mistake. I love you."

He curled his lips. "What can a lousy tramp like you know about love? Get out of here, Olivia! Get out of here before I kick you to pieces!"

He was nude and breathing hard.

She knelt, remembering the script, and looked up piteously at him. "Let me rest beside you. Please . . . your body is so slender and cute . . . so exciting to me."

She pressed her face into his crotch and sobbed as she embraced his legs.

He slugged the side of her head and she screamed as she toppled backward. She spread her legs so she'd fall to expose the crimson lining of her organ.

She lay blubbering, begging him over and over, "Please say you love me! Please say you love me!"

He screamed over and over, "Olivia, you slut, I hate you!" He beat himself inside his fist to the rhythm of her wailing.

He climaxed. His legs trembled as he stood over

her and fouled the bridal gown. Glistening with sweat he staggered backward and fell panting across the bed.

She stripped off the gown and kissed his lips as she lay down beside him. She stroked his temple and dabbed tissues at his brow.

He said breathlessly, "Damn that was good! . . . Ida, you were just great."

She crooned, "So were you, Larry Sweetie."

He got up and went to the bathroom for a shower. She lay back to enjoy a cigarette until she would shower. Then for an hour or so they would pet and fondle each other before saying good-bye.

Inside the motel office, the Bull armed himself with a hatchet to carry out Collucci's beheading clause in the contract. The Fox gripped a length of lead pipe and stuck a thirty-eight pistol, with attached silencer, into his jumper pockets. They locked their street clothes in the office and crept through the darkness toward the only light for miles around.

Ida stiffened in bed, a cigarette dangled from her frozen face. She was almost certain she'd heard a noise above the shower racket. It had been just outside the door, something like the sound a basketball player's shoes make in sharp braking.

She had one foot on the floor pointed for the shower when they oozed through the door. The Fox scowled and aimed the thirty-eight at the center of her forehead. His brother shushed his own lips with an index finger. She felt a shriek of panic building up.

But she was amused at her last thought before

her mind bank exploded. The fat round silencer at the muzzle of the thirty-eight reminded her of her pa at the movies. He had taught her at five to sneak her hand so smoothly under the straw hat on his lap that Ma and none of the kids ever knew she played with Pa's tool.

She was dead with three eyes staring up at them from the floor. But the Fox pumped a slug into her navel when they passed.

They stood at the half-open bathroom door. Steam swirled around their heads when they stepped inside. They stood loosely watching Cocio's shadow through the curtain, soaping itself.

Cocio reminded himself to take some mint sherbet home to Mama Victoria. He threw his head back and raggedly sang a few lyrics of her torch song. They laughed out loud to see his pipestem frame shake with the effort.

Cocio's throat locked. He stood very still and cocked his head to one side like a baby chick listening to the rustle of a weasel. Tile squeaked their boot soles as they came to the shower. Cocio knew instantly his only chance was to somehow get past them to the forty-five in his overcoat pocket.

He stepped from beneath the shower head and turned off the cold water. Hot water hissed from the head, and a mist of steam enveloped Cocio. He whipped back the curtain at the same instant that he punched up the shower nozzle with the heel of his hand.

They threw their hands up to their faces against the scalding spray. He leaped for the thin space between them at the moment they ducked down and rushed him. The impact knocked him to the flooded tile.

They seized his throat and privates, but their hands slipped off his soapy body. He rolled toward the door as they cursed and stomped him. The Bull hacked down at him with the hatchet and lost his balance on the slippery floor and the hatchet clattered to the tile.

Cocio rolled and snatched up the hatchet. The Fox stepped back and fired at his heart. He turned quickly and the bullet shattered his left buttock and skidded him through the flood of hot water to the doorway.

He pulled himself to his feet in the mist of steam. The Bull grabbed his ankle. He chopped the hatchet at the Bull's skull and sliced off a hunk of scalp and hair. The Fox fired again and gouged away Cocio's right cheek.

The Bull squeezed his wound and rocked on his knees in pain as Cocio reeled into the bedroom. The Fox glimpsed him through the mist and pumped a dumdum that shattered Cocio's tailbone.

He crashed to the carpet. The Fox rushed and kicked away the hatchet. He aimed down to put a slug though Cocio's head. The Bull barged from the bathroom patting his leaky head and scalded face.

He grabbed his brother's shoulder and spun him around. "No! No!" he exclaimed in Sicilian. His black eyes rolled back toward the bathroom. "That one should taste his own medicine."

The eyes of the Fox oscillated at the idea. They

dragged him by his heels to the shower. He sprawled on his stomach moaning as the Fox leaned in to the shower to cut it off and to plug the tub. He turned the hot faucet on full volume. The bathroom resonated with Cocio's high-pitched whimpering and bat-slugging-the-ball kind of pulpy cracking sound as the Fox smashed down the lead pipe on Cocio's shoulders, back and ribs. The Bull snatched and wielded the pipe until shards of bone popped through Cocio's flesh like the quills of a porcupine.

They hefted Cocio and balanced him on the rim. They stepped back and let him tumble in. His eyes protruded and he bellowed hoarsely in the boiling shock. His hands feverishly paddled the water pooch-fashion before he lunged from the tub and fell quivering to the floor.

They hefted him into the tub again. He whistled shrilly through his teeth and feebly tried to escape again. His head hung over the tub rim. His tongue lolled out black and bloated. The walls of tile reverberated with their laughter at such a funny sight. The Bull hacked with the hatchet until the head bounced on the tile, free of the stump.

They fished up "its" ankles in the scalding claret with a toilet brush. They pulled "it" out and dolled "it" up with red panties to satisfy Collucci's faggot clause in the contract.

They drained the tub and stepped in to cold shower their faces and bloody boots and jumpsuits. They lashed towels around "its" ankles and hung "it" stump down from the shower nozzle.

They giggled and rained spit and urine on "it" as

they had the corpse of Mussolini hanging in the square when they were children.

They went into the bedroom and Ida Schmidt's gigantic blue orbs accused them through a mask of gore. They mummified away the ugly sight with the bridal gown.

They went to the motel office. They smeared their burning faces with Vaseline from the motel's first aid kit. The Fox bandaged his brother's scalp. Then they cooled their gullets with soft drinks before they packed their working gear and dressed for the street. They chattered gaily in Sicilian on the way to their car, concealed up the road.

In the opposite direction, two hundred yards away, Collucci watched them from an abandoned cider stand. A serviceable used Cougar purchased by Angelo under a fake name was parked behind the stand. Collucci left through the back of the stand, carrying a starlight-scoped magnum rifle he had brought along to use just in case Cocio somehow managed to elude the terrible Bomatos.

He sat listening to the purr of the Cougar until the Bomatos' tail-lights faded away. In high spirits, Collucci pulled onto the highway. As he approached the motel, he fought off an almost irresistible desire to view the job on Cocio in his mirrored hate nest.

Tonelli's next and I'm doing the job on him. Sweet it will be! he thought, as he flogged the Cougar toward Hilda's blueberry pancakes.

CHAPTER TWENTY-TWO

The morning after Cocio's death, his employees arrived and discovered his corpse. The police were called in, and Lieutenant Paul Porta notified Tonelli immediately.

Tonelli and Bellini hastily arranged a conference. They sat on the penthouse patio in the womb of tinted plastic bubble that retracted for balmy days. The filtered sunlight was golden damask on the alabaster tabletop at which they sat conferring in Sicilian.

The crystal goblet of ruby vino at Bellini's lips shot sparkle like a diamond chalice, as he paused in his defense of cool objectivity, in consideration of Cocio's death, and the probability of Jimmy Collucci's hand in it.

Tonelli said with an agitated face, "I'm asking, who the hell in all of Chicago . . . in the world, would have the nerve and filthy hate to do a job like that on Francesco? . . . except Giacomo Collucci? For years I have caught, in his eyes, his hate for me."

Bellini shook his head. His fingers crawled the goblet. "I know him. He's a dandy. He wouldn't slop himself up on a job like this."

Tonelli leaned forward. "Then he put the slop in the contract he gave the sonuvabitch that did the job on Francesco, which is going to kill Victoria Cocio."

Bellini smiled. "Then you admit there could be one other than Giacomo who could have done the job on Francesco? There could be more . . . like fleas on a mutt. That is why we must move with cool heads."

Tonelli sailed his hands through the air. "You sound like his lawyer, Papa Luigi. Don't forget a tiger gone insane will destroy anyone. And especially his trainer."

Tonelli lit Bellini's cigar and a cigarette for himself.

Then Tonelli said with a rueful face, "What a shame my *soldati* didn't kill him when he did that job on Olivia. A young girl's heart can mend quickly."

The remark raised Bellini's eyebrows and Tonelli's caution. "Not always, Giuseppe. He didn't hit her pants and run. They got married. But we are dancing in wasteful circles around our problem . . . I'll go along with your argument that he is sick and dangerous with the power fever. Any solution ideas?"

Tonelli's caution was overridden by his generation of hatred for Collucci. "Let's broil the names of the others out of him and have him finished like Francesco was."

Bellini's eyebrows took flight again. "Olivia and Petey?" Bellini said softly.

Tonelli took a deep breath. "Petey can forget him, and Olivia stopped swooning years ago . . . He's just a bad habit they can break."

Bellini said, "No, Giuseppe, our first move must be smoother than that. This affair is rotten with many unknown pitfalls and threats, not just for ourselves here in Chicago, but also for the National Commission.

"I know him inside out, and if Giacomo made the move on Francesco, he's dreaming beyond just the control of Chicago. He's not so stupid he'd do the job on both bosses, one a member of the Commission, unless he was dreaming the biggest dream there is . . ."

Tonelli said, "You mean . . . try for the Commission?"

Bellini nodded solemnly. "I mean that. He's got to know he wouldn't stand a shine's chance with just local *soldati.* So, he has put together, or must put together, a plan for a mass setup of the Commission with other greedy turks in all of the families across the country."

Bellini shook his head. "No, we have no proof to show the Commission that he threatens them. And too, you and I are in a most delicate position . . . You allowed him elbow space to become a threat . . . And I brought him into the Honored Society."

Bellini sipped from the goblet before he went on. "We must keep his actions covered around the clock, until we get the hard proof for the

Commission."

Bellini shrugged. "Maybe he's clean. Maybe he's just dirty with Francesco's death, and has not put together the big plan yet. I'll put the best spy firm in town on him ... Maybe we can solve our problems ourselves in a quiet way."

Tonelli nodded and said, "What firm?"

Bellini said, "Barrantino's the best, and as you know, the size of his debt to you means we will have insurance that nothing of the investigation will leak."

Tonelli suddenly grimaced with pain and he rested his head on the table.

Bellini rose and went around the table. "What is it, Giuseppe?"

Tonelli raised his head and held his jaw in his palms. He mumbled through his teeth, "The root canal I got several years ago to save my lousy teeth is not standing up. For a month I've been dropping codeine pills like popcorn to keep down the pain ... Every one of them has to come out."

Bellini said, "Until Barrantino gives us a full weather report, I wouldn't expose myself unnecessarily if I were you."

Tonelli got to his feet.

As they stepped down into the living room, Tonelli said, "My dentist will do it here or I will slip into his office after his building is closed one evening soon."

They shook hands and Bellini left the penthouse for Barrantino's firm of sureshot spies.

At the moment of Bellini's departure, Mayme Flambert sat baldheaded and invisible behind a soot-blackened window on the third floor of a tenement rooming house. Half of her time she spent imploring the Voudoo Gods to help her arrange Collucci's death.

They had gabbled the promise that it was already arranged to happen before her eyes.

The rest of her time she spent pressing powerful binoculars against a clear section of window glass and sweeping the front of the Voudoo Palace, half a block away.

Ten days after Collucci got Cocio scratched, Taylor lay in his bed recovering from his wounds and the amputation of his legs at the upper hips. His powerful will to live was really responsible for his survival, his doctors agreed.

He had steadfastly refused to let himself slip beyond the pale while Collucci lived. He existed in a constant state of blind rage at Collucci for the helplessness of his ball of a body, and deep depression.

He was convinced that as a hopeless cripple, he was not fit to lead the Warriors. He felt that someone whole should succeed him. He thought and lived only to kill Collucci.

He was staring at the ceiling, wondering if the motorized wheelchair Dew Drop and Ivory were putting together could be used somehow to take him to at least gunshot range of Collucci. Bama interrupted his thoughts with homemade sweet potato pie, Taylor's favorite dessert. Taylor frowned and refused it.

Bama sat on the side of the bed in silence for some time before he said, "Jessie, Rachel and Fluffy have been calling me for days. They want me to reconnect your phone. They also asked me to try to get you to withdraw your order not to let them enter the Zone. Why don't you let them in, Jessie, so they can stay with you?"

Taylor said, "Fluffy ain't got no business spoiling her tender life staying around no ugly sight like me. And Bama, you forget Rachel got in the wind when I was whole . . . 'sides Rachel's aching to be rich down south. So Bama, if you put out some feelers . . . maybe I can be with the funny peoples in the circus, and make Rachel a muckety-muck nigger down in Atlanta, Georgia. I ain't jivin' . . . they could call me 'Beach Ball Boy' with no legs even."

Bama shook his head sadly at Taylor's bitterness.

He said gently, "Whether you believe in Him or not, Jessie, you need Him to help you pull back up. Ask for Him . . . He'll show you, sure as you're born."

Taylor glared at Bama, "Don't throw the 'Beach Ball Boy' no shit balls to juggle. If He's up there, why He let that Mafia man do me like this? Bama, 'splain it! Why He let him, Bama?"

Bama said, "You got nearly the toughest break. But the toughest would have been dying and leaving the Warriors without you. Jessie, He saved you to finish what we started for the people."

Taylor laughed. "You mean, Bama, He ain't got the mother wit to know a cripple ain't in no shape to help nobody, myself even."

Bama got to his feet and said, "We'll talk another time, Jessie. Can I get you something? Do something for you?"

Taylor said, "Yeah, Bama, you can leave me alone so I can meditate in some peace. I'm gonna move down to a bunker soon as Dew Drop and Ivory Jones get my special wheelchair together and fix me up some living space down there."

Bama said, "You know we've got a psychodrama test hanging for Kong and Charming Mills . . . I'll need you."

Taylor said, "Don't worry about it, Bama. I'll be down there waiting when you need me for that."

Bama turned and went away. Taylor stared at the ceiling and turned his thoughts to Collucci.

Charming Mills and Kong's cousin, Buncha Grief, were casing the area around Double Head's numbers bank for a shifting stake-out of Paul Porta's gang squad. Mills spotted a stake-out behind a billboard right across the street from Double Head's pot of heist gold.

Buncha Grief said as they sped across town, "Charming, we gonna get hot and rank the Double Head score. Let's lay off for a while and score when the police got their pants down."

Charming dropped off Buncha. He felt good, on his way back to the Zone to report to Kong, that the going up against Double Head's machine gun had been postponed indefinitely.

CHAPTER TWENTY-THREE

It was two weeks after the big Cocio snatch. Collucci sat sprawled out on his easy chair behind the locked door of the study. He had perfected the Dinzio swagger that he needed to invade the penthouse.

He spent most of his time here of late. He had even slept, for the past week, on the sofa in the corner. Olivia had grown very irritable and her flailing nightmares prevented the rest he needed to stay alert and alive in the rush of risk and death.

He had a week ago installed tiny transmitters in Olivia's bedroom and phone. He monitored the input with a receiver and tape recorder locked in a desk drawer.

He'd decided it was Bellini's doomsday senility vibes and his frequent visits that had put Olivia out on an emotional limb. He'd dreaded something else that day. He was ready to put Bellini to sleep at his first wrong move.

He wasn't worried that Bellini would break his oath of silence to Olivia, or anyone outside of his Honored Society. He also wasn't worried, at this point, about the Commission. He felt he could make the move for Tonelli, for he had also correctly surmised the basis of the reluctance of Tonelli and Bellini to take any suspicion to the National Commission without hard evidence.

He heard a buzzing of the monitor, and knew Olivia's phone had rung. He watched the activated reel of tape spin as it recorded the call. He played it back when it stopped. He listened to dull chitchat between Olivia and Tonelli until near the end of the call.

Then he was excited to hear Joe Tonelli say, "I've got to get off the phone. My mouth is killing me."

Olivia said, "Papa, please get them all out."

He said, "I am, tomorrow night."

She said, "What hospital?"

He said, "My dentist is going to extract them in his office, after hours."

She said, "Give me the phone number."

He said, "I'll be out from the gas and out of there in no time."

She persisted. "I still want the phone number, Papa."

He said, "Wait a second."

He gave it to her and they said good-bye.

Collucci looked at six P.M. on the study clock. He dialed the number, and a PBX operator told him the dentist had left for the day, and the medical complex building would shortly be closing.

Collucci wrote down the address of the complex. Then he went to the apartments behind the mansion.

He got Angelo and went to the Rizzo brothers, who were drinking beer and dogging around with their girlfriends in their apartment over Angelo's.

The Rizzos sent the girls away as soon as Collucci and Angelo showed. Collucci sat with them until midnight, perfecting Tonelli's scratch-out down to the most minute detail.

Taylor jailed his mind in his hate hermitage beneath the Zone on the same afternoon that Mario Rizzo picked the lock on an important door. It was the door of a vacant suite on the second floor of the medical building that housed Tonelli's dentist.

Angelo waited a half block away in the Cougar Collucci used when he secretly backed up Cocio's execution. Collucci, disguised as Dinzio, and the Rizzos waited impatiently in the empty suite for the building to close and Tonelli's arrival.

They heard the assistants in Tonelli's dentist's office across the hall say good-bye to the last patient of the day. They watched medical practitioners and their aides leave the building and swarm into the parking lot in the rear. Finally, an elderly black man, who was apparently the building custodian, shuffled away across the street.

Shortly, Collucci and the Rizzos saw Tonelli's Lincoln pull to a stop at a side entrance. Collucci was disturbed by the platinum flash of Consuella's mane inside the car. Everybody in the building, and all who entered it, would have to be put to sleep. Collucci chewed his bottom lip. He didn't want to orphan Consuella's twins. But neither did he want to postpone Tonelli's execution.

Two penthouse guards got out with Tonelli and Dinzio. Collucci smiled as he watched Dinzio's arm-waving protest to Tonelli. Tonelli waved the guards back into the car. The chauffeured Lincoln pulled away behind them as they crossed the sidewalk to the side door. Dinzio inserted a key, sent by messenger to the penthouse. They entered the building. Dinzio saw his boss into the dentist's chair. Then he left the office for a routine walk-around inspection of the building.

The Rizzos listened to the thump of Dinzio's feet on the rear stairway before they raced from the empty suite on rubber soles down the hallway. They peered down over the railing and sighted silencer-equipped forty-fives down on the top of Dinzio's head as he paused to light a cigarette on the first floor landing.

There was a melon-splattering-on-concrete kind of sound the dumdums made smashing in the lid of Dinzio's skull. The impact sat him down violently on his bottom. Dead. For an instant, he balanced there and swayed limply like a scarecrow in a windstorm. Then he tumbled into a dark heap on the floor.

The Rizzos went back quickly to the dental office just as Collucci stepped inside.

Collucci turned and said, "If he's under, make one of them bring him out before you . . ."

Collucci went to look at the street. The Rizzos went to the examining room and stood watching the backs of the dentist and his pretty brunette assistant as they gassed Tonelli under. The Rizzos pointed their guns.

Marty Rizzo said, "Keep your mouths shut and bring that guy around, fast."

The couple spun around and nodded vigorously. The dentist tremblingly injected Tonelli with a powerful stimulant. The Rizzos stepped close and pumped neat holes into the backs of their heads. They fell forward and shook the floor.

The Rizzos saw Tonelli's eyelids twitch. They rushed to tell Collucci and covered the street while Collucci went to scratch off Tonelli.

Tonelli's eyes fluttered open and locked on Collucci's face, which was Dinzio's face except for Collucci's light eyes. Tonelli's tongue explored inside his mouth.

He said with great irritation, "My teeth! I still got my goddamn teeth! Get that sonuvabitch back here to my teeth."

Collucci threw his head back and laughed like Dinzio.

Tonelli frowned and said sharply, "Go on, Dinzio. Obey me!"

Collucci said in his own voice, "Relax, I am here to solve all of your problems."

Tonelli turned up his still handsome face, composed except for wide eyes staring into Collucci's.

Tonelli said, "I hope you are not waiting to harm Consuella. She is innocent and a good mother . . . she has also given me much pleasure."

Collucci remembered that Olivia's mother had been Tonelli's first cousin.

Collucci said in Sicilian, "A filthy two-headed snake like you could get more pleasure with his sister or his mother in his bed."

Tonelli's face was impassive as he tensed and gauged distance for a lunge at Collucci's magnum. Collucci stepped forward quickly and pressed the gun snout against the bridge of Tonelli's nose.

Collucci stage-whispered, "I've got a human heart . . . maybe I won't pull the trigger if you can move me with some reasons why you should live."

Tonelli's up-turned face was radiant with contempt, "You expect Giuseppe Tonelli to beg a piece-of-shit punk from the Westside for his life?"

Collucci's teeth bared as he punched the snout of the gun into the center of Tonelli's forehead.

Tonelli said softly, "Please, not my face . . . for Consuella and Olivia . . . the funeral."

He pointed a finger over his heart, "Here." he muttered.

Collucci said, "You haven't got a heart, cocksucker! That night outside Olivia's bungalow, you gave your *soldati* orders to crush my face because we were in love. For that, I will blow out the windows of your dirty soul."

Collucci literally stabbed the gun snout through Tonelli's right eye socket before he pulled the trigger. Then he stabbed into the left eye and blasted inside the shattered head again. Tonelli flopped about in the chair for a moment. Then he fell back, stilled.

Collucci and the Rizzos left the building through a rear door. Angelo was parked there. They stuffed the corpses of Tonelli and Dinzio into the trunk for burial. They crammed into the Cougar, and Angelo pulled away.

Collucci was exhilarated. He glanced at six P.M. on his wrist. Spino, his representative, should at the moment be putting it all together for his dream, in a sit-down with the representatives of dissatisfied Mafiosi in families across country. All waited impatiently to assassinate their way to more power and riches through the establishment of a new, young National Commission.

Angelo glanced back at Collucci's face. Collucci's thumb and index finger made a circle for Angelo, that everything was peaches and cream.

But, a window curtain fluttered in a hotel facing the rear of the medical building. Behind the curtain, Barrantino, photographer and wizard of snoop, packed away camera and telescopic lenses. He left the hotel in frantic haste to deliver his pictures and report to Bellini.

CHAPTER TWENTY-FOUR

Collucci boarded a plane for Rome as Bellini's New York-bound plane moved above a sunswept ocean of clouds. The plane was jolted for a moment when it dipped through a tidal wave of pearly clumps.

Bellini felt sweet death wish flutter a thrill in his belly pit. *So, let the big bird shake to pieces up here*, he thought, *my Angelita must be lonely waiting for me to join her.*

He sighed. He loved Olivia and Petey so very much. What an ironic pity, he thought, that he must present the death sentence evidence against Jimmy Collucci to the National Commission.

From the beginning, he'd always done everything within his power to bless the life of Jimmy Collucci with success, some power and money, he thought. Like a father he had followed and felt the highs and lows in his life. With great pride, he had observed him all through his wedding to Olivia and for years after. And he had been satisfied to note that he kept his union with even the spectacular Olivia properly secondary to his union with the Honored Society.

Like a fond father riffling an album for his favorite still, expressing the most joyously fulfilled moment, Bellini remembered the look on young Collucci's face that evening he had inducted him into the Honored Society. His face had been ethereal there in the candle glow of the secret ceremony after Bellini had let Collucci's blood and given him the sacred oath of silence and respect for the Honored Society.

Now, it is my obligation to persuade the Commission Court to entrust me with the responsibility to end Jimmy Collucci's life for breaking that oath. Perhaps, he mused, he'd strangle life from Jimmy Collucci with his hangman's knot technique of the hand garrote. Or maybe he'd use a version of what he had called his dish dome technique, since the fulfillment of his maiden contract.

He smiled ruefully to remember his kid pals coined "Dish Dome" as a nickname for him. A half-moon ridge of brass knuckle bone deformed the rear of his skull top. His mother had been rich and invalid. His stepfather had been cute and nineteen. The stepfather hated ten-year-old Bellini. He kept Bellini's ugly skull shaved clean of camouflaging hair to punish him.

Bellini crept to the living room one quiet midnight and stared down on his stepfather, passed out on the sofa from too much vino. Right then and there, for the first time, he put out a contract, to himself, on his stepfather's life. He arranged the drunk's head. Then he had bashed in the back of it with his bone half-moon until the stepfather drifted away in a forever coma.

Bellini smiled as the plane lurched down on Kennedy Airfield. He had set his mother free to enjoy himself, exclusively! The police had glanced at the stepfather's death. They saw it as just another drunk departed after busting his head open in a fall.

Bellini left the plane and spotted the limousine that would take him to the meeting with the Commission in a back room of a restaurant in Little Italy.

CHAPTER TWENTY-FIVE

Collucci walked on Rome air from the meeting that made his drug dream come true. He had decided to stay in Rome to rest and refine, for a couple of days, his plans.

He would, on his return, arrange to slip on Tonelli's mantel of power in his own name. He would find and use a clever way to take over the penthouse in Olivia's name. He would plan and make moves from the Tonelli fortress.

At that moment, Bellini sadly fastened himself into his seat for the return flight to Chicago. He had the granted responsibility to serve the Commission's death warrant on Collucci.

Only hours after Bellini's departure did the Commission hack out its major decisions on strategy for handling those traitors, deduced as such, and others already strongly suspected. They agreed to temporarily handcuff the plotters with heavy-handed surveillance and beefed-up protection for the members of the Commission. This was the strategy until Collucci, the apparent strong man of the rebellion, was executed. Then they would seize all suspects and give them a torture lie test. Then justice in the Commission's Court.

They also agreed to immediately send the most

efficient assassin team available to Chicago to back up, if necessary, or carry out the execution if Bellini had not accomplished it within a week.

In Chicago, Olivia had summoned Bellini after she had reached a momentous decision. Bellini hurried to visit Olivia for the second time in the week after he returned from New York.

It was the day after Olivia had held a small private memorial service for Tonelli after Bellini had convinced her Tonelli was dead and buried by Collucci's hands.

Bellini paid his cab driver and went up the walk toward Olivia, framed in the open front door. He noticed pieces of Olivia's and Petey's luggage stacked at the bottom of the staircase. Olivia greeted them coolly for the first time since he'd known her, he thought.

She led him into the living room. They sat down on the sofa. Bellini watched her read the front page of a newspaper headlined "Mafia War."

She lifted her eyes and stared accusingly at Bellini. "You, Jimmy . . . and Papa have the money for bonfires. This paper says you . . . the Mafia kill each other in greed . . . for money mostly. Why do you kill, even your friends and relatives, for it when you don't need it?" Olivia exclaimed.

Bellini dry-spat with violence.

Then he said, "Mafia! It's fabricated media garbage! Take the solemn word of your friend and your spiritual father. No such organization exists in these times."

The silence lay heavy between them as they stared into each other's faces.

Bellini's eyes and voice lowered in reverence as he spoke in a soft monotone. "There does exist an ancient and oppressed honored society of elite Sicilian strong men who vowed to forcefully conduct and protect their business methods, interest and families in a corrupt and vicious world. Their enemies plant lies in the press for the pub—"

Olivia's, "Please!" cut Bellini off slack-jawed. "You trusted me and respected my strength and intelligence enough to show me Papa's death pictures. I'm not a child! I'm a woman!"

Bellini tensed and hawkeyed her as she went to her purse and lit a cigarette. She glanced at Petey napping on the floor across the room on a giant pillow.

She strode back to the sofa and paced silently before Bellini for a long moment before she burst into a torrent of impassioned words. "I am so ashamed that all of my life I let myself, forced myself not to realize, not to see yours and Jimmy's and Papa's wretched world."

She paused, and her eyes were on fire when she continued. "I'm liberated from my stupid cocoon of delusion. I'm glad women have declared war on men to force their humanity. I'm thrilled to join that war to save the world's sanity for our children.

"You went to New York to make sure Jimmy joins Papa. All of you should be sent to join Papa . . . you are all enemies of sanity . . . of children."

Bellini flushed scarlet. He got to his feet and

faced her.

He said, "I will not let you insult me. You are very upset. I am afraid for you."

He raised his arms to embrace and comfort her. He stared with his mouth open as she cringed away.

He was hurt to the quick by the fear in her face and her words. "You won't have to kill me. I'd be too ashamed to admit I'd ever lived with your horror."

He choked out, "Before I would let myself harm you, dear daughter, I would end my own life."

She glanced through the window and said, "My cab is here . . ."

He followed her to the front door with a sad face. She opened it and beckoned to the driver.

Bellini said, "Why are you leaving your home in such haste?"

She pursed her lips and said softly, "My conscience wouldn't let me stay in the Church if I stayed here . . . with him."

The driver came past them, following Olivia's finger to the pile of luggage at the bottom of the staircase.

As Olivia went to wake up Petey, she said, "Petey and I need a cleansing."

They stood staring down at Petey mumbling in his sleep.

Olivia said, "I will use only my mother's money for Petey and myself . . . their money, Papa's and Jimmy's . . . all of it, I'll return it to the people who need it!"

Petey rode Bellini's back to the door.

Olivia said, "Our cab can take you to a cab stand."

Bellini scarcely heard her through the roaring birth of an exciting way to steal Collucci's life.

Bellini mumbled, "I'll get coffee . . . lock up before I go . . . all right?"

Olivia nodded and said, "Good-bye and good luck."

Olivia turned away. Petey dismounted and followed her down the walk to the cab.

Angelo sat idly at his apartment window behind the mansion while his ailing spouse catnapped. He saw the cab go by the driveway carrying Olivia and Petey, and a stack of luggage riding in the front seat.

He was surprised not to see Bellini in the cab, since Bellini's cab had left empty.

Angelo's moon face wrinkled concern. He remembered Collucci had Bellini under suspicion as a foe.

Bellini pushed the door locked. He searched the mansion to be sure he was alone. He settled into an easy chair in a shadowy corner of the living room to wait for Collucci, if it took a month.

At the fall of darkness, Angelo darted into the basement beneath the mansion. He listened to the stealthy sound of Bellini's feet as he pussyfooted about the kitchen floor perparing himself a hero sandwich to stop the growling in his belly.

.

CHAPTER TWENTY-SIX

Two hours after Collucci received Angelo's call in his hotel suite, he was airborne for Chicago. After his arrival at O'Hare Field, he took a cab to a loop hotel room. He waited for middle-of-day brightness before he called Angelo and warned him to stay undercover while he covered the back of the mansion.

At two-thirty, Collucci's cab pulled up in front of the mansion. Bellini flopped loose-jointed on the living room sofa and watched Collucci come through the front door. Collucci's right hand was jammed into his overcoat pocket and his eyes were wary.

Bellini let Collucci spot him before he smiled and rose to his feet. "Ah Giacomo, your trip gave your face such a soft rested look."

Collucci froze and dropped the suitcase he was carrying. He drew a magnum pistol from his overcoat pocket. Bellini came toward him with a bland face. Collucci leveled the gun and stood as if hypnotized as Bellini narrowed the space between them.

Collucci suddenly said, "You keep coming, old man, I'll blow you away. You poisoned Olivia against me, haven't you? Where have you sent my family?"

Bellini said, "Poisoned? Sent away? . . . Olivia has installed me as your house guest until she and Petey return from a little trip."

Bellini smilingly held his hands out toward Collucci, palms exposed. "See Giacomo, a guest does not arm himself," he said as he oozed forward.

His arms were up and aimed like hammer-headed battering rams. He should be a foot closer, he thought, before he could hurl up his double fists into his throat to crush it, or stun him for strangling. Bellini decided to sweet talk himself into striking range.

He crooned as he almost imperceptibly shuffled four inches closer to the target. "Angelita loved and trusted you, Giacomo."

Bellini smiled sadly. "Your name was last on her dying lips. For respect of Angelita, put the gun away."

Collucci's brain sent the message to his trigger finger at the instant he saw Bellini spring the hammer heads airborne for his throat. But Collucci's finger was numb against the trigger. Paralyzed! He stood there transfixed and actually stared into Bellini's mad eyes for a mini-instant before his finger jerked the trigger.

He sidestepped. As Bellini's dead body charged past, his stomach churned at the ragged exposure of bone and brain through Bellini's blown-away face. He went to Bellini's crumpled form.

Angelo came through the front door. They stood looking down at Bellini's corpse. Angelo crossed himself and started to say a rosary in an almost inaudible voice.

Collucci glared at Angelo and cut him off, "Stop it! Pull yourself together, Angelo . . . he's not the fucking Pope."

Then Collucci gazed at the pitiful head and said, "I had a big warm feeling once upon a time for that senile old fool . . . you know like he was my real old man. I promised to bury him beside his Angelita . . . I'll have to break that promise. Have one of the Rizzos get Labretti the undertaker's most elegant box . . . for him . . . with no paperwork tracing to the box."

Angelo said, "What a shame the old man had to go . . . anything else, Jimmy?"

The big vein in Collucci's neck puffed with emotion. "Don't look at me that way! What a goddamn shame it is that he tried to strangle me! I am not guilty of his death. He is . . . I didn't kill him . . . he trapped me with his senility. He killed himself!

"A thousand times you've heard me say it, Angelo. It's always the dead, the stupid dead who bear all the responsibility and guilt for their dying. I never felt one fucking thing for any of the others . . . except for Bobo Librizzi."

Collucci moved in close to Angelo with fanatical eyes. "Angelo, I swear to you that old fool . . . Papa, lying there, means goddamn nothing to me now. He's just like all the other cocksuckers that

278

deserved to be put to sleep."

He leaned his wild face into Angelo's.

His voice lurched and shrilled. "Believe it, Angelo! He's just another dead cocksucker to me now. You believe me, Angelo? Say something! Say you believe me! Say it!"

Angelo recoiled and said, "Sure, Mr. . . . sure Jimmy, I believe you! I ain't never doubted nothing you told me about your own personal feelings on important private stuff . . . have I, Jimmy . . . ?"

CHAPTER TWENTY-SEVEN

Spring hand come to Chicago. The grand lady sprawled ashimmer in her ball gown of neon. Collucci gazed out at her from beneath the penthouse terrace bubble. He sat in a high-backed chair covered in royal blue velvet, that rested on a raised platform. He was impatient for the stalled plan to assassinate the Commission to move again.

He spent most of his nights in his chair. There were many nights when alone, he ached for Olivia and Petey. He had spent, and was still spending, five thousand a week in his world-wide search for a trace of Olivia and Petey. So far, it was as if they had vanished off the Earth.

And he thought a lot about Bellini asleep in his five-grand box, buried on the rise behind his Sweet Dream Roadhouse.

The Rizzos and Angelo played rummy at a table before him. The phone rang on the table beside Angelo.

He picked up the receiver and frowned as he said, "Mack Rivers," and passed the phone to Collucci.

Collucci said, "Hello," and listened for a minute or less.

Angelo's ears flapped to hear Collucci say, "Mack, I've changed my mind about having them and their wives here. The best psychology is me over there to hype them up to full confidence that they got reliable protection for all-out operation of their businesses. What the hell, Mack, they will be doing business on the Southside, not here. I'll be there tonight after regular closing."

Collucci hung up the receiver.

Angelo said, "Mr. Collucci, excuse my big mouth butting in. I know the Warriors are fading . . . but Taylor is still alive and nuts. Please let the numbers bankers and big drug dealers come here like you first laid it out."

Collucci threw his head back and laughed. "Even Taylor wouldn't try for me on a skateboard. Besides, the jigaboo numbers bankers and dope dealers will go on crapping in their pants unless I prove, by showing over there, that Taylor's balls shriveled away when he lost his legs. I have to prove the Warriors and Taylor have become pussycats."

Collucci lit a cigarette. He gazed out on his kingdom. He thought about the irony of how Tonelli's trusted penthouse *soldati*, except for a couple, had assisted and welcomed his take over of the penthouse.

Yes, he thought, he had a secret overpowering reason why he must go to the Southside. He had to prove to himself he was not afraid of Taylor.

Two teams of assassins sent by the National Commission to kill Collucci had been trapped and disposed of by Collucci's aides.

A third team sat around the clock at a window in a skyscraper hotel two hundred yards away with an overview of the penthouse terrace. One of the assassins sat, ironically, zeroing in on Collucci's forehead with a starlight-scoped magnum rifle. He and his partner had waited for two weeks for a day or even a moment balmy enough to encourage the retraction of the three-inch-thick plastic bubble under which Collucci spent most of his time.

On the far Southside, the dope jackers bandit gang led for Kong by his cousin, Buncha Grief, had finally put the chips down on the Double Head policy bank safe, loaded with cash and cocaine.

It was the end of the dope jackers. They were bloody and lost with the death of Buncha Grief and almost the entire gang. The dead lay strewn about, all but chopped to pieces by Double Head's machine gun.

They had held the bank's employees at bay and cleaned out the safe. They were going down a narrow hallway to the street when above their heads, near the high ceiling, Double Head pushed up a hinged ventilator cover and sprayed the gang with his machine gun.

One member of the gang, leaking blood, managed to reach the getaway car driven by Charming Mills. As the getaway car shot away past the policy bank, Double Head let go a burst through the blasted-away hallway door.

A round of gunfire tore through Charming Mills' back and pierced arteries inside his chest. His wounded companion leaped from the car several blocks away. Mills was near death. He blacked out and crashed the getaway car into a sentry vehicle at a Zone entrance point.

Bama, a moment before, had heard on the radio

about the massacre of dope jackers at Double Head's policy bank. When he heard the crash, he jumped from his supper at his girlfriend's apartment fifty yards away. He reached the wreckage and Mills was dead. He had Mills' body taken to the hospital morgue.

At first Bama didn't realize that Mills' death afforded an opportunity to run Kong through a psychodrama test.

Bama, while searching Mills' two-room apartment on the first floor of the parsonage, had noticed the carpet felt oddly spongy beneath his feet, under a large table he moved. He pried up the section of carpet. Beneath it was a fat cushion of banknotes, which he guesstimated at no less than a hundred thousand dollars. He restored the room as he had found it and went to set up the trap for Kong.

Taylor was brought to stake out Mills' apartment. He sat on a mound of bedclothes in a large closet without his wheelchair.

Kong, waiting in Buncha Grief's apartment for his return from the Double Head job, heard the news flash Buncha Grief's death in the shooting. Kong hurried back to the Zone.

Bama told him of Mills' death. Bama watched Kong rush into the morgue for a brief moment. Then he went quickly toward the parsonage.

Taylor watched Kong key himself into Mills' apartment. Kong went directly to the table and pulled it away from the corner cache. Taylor let him rip up the carpet before he stuck his head and luger outside the closet.

Taylor said harshly, "Smitty, freeze!"

Kong's hand rattlesnaked for the thirty-eight special in his waistband as he whirled around. Taylor pumped two holes into Kong's chest before he could squeeze the trigger.

The impact punched Kong flat on his back, corners of Kong's mouth and his eyes rolled in agony. Taylor leaned and almost touched Kong's face with his own.

Taylor said gently, "Smitty, I'm sorry your evil crookedness caught up on you . . . Why you do it, Smitty? . . . Why you hating? Why you put the hurt to me and the peoples? . . . Why you do it, Smitty?"

Kong rolled his dying eyes up and stared into Taylor's face with such luminosity and psychotic hatred that Taylor flinched.

He recited it with grotesque care, like a monstrous child repeating a half-remembered obscene limerick. "You hurting? Motherfucker . . . I was a star nigger before you fucked me outta my top spot with my Devastators . . . shit . . . I been hurting and hating ever since. I'm glad the dago fucked up your pins . . . Nigger, I pulled his coat you was on the way . . ."

Kong heaved a liquid sigh and died, and his face was hideous with sick triumph.

Taylor was still beside Kong, drained and still staring at Kong's twisted face, when Bama wheeled in Taylor's chair. He was accompanied by Dew Drop and Ivory Jones, Taylor's personal orderlies. They silently followed behind Taylor as he drove his motorized chair back to his bunker.

CHAPTER TWENTY-SIX

Collucci and Angelo left the penthouse at two *AM* for the bash of confidence at the Voudoo Palace. When they arrived, the doorman unlocked the door and let them into a scene of wild revelry and celebration.

Twenty flamboyantly garbed numbers bankers and wholesale drug dealers danced and laughed with their wives and women. They spotted Collucci. The band stopped playing and the crowd shook the room with cheers and applause. Collucci and Angelo took ringside seats at the reserved table. The band started up the last dance tune before show time.

And in her tenement room up the street, Mayme Flambert put her binoculars aside. She went to the phone in the hallway and dialed Taylor to inform him of the changed location of the bash.

Shortly after, Ivory Jones and Dew Drop were preparing a van to take Taylor to an alley ambush position diagonally across from the front of the Palace.

Dew Drop said, "Ivory, I don't like it. What do you think?"

Ivory said, "There's nothing to think about, Drop . . . we gave Big T. our promise . . . he don't have to know we're gonna back him up. Take it easy, Drop. Everything's gonna be cool."

Dew Drop said, "I guess . . . you seen Bama?"

Ivory said, "We don't have to worry about him. He went to bed finally, after three days. He's dead."

Ten minutes later, Taylor sat hidden inside the van, with a machine gun on his lap.

The Rizzos, armed with high-powered rifles and rigged spotlight, installed themselves on the Palace roof, twenty minutes after Taylor was in position beneath a mountain of garbage and trash near the mouth of the alley.

Only Taylor's glittering eyes were visible as they locked on the front door of the Palace. He sat there and saw his life cover to cover, over and over again as he waited.

At the end of the block, Ivory and Dew Drop, armed with shotgun, rifle and handguns, crouched in the van waiting to back Taylor's attack.

At four-ten A.M., the Palace door opened, and the horde of rowdies burst onto the sidewalk. Taylor was coiled like a steel spring in his chair as he watched for Collucci to appear.

The sidewalk in front of the Palace was almost clear when Collucci, Angelo and Rivers stepped to the sidewalk. Taylor struggled from the garbage and mounted the machine gun on a steel apron bolted to the chair arms. He switched the chair into high gear. He plunged toward Collucci from the alley mouth with fierce face and bared teeth, into the middle of Forty-seventh Street.

The Rizzos illuminated Taylor with the spotlight. Collucci spotted Taylor an instant before he blasted off a burst. Collucci snatched Angelo into the gutter beneath the limousine.

Mack Rivers caught a stitching of holes across his forehead and dropped dead on the sidewalk.

The Rizzos deafening barrage popped spurting springs of blood on Taylor's chest and face. He was a shredded sieve when a blast blew off a chair wheel. The chair crashed to the pavement in front of the Palace.

Behind him, Ivory and Dew Drop opened up with shotgun and rifle fire. Their guns shattered the spotlight and killed Mario Rizzo, who smashed onto the sidewalk.

The other Rizzo's automatic rifle splintered the van windshield and gouged gaping holes in the chests of Ivory and Dew Drop. The van crashed into a shoe store and exploded.

Taylor, tied into the capsized chair, lay on his side, his head resting on the asphalt. The left half of his face was gone. His nose dangled like a misshapen finger across the gory ruin.

But still he gripped the machine gun butt, and his remaining eye had an eerie phosphorescence as it swiveled in the lopsided head for Collucci. It locked on Collucci and Angelo, at its level, cowering in the gutter beneath the limousine. Taylor bellowed. His hate and passion for vengeance aimed the snout of the machine gun. The bodies of Collucci and

Angelo leaped and cavorted under the impact of the flaming blasts that virtually chopped them in half.

Bama, in fake white whiskers and wig, moved through the gawkers and knelt beside Taylor. Taylor's eye swung up to Bama's face. A comet flare of el train light streaked overhead and haloed Bama's wooly wig an instant.

Taylor's Halloween pumpkin mouth burbled through an ooze of blood and entrails. "Willie tole me ... Mama darlin' tole me ... Bama tole me, even ... I shoulda knowed ... you was up there ..."

Then Taylor was dead and Bama wept.

The sex-fiend squealing of city death wagons sodomized infant day. Chicago, the gaudy bitch, had banged another carnal night away. Now the fake grand lady lay uglied in her neon ball gown. Sleazed in the merciless light. Her bleak drawers hung foul with new and ancient death.

THE END